CRIES OF JOY

Axl Malton

To Kirsty

Thanks for the support!
Enjoy!!

Axl Malton

For Haley

Prologue

July 15th

Anna sat on the sofa with her baby nestled safely in the crook of her arm; her free hand was working its way through the coarse hairs on the head of the family dog who lay beside her. It calmed her, and calm was what she needed right then.

The Prime Minister was on the TV. She couldn't hear what he was saying because she had muted it; she had too much on her mind to listen to what he had to say. Although it didn't take a genius to figure out that whatever he was talking about wasn't good news. His hair was a mess, the collar of his shirt was askew and the pit stains on his shirt were growing bigger by the second.

The living room was cast in crimson from the lamp with the red shade at the back of the room; she thought it looked like a sign, a warning of danger ahead. Of course, she'd been seeing the warning signs for a while now, but she had just ignored them, hoping the situation would resolve itself. It didn't, so she found herself having to take matters into her own hands.

Her stomach was doing flips, the beef stew and mashed potatoes they'd had for dinner was threatening to come back up.

Get a hold of yourself.

The voice spoke in her head, she was pleading with herself to stay calm, she'd been over and over this a hundred times. If there was another way out she'd take it, but this was her only chance to keep her and her children safe.

The sound of banging and crashing of metal on metal came from the basement; grinding and whirring sounds of power tools made the place that had once been her home sound more like a war zone. It had been going on for days. What he was doing down there she didn't know, but whatever it was, it scared her.

Anna looked down at her baby, six months old and as cute as a button. She called her Joy because there was no other name quite as fitting.

The sound of crashing metal stopped.

Joy woke, screwed up her face and puckered her mouth the way she did when she was about to let out a big ear-splitting cry. Anna moved her free hand from the dog, the lovable terrier they named Barney, and grabbed a bottle of milk she had prepared before they sat. Joy let out the first syllable of her cry before Anna touched the nipple of the bottle to her lips. Joy took it and sucked at the teat greedily. The silence of the room was broken only by the strong slurping sounds of Joy drinking her milk.

Anna heard the footsteps on the concrete stairs leading up from the basement. Her heart was thundering in her chest. She had a moment to wonder how the hell it had come to this. She sat in paralysing fear of her own husband.

Graham came out of the basement. His hair, which had grown long and wiry over the series of lockdowns, stuck to his forehead with sweat, his face dirty with black grease and coarse black hair. His constant scowling made his skin form deep wrinkles around his eyes and mouth. Anna watched him as subtly as she could, trying to keep her focus on Joy so that he would just walk past her and keep on going. She was waiting for him to leave. *Praying* for him to leave. As soon as he was gone, she could start packing for her, Joy and Mikey. Mikey was ten, the things he needed could fit in a carrier bag. She could deal with them being dirty, they could survive that. Joy however, would require a lot of baggage. Formula, Moses basket, nappies, wipes, baby grows. Babies needed a lot of things. You can't get away with a midnight dash when you have a baby to care for.

Graham walked through the living room, avoiding eye contact with Anna. Barney never lifted his head from his paws but let out a low growl. Graham regarded this with a sideways glance and ground his teeth as he walked past. His profile made him look like a Neanderthal, the way his brow creased and his bottom jaw protruded as his teeth ground together. He was tightly wound; he always struggled with the ability to hide his emotions. They were spread across his face like words in a book. He walked out of the living room and laboured up the stairs. She felt every thunderous step he took reverberate in her chest as if her heart was echoing to the sound.

Anna could feel herself starting to panic, reeling off the list of things she needed to do in her head. She'd threatened to leave him if he carried on and it was time to turn those threats into action. She wouldn't be held prisoner in her own home like some victim, too afraid of her husband to be able to make her own choices, or who she could and couldn't speak to. Hitting her was the final straw. He'd crossed a line he couldn't uncross and he knew it. She lifted her hand and gently felt the tenderness of her jaw and winced at the sharp stab of pain.

The sucking noises turned to whistles. Joy was done with her milk. With Graham out of the room, Anna grabbed the play mat and laid Joy down. Without a word, Barney leapt from the place where he lay so he could rest next to Joy.

The toilet flushed upstairs. Joy let out a small cry and lifted her arms up in the air, wanting to be picked up. Anna faked the best smile she could and picked Joy up from the floor, then rocked her in her arms steadily. Joy gripped Anna's finger and smiled up at her. Anna smiled back. When she heard Graham's footsteps coming down the stairs her smile wanted to fade. She forced it to stay where it was to keep the act going a little while longer. Joy was looking up at her, blowing cute bubbly raspberries. Graham came back through the living room and walked straight through to the kitchen. He opened the door that led down to the basement; his mask hung on the back of it. Since the pandemic began, people had walked around shops and public spaces with those paper masks surgeons and doctors wear. If not, they'd opted for those ghastly plastic visors that will no doubt end up polluting some ocean or another when it's all over. Graham wore a military-grade gas mask. It was the only thing that would truly work, he said.

People are living in a fucking dream world, he'd say. *This isn't over, this is just the beginning.*

'I'm going to the shop,' Graham mumbled at Anna, his keys jingling in one hand, his gas mask in the other. 'I won't be long.'

Anna nodded. She couldn't bring herself to speak, afraid her voice might crack. She wondered if he knew that she was *really* leaving this time. That she meant it. If he did, she had expected more of a fight than this. Maybe his fight was all gone? Maybe he knew it was over as much as she did?

Graham opened the front door and stopped. The way the dying sun blared in through the open door made him lose all of his features. He stood there, a silhouette and nothing more. The outline of his body looked misshapen. The mask in his hand looked as though it was holding the head of some horrific monster.

'I love you,' he said.

The reflex reaction in her tried to make her say it back – fifteen years of marriage will do that to a person. She managed to resist. Her throat was dry and by the time she was able to open her mouth and say 'bye', he was gone.

Joy began to make laughing noises that came out in short high-pitched spurts, projected rapidly like a nanny goat.

Anna rocked her gently, never taking her eyes away from the door. Her heart was picking up pace, her pulse was thudding in her ears. She expected the front door to slam open, Graham to realise what she was planning, and to put a stop to it before she had a chance. The truck engine roared in the driveway. She could hear the crunch of the gravel under the tyres as he backed out on to the road. A wave of relief hit her that made her realise how scared she had actually become of him. Instantly she wanted to head upstairs and start packing. The part of her mind that always taught her caution told her to wait. *What if he forgot something, his wallet or his phone?* If he caught her in the act, he might not be able to control himself.

When there was no sound for ten minutes, and she was sure he was gone, she headed upstairs.

She put Joy in the travel cot that was set up on her side of the bed. The suitcase was on top of the wardrobe. She stretched, standing on her tiptoes, managed to get a strong finger to the corner of the case, and flipped it over to the edge. It teetered there agonisingly before falling. Every second counted if she was going to get out now. She caught it and flung it on to the bed in one slick movement. The case lay open, ready in wait. She opened the wardrobe door and grabbed a handful of clothes and their hangers. The panic that rose in her chest was clouding any common sense, making her feel hurried and pressured. She tried to slam all the clothes in, with hangers still attached. The bag wouldn't close and she still had to get Mikey's and Joy's clothes in. Her face flushed, her cheeks began to burn, and she felt tears fill her eyes as desperation stuck in her throat. Joy began crying in the travel cot beside her.

'Shush darling, Mummy's trying to think,' Anna said, her voice full of panic.

Joy only cried more. Her little arms and legs waved manically as she laid on her back in the cot.

'Stop it! Just stop it for one minute!' Anna raised her voice a little, she didn't want Mikey to hear her yelling. It would put him on edge.

She opened the bag and removed the hangers from her clothes and threw the hangers back into the wardrobe. The clothes now folded in fine, leaving plenty of room for Mikey's and Joy's clothes. Not much, but enough so they all had two or three outfits each until they had a chance to get new things. She doubted they'd ever come back here. Joy cried again. Anna wiped the hair from her face and took a deep breath. She went over and pulled Joy from the cot. Joy instantly stopped crying and nestled her head into Anna's chest. Anna kissed Joy's head; her hair was as soft as downy feathers. When Joy began drifting to sleep, Anna put her back into the cot and walked out of the bedroom and across the hall. She headed to where the hallway turned around a blind corner on to the landing. When she saw Mikey stood there, she cried out.

Mikey looked at his Mum with his face screwed up in confusion. He wore oversized headphones that connected to his Xbox controller with a wire. A mouthpiece hovered over his lips like he was a helicopter pilot.

'Mum. What are you doing?' he said. He was sounding more like his dad every day.

'I just need to pack a few things into a bag. OK darling?' She pasted a smile on and hoped Mikey wouldn't see the worry lines on her face.

'Are we going away?' His faced turned from confused to excited. 'Are we allowed to go on holiday now?'

'Not quite. It's like a holiday. But it's a secret OK, we can't tell Daddy. It's just for us. We're going to stay at Aunty Bev's house while she's away. OK?'

His face turned back to being confused. He was about to speak when a small voice came from the headphones. One of Mikey's friends telling him to get his head in the game, the Nazi zombies were overwhelming the team. He pinched the mic with his thumb and index finger. 'OK, OK. I'm coming.' He looked at his Mum and headed back into his room. He left the door open to allow her entry.

She breathed a sigh of relief and went in. She tried to stay calm whilst she raided his drawers, taking underwear and t-shirts, two pairs of jeans. She smiled at him. He looked straight past her at the TV like she wasn't even there.

Good, she thought. His guitar stood in front of one half of the wardrobe door; she shifted it gently and opened the door. Clothes were stuffed in the drawers messily, she grabbed two t-shirts, pants and socks and put them in the bag. Relief spread through her. First step done. She felt like crying. She was so close to getting away.

'Mikey, I need you to turn that off now. We're going to be heading out in five minutes, OK?'

Mikey kept his gaze on the TV screen. Zombies were being blown to pieces, blood and gore everywhere. She wondered why the hell she let him play these damn things.

'Mikey!' she snapped, and pulled the controller from his hands.

'What?' he said, annoyed, as if she had appeared out of nowhere.

'Turn it off, we're going in five minutes.'

Mikey sighed and let his head fall backwards. He looked up at the ceiling and let out a despairing grunt like his life was over. He'd heard her though, and that meant he'd do as he was asked. He was good like that.

Anna went back into her bedroom and put a few baby grows in the bag. She ticked things off a mental list.

'Nappies,' she said out loud. She put a handful in the suitcase along with baby wipes and nappy cream. Joy was asleep. That gave Anna some respite. She looked out the window and saw the driveway was still empty. There was still time to get away now, but she had to act fast.

'Where are we going? Where's dad?' Mikey said, appearing at the bedroom door.

'Your dad's out, we're going to get in my car and we're going to drive to Aunty Bev's.'

'Why?'

'Just because. Go get your shoes on.'

'We're going now? But it's getting dark out.' Mikey looked shocked.

'Yes, right now darling. We have to go now.' She felt the urge to cry again.

Something about the look in Mikey's eyes. The confusion that would soon turn to hurt when he found out what they were really doing. How could she tell him what his dad had done? That he had hit her? She couldn't think that far ahead. Maybe there was a way to avoid telling him that part of the story and just opt for a vaguer *"Sometimes people just grow apart."*

Graham's truck roared on to the gravel driveway outside. His headlights were flashing in through the bedroom window. Anna snapped her head towards the sound and felt her heart pounding. Joy woke and began crying. Fear rose in Anna's throat, making her feel sick. She ran to the window; her arms and hands were trembling. Graham sped in, sending gravel flying everywhere. His tyre tracks made wavy lines like he was out of control, his truck parked on an awkward angle in front of the house.

'Mikey, get back to your room!' She hurried Mikey into the hall, grabbing the suitcase from the bed as they went.

'What's the matter?' Mikey asked.

'Just get into your room, don't say anything to daddy about us leaving. He doesn't need to know.' She put the suitcase in Mikey's wardrobe behind his guitar and went back to her room. *How did he know,* she asked herself. He had to know, why else would he come back so soon? She went back to the window and looked out. She couldn't see him in the truck. The truck door was left open. In the last of the dying light, she could make out a bloody handprint on the driver's door.

Her lip began to tremble. As if sensing something in the air, Joy stopped crying. The house gave off a deathly silence that ramped up the tension in Anna's muscles. Steadily, Anna made her way out of the bedroom and down the stairs, keeping a firm grip on the handrail, feeling she needed it to keep herself upright if Graham was to burst in.

When she reached the bottom of the stairs, still gripping the handrail so hard she thought there'd be fingernail marks on the white gloss paint work, she could hear Graham outside the door. He was grunting or panting heavily, although it sounded muffled, like something was covering his mouth.

The front door burst open; Anna was glad she managed to keep hold of the handrail. Her knees buckled and she cried out as the door smacked off the wall, the handle leaving an indent in the plaster. A family photo fell from the wall and smashed on the hallway floor, sending glass spraying across the hardwood. Graham, stood there with his hands by his sides, his fingers curled like claws. His shirt was covered in blood as well as his arms and fingers. The thighs of his trousers were drenched in red. He still wore his gas mask; blood was smeared on the visor in lines and streaks from where a hand had attempted to wipe the blood away.

He slammed the door behind him; the latch made an audible *chunk* sound as the lock engaged. He fell against the wall, then he slid down to the floor, holding his hands in front of his face, looking wildly at the blood as if it were alien to him. He screamed, a horrifying scream full of agony and pain that sent a shiver down Anna's spine.

Slowly, she walked towards him. She felt her knees tremble with each step. With a small, quivering voice she said: 'Graham?'

'It's here,' he said. 'We're all going to die.'

Chapter 1

Two weeks earlier.

July 1st

The pots were piled high in the kitchen sink. Graham was down in the basement, doing whatever the hell it was he did down there all day, sometimes all night. Anna had just managed to put Joy down for the night. Although she hadn't taken much of her bottle, so the chances were it wouldn't be long until she woke crying for some more. The pull of the sofa, the TV and a glass of red was almost too tempting to resist. But Anna couldn't relax knowing the kitchen was a state. The cooking duties were never shared, so why would the clean-up be? They'd been in lockdown for five months, the going rate for a national lockdown these days. They were all at home, all contributing to the mess, yet neither Mikey or Graham thought to wash a pot. A woman's work is never done. *Ain't that the truth.*

She filled the sink with hot water and soap. Watched it slowly fill with suds. She scrubbed and wiped, stacked everything on to the drying rack. When the last of the pans were done, the sides cleaned with anti-bac wipes and the floor mopped, she dried her hands on a tea towel and headed into the living room. She kicked off her slippers, the soft ones that formed a cushion around the soles of her feet, and sat on the sofa. Instantly feeling the day's stresses wash away, her back muscles began to loosen, her feet pulsed as, for the first time today, they were relieved of the weight they had been carrying.

A bottle of red sat patiently on the side table, accompanied by a glass with a long thin stem. She poured a glass, not a quite a large, just enough. Anna wasn't a big drinker, but she found the one glass after a long day helped set her into relax mode. Lockdown had made it harder to differentiate between one part of the day and another. Time seemed to blur into itself. Separated only by time to sleep and time to eat.

They did have a routine in the beginning. When to do chores, when to do home-schooling, play-time with Joy, and when Joy was napping, Mikey and Anna baked brownies and cupcakes.

She tilted the glass to her mouth. As the first drops of wine hit her lips, she sighed with the ultimate satisfaction that only a good drop of red can bring. Barney, the family's wiry-haired Jack Russell, padded through from the kitchen, stopped and turned his head to look at Anna. They made eye contact, then he turned his head and went upstairs. No doubt to sit in Mikey's room whilst he played on his Xbox. Anna let out a little laugh. That dog was so protective, it was like he walked around the house on a night checking on everyone before he went to sit down, like a parent with sleeping children.

She flicked on the TV; the news was on. The headline that ran endlessly along the bottom of the screen read: *End of Lockdown?* Her eyebrow creased at the question mark. It should be a statement, not a question. They were gearing up for the 13th of July. That was when lockdown was going to end. They only had twelve days to get through before life could return to normal, or whatever the normal left to them was.

The Prime Minister came on screen. His hair was a mess, his face gaunt and drawn with exhaustion. He sat behind a mahogany desk; a wall of books flanked his sides. 'Good evening. It is with great pleasure that I am able confirm that plans to come out of the latest lockdown are set to go ahead, in twelve days' time on the 13th of July. I *do,* however, say this with an air of caution, due to growing evidence of a highly infectious variant, newly discovered in Eastern Europe. A case of which may have been detected here, on British soil.' He coughed into his fist; his face turned red as he spluttered more rasping coughs. 'Excuse me. I'm quite alright, just a tickle.' He laughed it off, although the laugh seemed forced. Anna had seen this picture a hundred times before. False promises that aimed to give the public hope of a normal life once again, before dashing their dreams with a prolonged isolation period. Still, she remained hopeful. It was bound to drive a person crazy were it not for the hope that there *would* be an end to all of this.

The Prime Minister continued: 'As it stands, we are able to go ahead with lifting the restrictions, and I sympathise with all the suffering businesses, tradespeople, shop owners, children missing out on school, everyone missing seeing their friends and relatives. I do. I want this to be over as much as all of you, but we must proceed, with caution.' The Prime Minister hit his fist on the desk to emphasise 'with caution.' He continued: 'Should another variant spread, the results could be catastrophic. Any news on this new variant will be made public in due course as we learn more. Good night, stay indoors and, most importantly, stay safe.

The camera switched back to the newsreader. Anna flicked the set off and drank another sip of wine. Swilling the aromatic liquid around her mouth, feeling it swim around her tongue, she closed her eyes and felt herself relax.

She heard a cry and sat upright, instantly snapping out of her relaxed state to attend to her baby. Only, when the second cry came, she realised it wasn't Joy or even Mikey. The sound was coming from the basement. It was Graham. Deep, racking sobs echoed up from the basement stairs, amplifying his cry of pain.

Anna got to her feet, set her glass down on the side-table, and headed into the kitchen. 'Graham?' she called down the stairs through the basement door in the kitchen.

No answer came, but his sobs seemed to be dissipating. Anxiously, she went down a step and called his name again. 'Graham?' Still no reply.

He had told her, under strict instructions, that she was not to enter the basement. If they were going to survive this lockdown with any semblance of sanity at the end, they needed to respect each other's privacy. The basement was his sanctuary, a place where he could escape the numbness of the family home and do whatever entertained him so much down there. He chose to be down there more often than up in the real world with the rest of them. Anna conceded this, in hope they could just get through to the 13th when they could all return back to normal. His sobbing had worried her. She had seen how much he had been struggling over the past few months, angry outbursts one minute, deep mournful sorrow the next. He wasn't a well man. His mental health had once been so robust, so impenetrable, but since the death of his father, another soul taken by this dreadful disease, Graham had suffered greatly.

She decided to go down the rest of the stairs and at least knock on the door that separated the stairwell from the basement. Every step of the concrete staircase had a sharp neat edge and was extremely steep. Graham had promised to fit a handrail to make it easier for climbing up and down them. That was eight years ago, so she didn't hold out much hope of him getting round to it anytime soon. She had visions of Mikey, excitedly running in from outside, wanting to go down and see his dad, to tell him about some achievement, and running so fast he tripped and fell down the steep concrete stairs, landing against the wall at the bottom. Lying there, twisted and broken.

She closed her eyes against the thought and carried on down to the bottom. She rapped her knuckles on the door. She heard shuffling from behind it, like boxes being dragged along the floor. The basement was mainly used for storing old memories, old gym equipment they never used, and old toys and records.

The door handle rattled. She heard the sound of deadbolts being slid back on the other side, deadbolts that she was sure had not been there before. The door opened a fraction. Graham peered out from behind the door, only his wet, bloodshot eye was visible through the crack in the door.

'What?' he snapped and then cleared his throat.

'I was just checking if you were, OK? I thought I could hear crying?'

'Of course, I wasn't crying.' He tried to laugh it away.

'It just sounded like -'

'I wasn't fucking crying. Leave me alone.' He slammed the door and bolted it again.

Anna stood, her arms outstretched - *what the hell was that?*

His constant snapping and shouting, taking everything out on her like this, made her feel like it was all her fault. It wasn't her fault and she was sick of Graham making her feel like it was. It was getting too much. There was only so long she could let it go without saying something. Graham was a grown man with responsibilities and a family of his own.

'I know you're still grieving over your dad, but you can't carry on taking it out on me!' she shouted, and slapped the door in frustration. She started up the stairs, feeling agitated. When she reached the top and walked into the kitchen, she heard the bolts of the basement door slide back and the door swing open on its rusty hinges. Graham's footsteps were loud and hurried as he ran up the stairs. When he came into view he marched towards Anna with a face like thunder; the dirt on his cheeks had thin white lines where tears had fallen.

'Don't you dare talk about my dad!' Graham charged over and stood up to Anna, forcing her back against the kitchen worktop. He towered a whole head above her, she had to crane her neck to look up and make eye contact with him.

'Who the hell do you think you're talking to?' she snapped back, trying to sound as if she wasn't scared of him at all, like it used to be.

'If it wasn't for you, I'd have been able to see him before he died.' Graham was panting, spittle gathered in the corners of his tightly drawn lips.

'You're saying it's my fault?' Dumbfounded, she put a hand on her chest and felt the rapidity of her heartbeat. She moved away from him and stepped backwards towards the living room. 'We were in lockdown; we still are in case you haven't noticed. Besides, we knew he had the disease, we couldn't risk visiting him.'

'Yeah, you keep telling yourself that. You never liked him. Admit it.'

Anna creased her brow, 'Yeah? Well neither did you. Your father was a horrible man who forced your mother into a life of secluded misery. Still, I wouldn't wish a lonely death on anyone. But we had to look after *our* family. I was pregnant, about to give birth. It was too risky; it could have killed me and Joy.'

Graham shook his head. 'You talk shit. The virus back then was nothing like what it's turning into now. You've never had any respect for me. I bet you loved the thought of him lying in his bed, alone, struggling for breath.'

Graham. Don't be so vile.'

Something in his eyes flickered, like the redness of a hot ember. 'Fuck you.' He pushed her with such force she fell to the sofa, spilling her glass of wine on to the carpet. A red streak splattered across the floor and soaked in.

Anna looked up at Graham in shock and horror. He had never gone so far as to lay a hand on her before; the threat had been there, the *want* had been there too, which was just as terrifying. She never would have married a man who was capable of it. Especially one who looked at her the way he was now. There was no regret in his eyes for what he had done. If anything, what Anna thought she saw was a want to do more. The way his clenched fist twitched by his side made her think he *would* do more. Suddenly, she felt extremely vulnerable in her own home where she should feel the safest of all places.

Then a wash of regret came over his face. His lip quivered as if he was just seeing what he had done for the first time.

'I'm sorry...I'm so sorry.' He turned and darted back down to the basement, slamming the door and sliding the bolt back across.

Anna, who unknowingly had been holding her breath all this time, let out a huge, relieved breath and turned hot with the flush of relenting panic. Tears filled her eyes and a lump formed in her throat. In that moment she didn't think her heart would ever slow down. She forced herself to take deep, shuddering breaths, in the hope that it would calm her.

Her heart began to slow, the small black dots that had filled her vision dispersed. When calm, she picked up the spilled glass, and found the cleaning products under the sink. She felt a strange anxiety in the pit of her stomach that lasted for the rest of the evening. Not in memory of the push, or the force he had used against her, as if she was a man of equal size to him. But because she couldn't shake the feeling that what had happened was only a warning for what was yet to come.

Chapter 2.

July 6th

One week left until lockdown was lifted. It couldn't come soon enough. Anna was sat at the dining table in the kitchen, which was nothing fancy, just a round table you would normally find outside of cafés where people would sit with a coffee, smoking a cigarette and reading the newspaper. Anna enjoyed the family eating together, but wouldn't have classed herself as a traditionalist by any stretch, so if Mikey or Graham wanted to eat their dinner on their laps in front of the TV when a game was on, she was happy for them to do so.

She had lived her own childhood being brought up in a house where women had their roles and men had theirs, and at the end of every day her mother would ensure that dinner was on the table for the moment when her dad would walk through the front door. Six o'clock on the dot. Without fail. It wasn't as though Anna's mum felt forced into that role, she enjoyed it, it was what she had grown up with from watching her own mum and she felt she wanted to carry it on. And that was fine with Anna, do whatever makes you happy. That was her motto. She just didn't want to live her own life so regimented and labelled with strict roles, allocated only by gender, not by skill or personal preference. Sometimes she would cook, sometimes Graham would cook, (although she did prefer to cook as Graham possessed very little in the culinary skills department) and they had dinner at different times depending on what everyone was doing or feeling that day.

She knew her mother and father were happy for her to live that way, they even said it was refreshing to see her create her own family dynamic, that she had a mind of her own and she wasn't afraid to use it. They were proud of her, and they had made sure to tell her that every time they visited, before they passed away five years ago. When they did pass, it had left Anna with no family; she had her own unit, Graham and Mikey, and now Joy, but no other siblings, no cousins, aunts or uncles to speak of. She had few friends, the only one of which she'd actually consider a true friend was Beverly Cage, a woman that her children would affectionately name Aunty Bev, even though there was no blood relation there at all.

Anna sat on the laptop, a ten-year-old machine that was so slow Anna would turn it on and go make a cup of tea, knowing that when she got back, it would still be loading the log in page. She was checking the online banking, trying to get a grip of their financial situation. She had been planning to do a birthday party for Joy; because she was born in the last lockdown (that ended briefly for two weeks before the new lockdown took over) they hadn't had a chance to celebrate with anyone. Her and Bev got their heads together and decided a summer barbecue would go down a treat. Bev had two girls who adored Mikey, they could play in the garden while she and Anna sat and had a few mocktails and a good ol' catch up.

She clicked on the joint account and saw their funds were lower than she had expected. A lot lower. She muttered a few choice words to herself and clicked to view the statement. Scrolling down, she could see several abnormally large transactions had taken place at the supermarket. The lockdown rules stipulated that they were permitted to go to the supermarket for groceries and essential items. Graham did most of it, but when he came back, he didn't bring anywhere near enough bags to amount to that spending.

Guess we'll have to take mocktails off the list.

She shut the laptop and crossed her arms. Barney got up from between her legs and started circling around her and sniffing her feet. Then, as if he had found a brand-new spot, he laid back down between her legs. She wondered whether to confront Graham about the missing money, ask him what the hell he had spent that amount of money on at the damn supermarket. Normally, it wouldn't be a question; she'd have hollered for him to come see her so they could discuss it and figure out what had happened, how they were going to make allowances the following month to ensure all the bills were paid. That was something they had to do now, now that they relied so heavily on the benefit system since Graham's business collapsed, and then the job he got afterwards let him go. The memory of last week, when he had pushed her to the floor and stood over her with hatred in his eyes, the way he had spoken to her, made her pause and think of another way to approach it, in the hope it wouldn't anger him. Not that it would, he wouldn't do it again. He had promised her he wouldn't, told her he was so sorry, sorrier than he had ever been in his life, that he didn't know what had come over him to do such a horrid thing. He'd begged her for forgiveness and it appeared genuine. After being with the same person for so long, you tend to have a sixth sense about these things, or so Anna believed she did.

She decided to leave it. The light on the baby monitor lit up, and then the sound of Joy crying came through the speaker. Barney lifted his head from his paws, his eyes wide and on high alert.

'It's alright boy. I'll go get her,' Anna said, and ruffled the long hair on his head. He rested his head back down but kept his eyes open. Anna went up to get her. Joy filled with happiness the moment she saw her mother enter the bedroom and pick her up out of the cot. She smiled and waved her arms around playfully. Anna made Joy a bottle and fed her it, then sat at the kitchen table. Barney, who had been with her all day, moved back to lie between her feet under the chair and rested his head on his front paws.

Mikey came thundering down the stairs. He bolted through the living room, his long blonde hair flowing behind him as he ran.

'Hey, where are you going in such a hurry?' Anna said smiling.

'Outside. It's so hot. I'm going to play football for a bit. Where's Dad?'

'He's downstairs.'

Mikey rolled his eyes and Anna smiled. Mikey rubbed his finger under Joy's chin as she drank. She stopped sucking and smiled at the sight of him. Anna removed the bottle from her mouth and sat her up. Joy reached as if to grab Mikey; he put his finger out and she grabbed it, then pulled it towards her and started clamping down on it with her sloppy gums.

'Eww gross.' Mikey pulled his hand back laughing.

'That's just how babies learn.'

'It's still gross. Can I ask Dad if he wants a kick about?' Mikey started putting his shoes on.

He had already started for the basement door as Anna thought about what to say.

'OK, knock before you go in though. And please, for the sake of your old mother's heart, take extra care going down those stairs.'

'I know, I know, I'll fall and break my neck,' Mikey laughed. He opened the door onto the stairs and went down, looking back at Anna and pretending to lose his balance. Anna gave him a reproachful look and he grimaced playfully. At the bottom of the stairs, he knocked on the door. Graham didn't answer so he knocked again.

Upstairs, Barney started growling. Anna leant to one side and stroked his back; he stopped when she touched him.

'What?' Graham said. Mikey hesitated – his dad sounding so angry caught him off-guard.

'Dad? I was wondering if you wanted a game of football in the garden.'

'Argh!'

Mikey heard something being slammed down on a table behind the door, then footsteps heading towards him. The door opened, only enough so Graham could stick his face through.

'What is it? I'm busy in here!'

'Um, er, I'm going into the garden to play football?'

'So?'

'So, do you wanna play? I'll let you be in goal?'

'No, I don't want to play football. Go play by yourself.'

Mikey looked dejectedly down at the floor. 'Oh, OK.' He turned to head back upstairs. His footsteps were slow and sad and his head was bowed low.

'Mikey?' Graham called after him.

Mikey, turned and looked back at him with a smile on his face, 'Yes Dad?'

'Don't act like a spoilt brat. You're a big enough boy to know sometimes adults are busy.'

'You're always busy,' Mikey said quietly, but loud enough that Graham heard.

Graham's face flushed; his cheeks began to redden. He stepped out of the doorway. 'Yes, I am always busy. Busy doing everything I can to help us. When the time comes, you'll be glad I was so busy instead of wasting precious time playing stupid little games out there with you. Now piss off out of my sight and don't disturb me again.'

Mikey nodded and ran back upstairs.

'And grow the hell up!' Graham shouted before slamming the door.

Anna stood when Mikey came into the kitchen and shut the door to the basement. She went to give him comfort but Mikey turned away. He kicked off his shoes and ran back upstairs. Anna walked over to the top of the stairs and saw Graham standing there, panting heavily. He looked up and saw Anna looking down on him in disgust.

'What?' He gestured with a shrug of his shoulders and shook his head. When Anna only answered with a look of disappointment, he waved a hand at her dismissively, before going back into the basement and locking the door.

Chapter 3.

That night Anna gave Mikey tea in his bedroom. Told him to eat his pizza whilst playing video games with his friends. This earned her a few 'cool mum' points, which always came in handy. Barney had been running round and round her legs all day downstairs. He was never normally so needy, especially not with her, but today he couldn't seem to leave her alone. He was a lovely dog, and she cared for him dearly. As nice as it was to have her own personal guard dog all day, she was relieved when he chose to sit in Mikey's room for the evening.

She put Joy down at eight, kissed her on the cheek and put her dummy in. Joy's eyes were already rolling, wrapped snuggly in her blanket and showered with love. She would sleep peacefully until the early hours when she would wake for a bottle, then sleep again until the sun came up.

Anna went downstairs and laid the dining table ready for dinner. The table sat to the left of the open plan kitchen, in front of the French windows that opened up on to the garden. No flowers or champagne propped in an ice bucket, just a few candles to create an atmosphere. She was hoping that putting a bit more effort than any other evening would help to pull Graham back from the pit he'd fallen into. He came up when she set it on the table, an excellent cut of sirloin, mashed potatoes and green beans. Anna was sat at one side waiting. She'd put a touch more make-up on after she tucked Joy in. She always liked to look her best but during lockdown, she supposed she'd let it slip a little. She didn't receive much inspiration for getting dolled up and setting out a romantic meal for her husband, who for the past six months hadn't seemed to give two shits if she was even there or not. He'd let his appearance slide dramatically. Anna didn't think of herself as a shallow person who'd be bothered by such things, but just over a year ago he looked like a swimwear model. His attitude was the real turn off. His anger and his inappropriate way of dismissing Mikey. Her thoughts had been mainly focused on the subject of divorce. Something which made her shudder, just at the thought of the word as she said it in her head. Never out loud, that would make it too real. It dominated her mind more than she wanted to admit, even to herself. The meal was a step in the right direction. She owed it to the children, she owed it to their fifteen-year marriage, she owed it to herself to try and make it work. If she had to walk away, at least she could say that she'd tried.

Graham pulled his chair out without even glancing in Anna's direction. She supposed it was too much to hope for, that he would notice she had made an effort. A bit of extra lippy, had done her hair nice. Still, was it too much to ask, for a simple, *hello, how are you?*

He sat down, grabbed his fork and swapped it into his right hand and shovelled the mashed potatoes into his mouth, chewing loudly with his mouth open as he ground his teeth and swallowed. Anna could hardly look at the way he kept shovelling the food in, as if he was starving and he thought someone was going to take it away from him any second. Globs of mash splattered his cheeks; next he moved on to the green beans. He grabbed the saltshaker and sprinkled so much salt on you could scoop it up with a spoon, and ate them in one mouthful.

Anna picked up her own cutlery and began to cut a piece of steak. She didn't cook steak often, that was also a treat. She saw as she sliced through the meat how juicy it was, the insides perfectly pink, the outside seared and slightly blackened. She chewed and felt it melt in her mouth. When she looked back at Graham, he was mopping the juice left on the plate with the remainder of the potatoes, and then he stood. Wiping at his mouth with the back of his hand, he grabbed the bottom of his shirt and lifted it up to dab the meat juices from his lips. He dropped the shirt and spots of red and brown had soaked into the white cotton.

'Well?' she asked as he dropped his plate into the sink and walked back towards the basement door.

'Well, what?'

Anna put her cutlery down and ran her hands through her hair. 'For God's sake Graham. I've just cooked us a meal, set the table, even lit a damn candle, and you didn't even notice I was sat opposite you.'

Graham shrugged. 'What do you want me to say? There is so much going on in the world right now. You know there's a disease out there that is spreading like wildfire? Mutations are getting more and more dangerous, becoming more fatal and affecting a much larger group of people.'

Anna looked perplexed, she wondered how he hadn't taken on anything she had said. She thought he might at least feign an apology but he was carrying on like he didn't even care. 'And what are you planning to do about it? Huh? Instead of worrying about that, maybe you should worry about your own family.'

'I AM!'

'We're falling apart! This isn't a life; this isn't a marriage.' Anna pointed back and forth between them both. 'I can't carry on living like this Graham.'

He stood silent and rocked on his heels like he'd been stung.

'What are you saying? You want a divorce?'

Anna sighed and looked up at the ceiling briefly. She felt tears well in her eyes and tried to stop them before looking back at him. 'I think that's where we're heading. Yeah.' She bit her lip.

'I'd do anything for this family. Anything!' he shouted at her. The vein in his neck pulsed.

'You won't even play a game of football with your son.' Anna was crying now. Her tears were falling down her cheeks and she wiped them away as soon as they fell.

'When the shit hits the fan, then you'll all be glad of my work.'

'Work? What fucking work! You're not doing anything. You sit down there all day, all night sometimes. Leaving me to do all the housework and look after the kids and the dog.'

'Those are your jobs,' Graham snapped.

Anna gasped in shock before laughing and covering her face with her hands in frustration. 'Don't even start that bullshit, that's never been how we've done stuff in this house. My parents were like that, your parents were even worse for it, but that's not us. Don't turn into your dad.'

'Fuck you. You're going to have to drop your feminism bullshit if we're going to survive this. I'm the one who's going to save us all.'

'How are you going to do that? Does it have anything to do with spending all of our money on shit at the supermarket? Huh? I've seen the bank statements, Graham. So don't look at me like that.'

Graham's cheeks flushed red, 'You're checking up on me? You're checking up, on me?'

'Don't give me that. What have you spent it on, Graham?'

'None of your fucking business.'

Anna stopped herself from continuing this pointless back and forth. She shut her eyes and clamped her lips together. Her arms spread wide as if asking the Lord for strength.

She spoke softly. 'Graham, if this carries on. I will leave. Maybe just for a break, nothing...final. Just so we can have a bit of breathing space, see if this is what we want.'

Graham pushed the dining chair back under the table, making the table legs squeak as it moved along the tiled floor.

He gripped the chair and leant across the table towards Anna. 'Just you try and take my son away from me. Just you fucking try it.' He stared into her eyes as if he was waiting for her to make a move. The moment she did, he would lunge at her. This wasn't the man she'd married.

Slowly, she stood from her seat and kept eye contact with him. The room was silent aside from the ticking of the clock on the wall and the dripping of the tap. Graham was squeezing the chair, his knuckles turning from red to white as he clenched. Anna felt her eyes sting and begin to water.

In a flash, Graham slammed the chair into the table and turned away. He opened the door to the basement and walked slowly down the stairs.

Anna carried on watching him as he went. Her muscles had stiffened like she had been turned to stone. When he was gone and she heard the familiar sound of the deadbolt being pushed into the lock position, she relaxed. After a few deep breaths she began to clear the plates. As she began running the tap and filling the sink for the pots, her mind began racing through what had just happened. She found it curious that he had said, *'Just you try and take my son away from me.'* Not *my children,* or *my family.* Just *'My son.'* Like Joy wasn't an issue. The end was near for them. Right now, all she could feel was anger, anger and fear. Anger at how little he seemed to care about any of them, not just their marriage, and fear because she no longer knew what her husband was capable of.

Chapter 4.

Anna was patting Joy on her back, whilst walking backwards and forwards in the kitchen, Barney swerving in and out of her legs as she took each step.

'Come on baby girl, get it out.'

She patted her back some more until Joy let out a great belch for such a small person. Anna held Joy out in front of her. She was now smiling instead of griping and grimacing.

Her phone rang. The name flashing up on the screen was Beverly Cage. This brought a smile to Anna's face before she even answered the phone.

'Bev! So glad you called. How are you? Still on for Saturday?' Anna sat at the kitchen table. A muffled sound of distorted electric guitar came from upstairs. Anna looked up to the ceiling as if she'd be able to tell Mikey to turn it down through some telepathic signal. It didn't work.

'Yes of course. I can't wait to meet little baby Joy! I can't believe she's six months old already, I've missed so much!'

'I know, she's getting so big. Still, she's not started crawling yet, so maybe you can get her to do something, because I sure as hell can't. When Mikey was six months he was already off. If he couldn't crawl, he'd just roll to wherever he wanted to be.'

'Mine were the same. Damn, I can't tell you how much I want to get out and see the world again. How are you coping, how's things your end?'

Anna paused. 'Things are...things are good. Stressful, you know, what with money and being cooped up for so long,' She tried to sound cheery but struggled to sound convincing.

33

'Anna. You know I know you too well to lie to me. Go on. What is it? Is that husband of yours behaving? I hope he's doing his share of the night feeds?'

Bev, as well as being the only real friend Anna had, was a few years older, and -although Anna would never admit to it- Anna saw her as a kind of honorary mother figure. Having lost her mother a few years ago, she had no one else to just pick up the phone and call when she needed help or advice.

It was something in the way Beverly asked about Graham, how she asked if he was pulling his weight, helping with the night feeds, that made Anna start to cry. Bev had said those things only half-seriously because, why wouldn't he be helping? Why would he leave everything to her? Not just for a couple of days, or weeks, but for Joy's whole life, he had done nothing to help her. It was like he refused to have anything to do with Joy because if she wasn't in Anna's stomach when his dad got ill, maybe he could have gone to see him before he died and he didn't want to help Anna as some kind of punishment?

'Anna, what's wrong?' Bev sounded concerned now.

Anna told her about Graham's behaviour. She was getting increasingly more nervous that he might be listening in. She spoke quietly, rocking Joy in her arms. Joy slept. The swinging motion had a hypnotic effect that she couldn't resist.

Bev was shocked at Graham, shocked and disgusted.

'What should I do?' Anna said.

'You kiddin' me? Get the hell outta there! That man is abusing you and those children. We're all suffering from this lockdown, what makes him think he's so special? If he can't be a man and stand up and take care of his family, then fuck him.'

Her anger brought out an accent that sounded as though she was fresh from the ghetto, not the gated community in the suburbs where she actually came from. Bev had grown up in America until her early twenties and although the strength of her accent had diluted over her time in England, it came out in full force when she got mad. It never failed to bring a smile to Anna's face.

'We've been married fifteen years Bev.'

'And still, he treats you like this. After all this time.' She made loud tutting noises. 'If he's been as angry as you say, mark my words. He'll hurt you, Mm-hmm, you mark my words, dat mutha fucka about to beat on you. Maybe even those kiddies. Take that break you suggested. I'm going away for a little while; you can always stay at mine if you need to.'

'You're going away?'

'It's a work thing. I'll tell you about it on Saturday. Tell me you'll think about it?'

'OK. I'll think about it. Thanks Bev. I don't know what I'd do without you.'

'And you'll never have to find out. Take care Anna, much love. See ya Saturday.'

She hung up and Anna felt a small relief that she had told someone and Bev had responded perfectly. Giving her a way out, a place to stay and a shoulder to cry on. She didn't like the thought of being in Bev's house without her being there, but hopefully it wouldn't be for long. Graham would come to his senses when she was gone. Then with a bit of mediation and with the aid of the world returning back to normal, they'd work it out.

Chapter 5.

Anna stood looking in the bathroom mirror. She spun to stand sideways and pushed her belly out. She pinched the roll of flab that had developed over lockdown and looked at herself dejectedly. She turned forward and decided to wear a long dress for the party instead of the shorts and t-shirt she had planned. Pulling at the skin under her eyes that seemed to have got looser over-night, she put her hands on the sink and leaned to get a closer look at herself. Her face was smooth and soft; aside from the bags and loose skin under her eyes, she had still managed to retain most of her youth. In a stark comparison, Graham looked to have aged twenty years during this lockdown. His long, scraggy hair was greyer; even his beard was mostly grey now, no black left aside from the odd strand that outlined his lips.

He was ten years older than she was. He'd been thirty when they met. She was barely out of her teens when he'd picked her up at a bar and whisked her off her feet. Ten years is nothing, they both said. Now, the single decade seemed to have turned into a great gulf, as if not only they weren't the same generation but they weren't even from the same century.

Anna was just finishing applying the thick layer of make-up to her face when Graham walked in. Something she wouldn't have batted an eye at a year ago, now felt as though her privacy was being encroached upon. She felt vulnerable and uncomfortable with him barging in when she was in there.

'What time are they coming?' he said.

'Lunch.' Anna turned back to the mirror and puckered her lips; her hand was shaking slightly as she applied her lipstick.

'You've told her. Haven't you?' Graham looked at her via the mirror with hard eyes.

'Told her what?'

'That we're going on a break. Or rather, you're going on a break. That you don't want to be with me anymore and you're trying to take the kids from me.' To Anna's surprise it looked as though his eyes were filling with tears and his voice sounded as though it was on the verge of breaking.

'Graham, I don't know how many times you want me to say it. That is not what's happening here. We need time apart to see if we'll come back together again. You need space from me, and quite frankly...I need space from you.'

Graham ground his teeth. He moved to stand behind her. His entire frame looked big enough to swallow her whole.

'I'm sorry it's come to this. I've just not been coping. I'll do better. I promise.'

Anna looked back at him with sympathy. 'I know. But things haven't been right for a long time. A break is just what we need.'

Graham's face changed as if he'd removed a mask. 'You're making a mistake.' His voice sounded soft but there was a venom underneath it. 'You know that. When the world crumbles, you'll know you made a mistake.'

This again.

'Let's not think about it now. Can we please just have a nice belated birthday party for Joy?' Anna carried on looking forward, afraid to look away and catch a glimpse of the anger in his eyes. Graham hovered there for what felt like forever before he made a move. He clasped his hands on to Anna's upper arms. His thick fingers felt big enough to crush her arms like they were nothing but chicken wings.

'I'll go await our guest.'

He left the bathroom and Anna let out the air she was holding in and felt her heart palpitating in her chest.

Just get through today.

Chapter 6

Anna, with Joy in her arms, sat at the kitchen table talking with Bev. A good-looking black woman with long manicured fingernails and fantastically white teeth that she had bleached once a year, it made Anna conscious of her own appearance, she worried that she didn't look as good as she once had. They were surrounded by pink balloons; bunting hung on every wall with the words 'HAPPY (belated) BIRTHDAY' and 'IT'S A GIRL' written in shiny foil lettering.

Mikey ran through the kitchen with a water pistol in his hands, laughing and screaming as Bev's two girls, Kirsty and Zoe, chased after him with water pistols of their own. It was an extremely hot day; now lockdown was lifted, the whole country would be out celebrating in beer gardens, filling parks and enjoying barbecues with family for the first time in months.

Bev was wearing a thin buttoned shirt and some old gym shorts that looked more like hot pants. Anna wore a floaty dress that was both casual and elegant.

'So nice to finally be able to do this,' Beverly said, reaching out a hand and touching Anna and Joy.

'It's been so long, hasn't it? I just hope it will be over soon.'

Joy cooed and flapped her arms, trying to grab at Anna's smiling face.

'Well, you certainly gave her the right name, she is a bundle of joy, isn't she?' Beverly shone a bright smile in Joy's direction.

'Oh yes, she is. A handful, but it's all worth it. It's been so long since Mikey was this age, I'd forgotten how hard the night feeds were.'

Bev looked at her knowingly and tapped her hand. 'You'll blink and it'll be gone. Enjoy her being this age, they're only babies once.'

Graham entered from the door that led to the basement. Mikey had been pestering him to come up and play outside. Imploring him that he needed help against the two girls that were ganging up on him, explaining that if his dad would join in it would be two v two, evening up the odds. Graham had rebuffed him twice, telling him he was too busy. Anna's heart fluttered with relief when Graham came upstairs. If she was going to leave, she'd rather Mikey and Graham separated on good terms. His shirt was unbuttoned, revealing a well-fed beer belly, and he wore an old red bandana tied around his head like Rambo, gripping a Mega-soaker in his hands like he was a killer soldier on a covert mission.

He held a finger to his lips; Anna made a zip gesture over her mouth as he crept towards the back door. She thought it funny how different people can be in front of guests. Anna imagined if she hadn't already spoken about all of their problems and reached out for Bev's advice, Bev would be none the wiser as to their marital difficulties. Graham had turned into the Graham she had married all those years ago. How long it lasted, that was the issue.

He leaned against the door frame and peeked round the corner. He took two deep breaths, pumped the piston on the under barrel of the water-gun and jumped through the threshold.

'It's soaking time!' He fired a powerful jet of water that soaked Mikey and the girls; the girls screamed, Mikey cheered and lifted his hands over his head in celebration. Barney jumped to catch the water from the air.

Anna and Bev laughed and shook their heads.

'Men. They never grow up do they,' Bev smirked.

'It's so nice to see him joining in. It will mean so much to Mikey.' Anna watched them playing and smiled, even though what she was feeling was sadness.

Bev looked over her shoulder at Graham outside, then turned back to Anna. 'Go on then. How are you? Really? Have things got any better?'

Anna rocked Joy in her arms and looked down at her before looking up at Bev. 'I told him I was going to leave. That I'd take the kids, hell I'll even take the dog. I just want him to *want* us. You know what I mean?'

'Hmm mmm.' Bev pursed her lips and nodded, wide-eyed and understanding like she'd seen the same scenario a thousand times.

'He just sees it as I'm taking them away from him forever, that I want a divorce and I'm never coming back. And that's not it. Not yet at least.'

'Listen honey, you don't owe anyone anything. From what you've told me, you damn near raised these kiddies on your own for the past year already.'

'Six months,' Anna corrected her.

'Oh, I'm sorry. Just the six months. You always -' Bev stopped herself as she heard her voice begin to rise. She spoke again quieter. 'You always jump in to defend him. In these conditions, six months is a damn long time. Home schooling because of the lockdown, looking after a baby, your body still healing from giving birth, even making sure the dog gets enough exercise.'

'I know Bev. I know. I just - I just think he's struggling. Mentally. He's not been himself for so long. He thinks there's going to be another outbreak, something worse, something bigger than before. He's spending a small fortune at the supermarket and then spends all of his time down in that basement.'

Bev sucked her teeth and leant back in her chair. 'Dat man don't know how good he got it wid you.' Out came the accent.

'I don't think I could take another lockdown.'

Bev waved her index finger to dismiss the notion. 'It'll be over soon. The vaccine will have been given to everyone by next year, then there'll never be any need for another one. As for another outbreak? Pffft. Just a load of scare- mongering if you ask me. He probably read it on the damn internet, in some 'dumb mutha fucka' chat room.'

'I hope you're right; I thought the same.' Anna looked nervously over her shoulder, as if making sure she wasn't being watched. 'Then I read this.' She pulled out a newspaper that had been folded and stuffed under a heap of magazines on the coffee table. Bev picked it up and snapped it open.

The headline printed in block capitals across the front page read:

DEADLY STRAIN OF VIRUS HEADING FOR ENGLAND!

The article told of a new strain of virus that showed early characteristics of Ebola, with a much faster rate of infection and a mortality rate far worse than anything the world had ever seen. Cases had been confirmed as close as Europe and two unconfirmed cases in London and the Midlands.

'It's bullshit,' Bev said confidently. 'Scare-mongering to get us all to stay in. I wouldn't lose sleep over it.'

'Wish I had sleep to lose,' Anna said, nodding towards Joy who reached out and grabbed a tiny fist full of Anna's lip.

They both laughed.

'You'll be fine. You've got this little wonder, and a great helper in Mikey. My house is always there if you need a place to go. I'll give you a key now. Just say the word.'

'Thanks. I might take you up on it. I'll let you know.' Anna chewed her lip and looked back out at Graham playing with Mikey. 'I think I owe him a couple more days. See if he can turn things around.'

'You wanna see if things get back to normal on their own, huh?'

'Normal feels like a million years ago. We haven't had sex in..' - she tilted her head as she tried to figure it out - 'you know what, I can't even remember. It's been that long. He just doesn't look after himself. Hardly ever showers, doesn't shave, spray deodorant, exercise. He used to be so fit and healthy and now it's like he's an old man.'

Bev reached out and held Anna's hand.

'Has he hit you again?'

'He never hit me, Bev. I don't want you to think that of him. Sometimes, it just feels like he will. Like he's just one movement away from doing it. It feels like he can't stand me sometimes, like being in the same room as me and breathing the same air is offensive to him. I can't take it anymore.'

'You can't live like this Anna. It's not healthy, for you *or* the kids.'

'I know. I think I will take that key.' Anna dabbed at her eyes as tears began to gather and fall down her cheeks. Bev said nothing. She reached down into her purse, a Gucci or Armani thing, worth more than all of Anna's wardrobe put together. She pulled out a set of keys, pushed each one round until she found her spare, worked it off the key ring and handed it to Anna who put it in between the pages of one of the magazines.

Anna and Bev both sipped on their coffee, which had gone cold but was still drinkable.

Joy blew some raspberries, which drew the attention of both Anna and Bev.

'You know his dad died of it?' Anna said, now looking back out at Graham. He was drenched, his hair was slapped against his forehead and he was laughing. The smile on his face looked wrong, and the sound instantly filled Anna's mind with memories of all the good times they'd had together.

'Oh shit, I'm so sorry. When was this?'

'Just before Joy was born. He was all alone which makes it so much worse. I know Graham carries around so much guilt for not seeing him more. But we were shielding, I was pregnant, and we couldn't take the risk.'

'That is just awful. This damn virus has taken so much. Don't go thinking that gives him an excuse for the way he be treating you.' Bev pointed that over-used index finger at Anna with the long pink fingernail pointing towards her.

Anna waved her free hand in front of her face like a fan, as if to blow away the emotion. 'Anyway, look at me bringing the mood down, some "birthday" party. How is your work going? How's Rob?'

'Rob's doing fine, he just works from home all the time now, we've fallen lucky in that regard. I'm able to do some stuff from home, which helps, but I need to be out at meetings.' Bev was a shareholder in a frozen vegetable company that distributed worldwide. 'Speaking of which, my news. You'll have to share my place with Rob and my girls, because I go away tomorrow. Don't be too jealous. It's only in southern Italy!' She pulled her mouth open as if screaming excitedly like a teenager announcing their spring break plans.

'Lucky bitch!' Anna gasped spiritedly.

'I know I am. As much as I love home-schooling,' – she made a gun with her hand, placed it against her temple and pulled an imaginary trigger – 'I am so looking forward to laying on the beach and soaking up the Italian sun.'

'Working, of course.' Anna raised an eyebrow.

'Oh yeah, work, work, work. That's me.' Bev winked.

'Four weeks I'm there.'

'Poor Rob then, stuck with the kids all by himself for four weeks.'

'I know. I took pity on him and arranged for my mother to have them for the last two weeks. Gives him a bit of time to go out and play with his friends. He reckons he's going to take up running again so I bought him some bright orange Nike Airs, not that he'll ever use them. The most running he'll ever do is to the bar before last orders. At least if you're going to be there, the girls will distract Mikey from what's happening at home.'

'That's true. They do get on well those three, don't they?'

Anna glanced back towards Graham; the kids were running around him, firing at each other. Graham was stood motionless, arms by his side, still holding the gun in his hand, looking like some military statue of a fallen hero. He was staring up at the sky, watching the birds fly in expert formations above his head. He looked over his shoulder and their eyes met. His eyes were hard and full of anger. Anna lifted the page of her magazine to check the key was there.

Chapter 7

After the party Beverly got her children in the car and said bye to the Willow family. Through gritted teeth she gave a smile to Graham before hugging Anna and whispering in her ear, 'My house, is your house. Remember that.'

Anna thanked her and stood on the front doorstep waving until Bev had turned out of the drive and onto the road leading back into town. Mikey, who had been stood in front of Anna waving with her, ran back inside. Graham had gone back in before Bev had even turned the key and started her car. Anna stood out there for a moment, enjoying the sweet smell of the pine forest behind the house being blown over on the soft summer breeze that was warm on her skin.

Barney went running down the side of the hedge to the back garden, she could hear his sharp little bark, that sounded quite menacing for such a small and harmless little dog. The sun was glaring down on her, forcing her to squint her eyes against the brightness; the sky was a perfect blue, cloudless and crisp. Surrounded by nothing but fields, the only sounds were of the birds in the trees and the crickets in the long grass fields that flanked the driveway. This had always been a comfort to Anna, for she loved the countryside, and the smell of the clean, unpolluted air. Now though, as Beverly's car drifted out of sight down the winding country road, she felt isolated and alone, and an overwhelming sense of helplessness came over her.

Back inside, Anna set Joy on the floor to play with Mikey whilst she cleaned up the remnants of the party from the kitchen table and sides. There was still plenty of cake left after they'd all had a piece. Anna, wanting to celebrate in style, had taken the opportunity of lockdown being over, to go to the bakery in town first thing that morning and buy a great big chocolate cake that would have fed a party with three times as many people.

She headed into the kitchen to wrap it up and put it away so they could have a piece later, when she walked in and saw Graham sat at the table, forking the cake into his mouth.

Her initial reaction was to say something: *hey, what are you doing? Do you not think the rest of us might have wanted some of that?*

She held her tongue, which in itself was a new thing. That told her more than anything that had happened before how much Graham was having an effect on her. The fact she was being a different person than who she really was when she was around him. Out of (she hated admitting what it was) fear. The thought that she was living in fear of the man she had loved for so many years made her incredibly sad.

Graham plunged the fork into the mound of cake and shoved the chocolate sponge into his mouth in great amounts. Crumbs fell from his partially open mouth and chocolate icing smeared his lips. Anna found she was looking at him in a kind of grotesque fascination, the kind people have at freak shows or at the circus, feeling repulsed by what she was seeing, yet unable to look away. He looked like a patient at an olden day insane asylum; his long drawn, tired features and scraggy hair added to his lack of dignity.

He dropped the fork into the mess of cake. He'd left half of it, unfortunately it was the lower half. He had eaten his way through the top layer with the chocolate icing and marshmallows stuck on top, and left the dry sponge at the base. He wiped his mouth with the back of his hand, and then wiped the back of his hand on his jeans. He stood and went over to the fridge where he pulled out a bottle of beer.

'Did you enjoy that?' she said.

He pried the metal cap from the bottle with his teeth, then tossed the cap onto the worktop so it skittered towards the sink. 'The cake or the party?' he said, then began pouring beer into his mouth.

'Either.' She moved over to the table.

The tap in the kitchen sink was dripping, it made a metallic *dink* as the drop of water hit a pan that sat waiting to be washed.

'Cake was OK. A bit dry. The party was fun, it was nice to spend a little time with Mikey. You were right.'

She was stunned into a momentary silence at how normal he sounded compared to the state of his appearance. 'Good. That's really good, Graham.'

'Yeah, it is.' He looked to have been heading straight for the basement but now turned back towards Anna at the dining table. 'You know, I am sorry for the way I've been lately. I know I've been aggressive at times. But you know it's not me. Don't you?'

Anna nodded. She felt as though she'd been hit with something out of the blue with no word of warning. Things had been so bad for so long, could he really have changed in a day? Maybe lock down being lifted was all it took. His paranoia about an impending outbreak of a mutated disease seemed to have left his mind.

'Good. Because I know maybe I've, "not been myself lately",' he said with a smile that seemed sly and mocking, using his fingers as air quotes. 'But I think we *all* need to work on ourselves a little after lockdown.' He pointed at Anna's belly and smiled again.

The kitchen tap dripped.

Dink. Dink. Dink.

Suddenly Anna felt vulnerable again, and nervous. Graham had his head bent slightly and he looked at her with a menacing stare. 'Should you need me; I'll be in the basement.' He turned and slowly walked down the stairs, whistling a Rolling Stones tune Anna couldn't remember the title of.

When he was gone, she pulled out a chair and sat. Her hands and knees were shaking and her breath was short. Had he heard? Was he listening to her and Bev's conversation the entire time? If so, what would he do to stop her going? Would he hurt her? Hurt the children? Her mind was running with a thousand different scenarios when she looked at the stack of magazines and the day's newspaper.

The paper was gone, but the magazines were still there. She grabbed the one that she had slid the key into and flicked through the pages. Her heart fluttered in her chest when she didn't immediately find the key. She turned the magazine over on its side and shook it, flapping the pages open, and waited for the clang of metal on the table when the key dropped out. It didn't fall.

The tap in the kitchen kept dripping, the droplets seemed to be falling faster.

Dink dink dink dink

She must have got the wrong magazine; she worked her way through the stack of four magazines and found nothing.

'Come on come on come on.'

Dinkdinkdinkdink

Panicking, she flung them on the floor and began wildly ripping through them, tears welling in her eyes, on the verge of hysterics as she realised, he *had* heard them. He had found the key and taken it downstairs.

She sat on the kitchen floor; her trembling hands covered her mouth and genuine fear gripped her throat. Graham always told her she had a tendency to get ahead of herself, jump to conclusions: *get the wrong end of the stick,* as he would say.

She tried to calm herself down. Tried to think of reasonable reasons why he would have taken the key.

Maybe he just found the key and thought it was one of ours that we'd lost? It did look similar to our front door key.

He's taken it down and put it in his drawer with the other spare and random keys we have kicking around?

She knew it was none of those. She knew he had found out she was planning on leaving him and he was putting a stop to it without coming out and saying it.

She had managed to bring herself round, her heart was calming and she got to her feet and began collecting the dishes. She turned on the tap and began to fill the sink, glad to be rid of that *dink* sound from the dripping tap. She washed the pots and thought of the look on Graham's face, how he could smile and yet look so intimidating and unnerving. The way he had looked down at her stomach when he'd said, "*We all need to work on ourselves after lockdown.*" The Graham she had married would never have been so awful. He was a bully. That was what he had turned into, a nasty, evil, schoolyard bully.

'Mum? Can we have some more cake yet? Mikey called from the living room.

Anna turned her head and looked at the destroyed pile of chocolatey mess Graham had left on the table. She walked over and picked it up, then carried it over to the bin. She flipped the lid and dropped the cake into it.

'Sorry love. It's gone bad,' she called back.

It's all gone bad.

Chapter 8

*July 14*th

During lockdown, Anna had made good use of her time by learning how to knit and crochet. She'd spent a lot of her latter pregnancy stages in bed keeping rested. The way the hospitals were, the last thing she needed to do was to have a fall and need to be rushed in. The risk of catching the virus was too great, not to mention terrifying for her unborn baby. The last four months of her pregnancy had been spent making baby blankets, multi-coloured rainbow ones with matching hats, booties and scratch mittens.

Turned out she had a natural talent for it, if she did say so herself. No one had seen her work to judge it (yet) but she was quite convinced, when holding a finished piece up in the mirror, that she would easily pay money for it if she found it in a shop. The stitch was strong and professional, each loop identical. She had actually been quite proud of herself. She'd never put her hand to making anything before, for the same reason she could never get into reading novels of any great length: she didn't feel she had the time.

That was something lockdown had given everyone.

Time.

In lockdown she'd had time to learn more about her husband and her son then she ever would have without it. Being stuck in a house with the same people twenty-four hours a day meant you get to know things you would have otherwise missed. Like the way Graham picked his nose when he thought no one was looking, and knew all the words to Little Mix's Black Magic. She thought Mikey must be the class clown at school, all he wanted to do was play and laugh, he had Anna in hysterics with his impression of his head teacher

Mr. Silence, who had a great slug of a moustache and an unfortunate lisp that made him spit whenever he tried to say anything with too many S's.

Anna was sat on the sofa, Joy to her side, sleeping peacefully in the Moses basket. Anna had the TV on, but only for the background noise; nothing important or interesting was on but Joy slept better when it was on. Anna was twiddling her fingers, wanting to go upstairs to her craft room and crack on with her latest blanket.

She decided to go on and do it, figuring if Joy woke up, it wouldn't be too hard to get her back to sleep.

The headlights shone in the front room window as Graham turned into the drive. He hadn't told Anna he was leaving; she only knew he had when she heard the truck's engine fire up and speed out of the driveway.

She could hear him outside, his footsteps on the gravel walking round to the back of the truck and the boot door being dropped down. The hinges were old and rusty so they let out a loud whine as it opened and closed. He started grunting with great effort; clattering noises came from outside that sounded like metal clashing on metal. She jumped up and went to the window. He had parked the back end of the truck so it was out of view. Whatever he was unloading, he was taking straight into the basement from the outside hatch round the side of the house.

In normal circumstances, she would have gone out and asked him what he was doing; she might have even offered him a hand. She decided to leave him to it. She gently picked Joy up from the sofa; the dummy in her mouth started moving back and forth as she suckled from being disturbed. Anna carefully took her upstairs and into her craft room.

Anna checked on Mikey before getting settled with the new blanket she had started a few days before. She found she was now craving sitting down and getting on with her crochet in the same way she imagined a crack addict would crave a pipe. When the lockdown had become exceptionally tedious, she found that sitting and mindlessly crocheting passed the time and cleared her mind. Mikey was fine, Barney was curled up beside him while he was playing on his game with a zombie-like expression on his face that mirrored the zombies he was killing on his TV screen. She asked him if he was OK and if he needed anything and was answered with a: 'huh? Nah.'

She placed the Moses basket on the floor beside her chair; with Joy now peacefully sleeping, all it had taken was the gentle rocking motion of her being carried upstairs to send her back off. Anna grabbed her wool and crochet hooks and slumped in her chair, possibly the comfiest chair she had ever purchased, it seemed to suck her in and wrap her in cotton wool, taking away all the aches and pains that stung her lower back after a day of housework.

She hooked the wool and threaded it through the loop, wrapped it round, swooped it round the hook once more, threaded it back, looped it again. It was repetitive; she could see why it wasn't for everybody, but she found it therapeutic. She wondered if she would have made it through these lockdowns with her sanity still intact, were it not for the crochet to retreat to when things got tough. There were always tough times, of course there were, there were tough times before the pandemic so of course there would be plenty during it.

The blanket was taking shape, this would be her best yet. It started as a square of red, then a border of yellow, then green, then blue, and now she was adding a row of purple. One more row and it would be done. She hoped to get it done by tomorrow night, then she could tuck Joy into her cot with a brand-new bed-time blanket. Made by her own mum.

Anna worked on her blanket for what felt like ten minutes but had actually been over an hour. She finished the row she was working on and put it to one side, ready to carry on the next day. Anna tucked Mikey in and gave Joy a bottle before settling her down in her cot. Joy was in her own room now, much to the anxiety of Anna. She had set up a travel cot in her bedroom so that if Joy cried in the night, she could bring her in with her.

Anna crept out of Joy's room, confident she would sleep for most of the night as she had drunk the whole bottle. She made her way downstairs and sat on the sofa in the living room, turning the TV on and hitting the mute button. The baby monitor was blinking beside her, and Barney, who had tired of watching Mikey kill zombies, curled at her feet. His wiry-haired muzzle nestled into the gap between his two front paws.

Anna had little or no interest in TV these days, but it felt wrong somehow, sitting on the sofa and it not being on. All she really wanted to do was sit. She stretched out her hands and clenched them into fists; her fingers felt as though they were getting crotchet-induced arthritis. Her eyes were drifting, the heat of summer was stifling, making her dress cling to her sweat-soaked skin.

The TV was mounted onto the wall above the fire place. She looked into the dark mouth of the hearth; the fire hadn't been lit for months. Inside was so black it looked like an endless pit that could swallow her whole.

That might be easier.

The longer she left it, the harder it was going to be for her to leave. He wouldn't let her go easily. That was becoming more apparent with each passing day. The way he looked at her, the way he spoke to her. He forced himself to smile and play with the children when others were here to see, but Anna knew. The rage inside him was bubbling under the surface. Ready to explode, and God help whoever got in his way when it did.

He had handled the first lockdown so well. If anything, he would tell people he'd *enjoyed* it. At first it was a novelty, like everyone was playing their own role in a Hollywood-end of the world-blockbuster. When the novelty wore off, that's when the loneliness crept in. The isolation became harder to bear, nerves were frayed and tempers rose. Never like this. He had never been so hard and bitter towards her before. He had his friends to bounce off the first time round; everybody needs friends they can vent to about their partners, otherwise no marriage would last because of the pent-up anger that comes from general, everyday annoyances. Graham had cut ties with his friends after his father died.

They didn't care enough. They weren't there for me.

'What were they supposed to do?' Anna would ask him. 'They couldn't leave their homes either, they rang and gave their condolences. There was nothing else they could do.'

Graham responded to this by telling her to *Fuck off*. Anna was stunned into silence when he did. They'd had crossed words before, but never sworn at each other and spoken with such venom. She put it down to grief and forgot about it until it started happening more frequently and then got to the point where they found themselves now. Broken and separate in their own home. One afraid of the other and wanting to leave, but so scared of actually doing it she was sitting in her own living room, with the TV on mute, feeling utterly drained and exhausted, both mentally and physically.

Anna had never liked Graham's friends, womanizing 'lads' who just liked to get drunk every Friday and Saturday night without a care for their own wives, but she wished they were still in contact with Graham now. They would be able to take the sting out of the tail. At least distract him with a few beers so she could slip away and get to Bev's house with Mikey and Joy. That was the goal she had to focus on. If she focused on how things could be easier...or if she did this different...There was nothing else she could do, apart from leave.

'Be brave,' she told herself, 'be brave, and tell him you're leaving. Tonight.' It had to be tonight because Bev was going away in a couple of days and now Anna didn't have the key. Graham might let her go out the door, but he wouldn't help her by giving her the key to her salvation.

Anna turned to look through the kitchen; she stared at the door in there that led down to the basement. When he next came up. That's when she'd do it. That's when she'd tell him she was taking the kids and getting out of here.

She heard a loud shout coming from the basement, which made her give a short yelp and clutch her hand to her chest. She got to her feet, straightened her dress, and moved into the kitchen. She stopped when she heard footsteps thumping hard and fast behind the door. Her heart jolted and the door sprung open. Graham stepped through; his face and hands were covered in black oil smears. A fresh blister had risen on his index finger.

'What are you wearing?' Anna didn't mean to sound judgmental; it just came out that way. He was wearing a dirty vest with the classic Rolling Stones logo on it, the big-lipped mouth with protruding tongue. It looked like it was medium size when he took an extra-large. The bottom of his belly hung under the bottom seam, flopping over the waist band of his jeans.

'It was my dad's. Is that OK with you?' he snapped. She could see his eyes were glistening in the fluorescent kitchen lights.

'I just don't know why you're wearing it. Do you even like the Rolling Stones?'

He huffed. 'Shows how much you know me'.

Anna felt the muscles in her neck and shoulders tighten. There was nothing she could say to him when he was like that, so she walked back into the living room and sat on the edge of the sofa, her hands placed on her lap, knees together, and waited. Mentally preparing herself to tell him.

She heard the familiar rattle of beer bottles clanking together in the fridge as the pack shifted when Graham took one from the bottom of the pile. He walked back in and sat in the armchair. He was staring at Anna. Staring hard and cold; even when he upended his bottle to drink, his eyes were still fixed on her.

Anna opened her mouth to speak when Graham parted the bottle from his lips and said, 'Were you going to tell me?'

'Tell you what, Graham?' She shifted uncomfortably in her seat. A small part of her still hoped he hadn't taken the key and knew she was going to leave. Barney kept his head rested on his front paws but his eyes were looking up at Graham warily.

Graham laughed, the kind of laugh that came just before a revelation of deceit; humourless and harsh.

He reached his hand behind his back and pulled out the key from his back pocket. He held it up; the shiny metal surface sparkled in the light that came from the lamp at the back of the room. 'You were going to leave. Weren't you?'

'Graham...Please, listen,' Anna stuttered.

'You were just going to take *my* kids without telling me, and leave me here, alone. Bev give you a key to her house so you had somewhere to go, huh?' He was snarling, his eyes fixed on hers in an intense stare.

'I *was* going to tell you. I promise -' Anna stood.

'Your promises don't mean shit.' Graham threw the key towards Anna; she yelled out and dodged, lifting her hands instinctively over her face. The key hit the back of the sofa and rested beside her. She looked at it – a voice inside was screaming at her to grab it quickly, but her muscles wouldn't respond. They were stiff with fright. Barney got to his feet and let out a long low growl.

'Graham, we aren't working. You must see that we can't go on like this? We don't even see each other anymore, you're always in the basement. When you come up for food you eat as quick as you can so you can get back down there, you have very little to do with Mikey and you've barely spent a single second with Joy.'

Graham waved a dismissive hand towards her.

'We need time apart, time to clear our heads-'

'You've said all this shit before. You just want to get out and find someone else. Don't you? Admit it!'

Anna looked at him, shocked and hurt. 'Of course not! That's not what this is!'

Graham moved towards her. 'You're a vain, superficial bitch. Yeah, I've put on a few pounds, maybe don't take care of myself like I used to, but I'm still your husband. You should give me more respect.'

'I do respect you -'

'Bollocks! Maybe once, but not anymore,' He started laughing manically; his teeth appeared from behind his hairy lips, yellow and tobacco-stained. 'You think I don't hear you talking with Bev? Telling her how I don't look after myself, don't wear deodorant? You think I don't see the way you look at me like I'm some gross tramp who just walks around *your* house?'

'It's not like that.' Anna started to cry.

'Let me tell you something, sweetheart. You're not exactly as fit as you used to be either. A little bigger around the waist, I see.' He reached out and grabbed her belly, squeezed hard with his thumb and index finger until she cried out and tried to pull his hand away.

She crouched over. Barney started barking at Graham's feet.

'Your arse is spreading too. I see you when you get out the shower and drop the towel, the way your tits swing lower, the way your thighs are covered in cellulite and stretch marks. Do I say anything? Give you dirty looks to make you self-conscious? No. But I'm telling you now.' He leaned in and put his face into hers. Anna cried and continued to try and release his grip on her stomach. 'You fucking disgust me.' He raised his right hand and struck her with an open palm, rocking her head back and sending a bolt of pain across her cheek. He let go of her stomach and pushed her to the sofa.

Anna sobbed, holding one hand over her stomach and the other on her face. Barney stood in front of her, barking and baring his teeth at Graham.

Graham started chuckling; he grabbed his beer and drank it in one swallow.

Whilst Graham's head was leant back, beer pouring down his neck, Anna put her hand on the key beside her and quickly put it behind her back. She sat herself up and got her breath back enough to talk again. 'I'm leaving. I'm taking the kids and I'm getting the hell away from you!'

Graham chewed his lip. He moved the beer bottle from one hand to other, lifted one hand and wiped the wetness from the condensation on his shirt. He closed his eyes and took a deep breath. He held it in for five seconds, then he blew it out and opened his eyes.

He started for the door and stopped at the threshold. He leant against the frame and ran a hand through his hair.

Graham turned back to face her. 'You want to know what I've been doing?'

'What?' She looked at him, confused.

'Downstairs. Do you want to know what I've been doing?' He bit his lip and raised his eyebrows.

She nodded.

'I'm preparing.' He flicked his eyebrows up and smiled.

'For what?'

'For what? she says. For what?' He mimicked her with a high-pitched squealing voice, that only served to embarrass her. 'For that! Are you stupid?' He jabbed his beer bottle towards the TV that was still on mute. The Prime Minister was on again, answering questions about the potential new strain that had been discovered. Then he started moving towards her slowly, slightly crouched to get on her eye level.

'The world is going to be hit by something far worse than anything we have ever seen. I've read all about it on the internet. What we've just been through in the past couple of years was merely a fucking *taste* of what's to come. People will be dropping dead in the street, there will be riots, anarchy, looting and murdering, raping, you name it. People are going to lose their minds and when they do –' He let out a low, rumbling laugh and poked at her forehead with his finger – 'you, and your simple little mind, won't have to worry because muggins 'ere will have taken care of all of us. I have stored enough food down there for us to last over two years, given the correct rationing. There are a million other things I have been working on, and looking into. But you don't need to know about that until it happens. Which it will.'

Anna shifted on the sofa, wincing against the pain radiating from her stomach. 'Graham. We won't be staying in this house for the next two years. The stuff on the internet is bullshit. Written by some angry-at-the-world arsehole living in his parent's basement. You have to accept that I will be leaving with the kids. We need time apart.'

Permanently, she thought, but dared not say out loud.

'You think any of that will matter? You think you'll be able to cope when shit really starts to go down? When the world falls to pieces and people are trying to break into the shitty little house the council gives you?'

'Graham. It won't happen.'

'You really think I'm going to let you break our family apart, when all this is going to happen? You say it's bullshit and, my God, I hope you're right. But if it's not, and you're alone with two kids when desperate men are ripping at the door, breaking in through the windows to fuck that tight little ass of yours, you'll wish you'd never left me. You'll be fucking *praying* that I'll come and save you then.'

'Graham, you're scaring me.' His face was in hers now; she recoiled, trying to get away from the smell of oil, beer and stale cigarette smoke. She moved a hand to Barney, who was now vocalising a defensive rumbling growl at Graham.

'Good!' his face shot into a wide psychopathic smile. 'That's good, darling, you should be scared.' He grabbed the back of her head and pulled her closer to him.

God he was strong; he might have put on weight but he still had a raw power in him. 'Things *are* going to get scarier, but that's OK. You have me, and I'll make sure no one can get in and hurt us.' He kissed her. She didn't want to kiss him back, but that didn't matter, he pressed so hard into her she would never have been able to pull away. He let go of her head and moved back from her. 'I'm going back downstairs now. Should you need me, don't come down.' He winked and licked his lips before straightening up. He was about to leave the room when he stopped and turned back. 'Almost forgot.' He bent down towards Anna, looked her in the eye and reached behind her, he grabbed something there, then when his hand reappeared, it was in a clenched fist.

Anna's eyes closed in despair and her heart sank.

Graham's fingers opened like the petals of a poisonous flower, inside was Bev's key. He smiled and put it in his pocket. 'You try to leave me... I'll fucking kill you.' His smile held no humour in it. He was serious and she knew it. He turned and ran back down to the basement.

Anna started to cry. She did so quietly, not wanting him to hear her and come back. Barney rested his long-haired head on her lap.

Chapter 9

July 15th

The next day Anna woke early; the sun was just rising so she knew it was a little after half-past six. She made a fresh bottle for Joy, who was nestled safely in the crook of her arm. Anna mixed the milk powder into the bottle, shook it and placed it in a bowl of cold water to cool. Barney was circling her feet and scratching at the back door, so she let him out and sat at the dining table. Joy was wriggling and cooing happily in her arms. Anna stifled a yawn and felt the pulling pain of her jaw where it had begun to swell.

She picked up the bottle and splashed some milk from the teat onto her wrist to check the temperature. She did this three times until it was right, and then she gave it to Joy, who reached for it desperately. Joy had slept from one A.M. last night, the longest she had done since they brought her home.

Progress.

Still, six-thirty in the morning was too early for any normal human to be up and out of bed. She glanced to the door that led to the basement. The door itself had been made of solid oak, about two-hundred years ago by the looks of it. She was sure that when it had first been made it would have been a fine piece of craftsmanship, now it was just a battered lump of wood with a handle that filled a hole. She could hear the faint clangs and the unmistakeable sound of a power drill coming from down there. Graham hadn't come to bed. She was nervous he would try, but after last night, she was glad he hadn't. She went back to her thought of how six-thirty was still too early for normal people to be up, and wondered what time Graham had woken or if he had even slept at all. He can't have found anywhere comfortable to sleep down there, she thought, in the cold basement with nothing but a beaten old chair and concrete floors.

His speech last night had frightened her, not because what he spoke of could be true, but because it was so apparent that he believed it. These websites, chat forums or whatever they were, were no good for anyone. A bunch of lonely idiots making shit up as they went along.

'The vaccine has hidden microchips'

'The virus is just the government's way of culling the population'.

Get a grip.

The thing that angered Anna the most about it, was that people *believed* them. People lapped it up, especially those who struggled with mental health issues. It seemed easier to find these conspiracies as a way of explaining the horror that was happening in the world, because something like this couldn't just *happen,* could it. Someone had to be responsible, someone had to be blamed.

Sadly, she was coming to realise that Graham had been sucked into it; his mental health was fragile at best. It was something he was going to have to figure out on his own. After last night, she couldn't stay in this house with him. It was all she could do not to grab the kids and run away now.

You try and leave me...I'll fucking kill you.

It wasn't just the words he'd used; it was the look in his eyes when he'd said it. The way they seemed to vibrate in their sockets as he looked down at her. They were the wide and unblinking eyes of a madman. He meant every word. That she believed, and it terrified her.

Chapter 10

Mikey was outside playing with Barney, throwing sticks, getting Barney to bring it back and drop it on the floor so they could do it all again. He was having fun, that was the main thing and it was good exercise for him and the dog. Getting used to repetition was something everyone had become accustomed to, some even found fun in the mundane things. Like throwing a stick to be brought back so you could throw it again. And again.

Joy was having a nap, she had been awake all morning playing on her play mat by the fireplace, shaking her rattles and chewing her teething toys relentlessly.

Anna, who was struggling to do anything around the house because she found herself in a constant state of anxiety, decided to let herself have a moment in the craft room. She could get halfway round her blanket with a fresh line before having to go make lunch and then get Joy up. That way she could at least do something productive whilst working on a plan to get herself and the children out of the house without Graham knowing. She had rung Beverly. Not once or twice, but every time she found herself out of Graham's ear shot, she dialled and got no answer. She hoped Bev hadn't gone to Italy early. She needed Bev to be there now that Graham had discovered and stolen the key. Rob would be in – how much Rob knew was the problem. If Bev hadn't explained things clearly enough, Rob might let them in and then call Graham and give him a heads up that his wife and kids had turned up out of the blue, just in case he was worried.

She tried to calm herself, she couldn't think straight when she felt like this. The anxiety was making her feel as though she was drowning, like she had a belt strapped tight against her chest and someone was pushing down on her ribs crushing her lungs.

Concentrate.

After a few deep breaths that made her feel a little light-headed, she picked up her wool and crochet hook and started. She was on red, finishing it the way it started; she found that it made it more aesthetically pleasing that way. While she was hooking and looping, her heart started to slow and the belt across her chest loosened enough so she could breathe easier. Her mind was beginning to drift into a thoughtless, empty dream where nothing would bother her, where no problems or troubles existed. Then she looked at the crochet hook in her hand. It had a larger handle then most, with an inscription that said, *'TO MY DARLING WIFE, ANNA, GET CRAFTING'.*

As soon as she had shown promise that she actually had a skill in her new-found hobby, Graham had researched and bought her this thoughtful gift. Every time she had looked at it, it made her smile, now she just wanted to cry. He had always been so thoughtful, so selfless and generous. It was as if he felt no love for her anymore, he was consumed by the idea that the world was going to end or the zombie apocalypse would kill them all. She shivered as she thought there was more chance Graham would be the death of them all.

'Mum! I'm hungry!' Mikey shouted from the bottom of the stairs.

Anna cringed in frustration. Then Joy started crying from the bedroom.

'Sorry!' Mikey shouted back up.

Anna put her blanket back on her desk, a desk that was covered in a shop's worth of crafting paraphernalia that was commonplace in any crafter's tool box. She took a deep breath to calm the frustration of now having to make lunch with a baby that should have been sleeping soundly for at *least* the next forty-five minutes.

'It's ok love. I'll be down in a minute,' She put the crochet hook down on the desk with the inscription facing up. *'GET CRAFTING'*.

Maybe later.

Chapter 11.

Mikey sat at the table, knife and fork in hand as he eagerly awaited his food. 'What we having mum?' he asked through his long blonde hair that kept falling in front of his face, forcing him to flick it back behind his shoulders. He had dreams of becoming a rock star, so allowing his hair to grow long was a natural first step in that process.

Anna removed a tray from the oven and turned to show Mikey what was in store for him. There were six fat sausages sizzling on the grill tray, cooked perfectly, the juices running and hissing at the bottom of the pan.

'ooo, sithaling sosageth, my favourite,' he said with his popular impression of his lisp-afflicted head teacher. Anna laughed. She plated up three of the sausages on his plate, along with a fried egg, baked beans and a slice of toast with lashings of butter.

'Wow, what a lunch. I'll be stuffed up to me neck when I finish this!'

'Stuffed up to *my* neck, you mean. Not *me* neck.' She looked at him smugly, correcting his grammar. She felt a little bit like a teacher now, since she had done so much teaching at home over the past year or so.

'Y'know what I mean,' he quipped and dug straight into his sausages like a boy that had been deprived of proper food for weeks. Anna watched him eat with a smile on her face. He was going to grow up to be a big strong man with the world at his feet.

Joy was back on the play mat, enthusiastically hitting the toys suspended from the foam arch over her head; she had still shown no interest in crawling so Anna was confident Joy would be fine lying there whilst she got her jobs done. Barney was by Anna's feet patiently waiting for the sausage that was surely coming his way if he was good.

Mikey was growing up quick; he had recently discovered music and picked up the guitar. (Another logical step to becoming a rock star.) He was getting good and Anna wanted to do everything she could to encourage him to achieve his dream; Graham, on the other hand, didn't want him to dream too high, or waste his time working towards an unachievable goal. Anna said to him, 'If you can't even dream, what's the point in doing anything?'. Graham had waved it off and, in the end, agreed to at least feign support for him. It was hard to keep Graham on side, what with the relentless repetition of Deep Purple's 'Smoke on the Water' riff screeching through the house. Whenever he played his guitar, the sound seemed to travel all through the house, from the top floor to the basement, so there was no escape. After months of excruciating wails of distorted guitar being played, badly, Mikey grasped it. Now it was a pleasure to hear him. Anna would even put in requests for him to play. He rarely accepted her requests though, he thought her taste in music was rubbish, or 'lame' as Mikey would say.

Mikey put his cutlery down on the plate in the shape of a cross; he had eaten the whole lot. Anna had a couple of eggs, scrambled in a pan. She grabbed a spoon and scraped a helping of butter from the tub and was about to add it to the eggs when she stopped. Her free hand moved to the purple bruise that had appeared on her belly from Graham pinching her, and she put the spoon down, deciding to have the eggs as they came, with nothing added. She sat next to Mikey and put a forkful in to her mouth and chewed the squishy bland lumps of egg and swallowed them down.

The news was on in the back ground; she tried her best not to listen to it, it all seemed to be doom and gloom on there nowadays. Her ears pricked up when the Prime Minister, reading from a typed-up piece of paper, gave an update on the new strain that had been reported in the paper. He said how it *was* worse than the previous strains they had encountered and that the government would keep the public updated as soon as they knew more, before again reassuring everyone to carry on as normal now most of the restrictions had been lifted, but to remain cautious. And then he gave a speech about solidarity and the good old British resilience that had seen everyone through these past couple of years. A chill ran through her spine and she moved closer to hear what else he had to say. Graham's words from the night before were ringing in her ears and suddenly carried more weight.

Over the past couple of years, she had seen the Prime Minister giving these speeches on the news more often than she would have liked. There was something in his face, the way the lines at the side of his eyes had grown deeper and more pronounced; the bags under his eyes were a deathly shade of black despite the make-up put on to try and cover them. Most of all, what she noticed about him was the expression on his face that contradicted his message of calm and national solidarity. It was the look of fear that had washed over him, a look that couldn't be covered up, no matter how much make-up they slapped on him.

That fear she saw on him was projected through the TV and into her. it crept up her spine and became physically visible from the goose bumps on her arm and the hairs standing up on the back of her neck. She didn't believe the rantings of the crazy people on the internet. She refused to believe it.

It couldn't be much worse than the last time. Could it?

Chapter 12

Graham finally emerged from his pit, still wearing that hideous vest that was too tight for him. Anna kept eye contact with him; the last thing she wanted was for him to see her staring at it, noticing the smears of dirt on it and the way his flabby belly hung from underneath it like a turtle's head peering out of its shell.

'Nice to see you up here with us.' Anna greeted him with a smile, the way her mother had taught her. Her face ached and the small lump on her jawline made her smile seem distorted. *This is how to greet your husband. Big wide smile, let him see those teeth.*

He looked towards her; she almost gasped when she saw how pale he was. His eyes had turned into black holes, his lips seemed blue, and the black grease stains smeared on his face were made blacker by the whiteness of his skin.

'Did you hear it?' he said.

'Hear what?' she said dozily, still staring at the death-like features on his face.

'The news, the Prime Minister was just on, talking about the mutated strain.' He lunged towards her and squeezed her arms tight. 'It's happening Anna. Quicker than I thought but it's happening. You can't ignore it anymore; you have to listen to me.'

Anna choked on her words as she tried to speak. She thought he might have made one last-ditch attempt to convince her to stay without threats, to apologise for hitting her but it was as if what had happened last night wasn't important. She supposed if he really believed what he was saying about this virus then why would it matter, when the end of the world was coming. 'I saw it.'

His eyes lit up with delight. 'So, you know? So now you finally know it's happening. Anna, this makes me so glad.

I didn't think you would ever believe me, but now you have seen it on the news you know I'm not crazy. You'll know now that everything I've done is for us.'

'Graham, we can't stay here.'

'We can,' he interrupted. 'I have a plan. I've worked it all out. We'll be fine, I promise.' He started pacing the room, running both of his hands back and forth through his hair; his eyes were wide and his face started to flush with colour.

She sighed and wiped her hand over her mouth, trying to hide her frustration. She wanted to scream at him, tell him he was crazy for thinking things were going to happen the way he thought they were, but held her tongue. The lump on her face began stinging and throbbing as a timely reminder.

He stopped pacing and stood with wide eyes looking out of the living room window at his truck that was still parked on a slant in the driveway.

'I'm going to do another run to the supermarket later,' he said, looking at Anna now. He moved towards her and carried on talking, but the way his eyes darted around made her think he was talking to himself more than he was to her. 'I should have enough provisions. But you can never have too many. Yes, get more. Lots more. Can't get caught out. Can't go out once it's started. That's how it'll get you.' He walked around the room in sharp bursts like he knew what he was doing, then forgot and stood still, then remembered, then forgot again.

He held a finger up to Anna and shook it. Sweat was pouring down his face and soaking into his beard. 'We can do this. We'll survive it, I swear to God Anna, when this thing hits and everyone is running around like maniacs desperate for a scrap of food, we'll be safe and sound in here.' He shot towards her and clutched her arms tight. Barney came into the room from the kitchen and growled low and protectively.

'I. Will. Save us.' His voice quivered with what sounded like excitement. The adrenaline was making his

71

whole-body shake. He let go and stood back a few paces. Barney came in and stood in front of Anna. Graham stroked at his chin and looked off in thought. 'I need to get ready before I go for more supplies. Everything must be checked and double checked!' he shouted and ran for the basement. He went flying down the stairs; his feet hitting the steps made a sound like rolling thunder that was over in a second before a door slammed.

Anna sat back on the sofa and breathed out a long, tired breath. Had he gone completely mad? Had this time in isolation driven him beyond the edge of sanity and into the darkness of complete mental destruction?

Then she realised she had her window. When he went to the super- market, she could pack a bag for her, Mikey and Joy. If there was enough time, she could get them all in the car and get away before Graham got back and realised. The last thing she wanted was for him to come home and for her to be trying to get the kids and bags in the car. God knows what he would do if he found them like that.

She reached for her phone and pulled up Bev's number. She hit the call button and waited for Bev to answer. Praying that this time she would answer.

'Hey you! So sorry I missed your calls, it has been mental here today trying to get sorted for my flight.' She sounded happy and excited about packing for a holiday, and who could blame her.

Anna had to calm down. The sound of Beverly's voice made her feel a lump in her throat and she thought if she tried to speak, she would just cry instead.

'Anna? Are you OK? Is it Graham?' Bev's voice now sounded grave and serious.

'I need help. I'm doing it, Bev. I'm leaving him. Me and the kids, we just need a place to stay, just for a little while,' Anna said, her voice little more than a whisper. She looked over her shoulder at the basement door, terrified that Graham would walk through it and hear her.

'What did I say? Anytime. You have my key, don't you?'

Anna was about to speak and tell her everything when she heard a noise coming from behind her in the kitchen. A low creaking sound like rusty hinges. She turned and looked behind her and saw nothing.

'Anna? You there? I'm getting on a plane, like now, my flight got bumped up.'

Anna tried to shake herself back to the conversation and what she had planned to say but the words wouldn't come out. Finally, she said: 'Yeah, I'm here. Will Rob be in if I need to come round?'

'Yeah, he's there, should be there the whole time. Kids aren't at school and he's working from home so it's not a problem. Remember: my house your house.'

'How much does he know?' Anna asked. She chewed her fingernails nervously. A habit that had always infuriated Graham.

'I didn't tell him much, or what Graham has been like, but told him not to be too surprised if you turned up with the kids.'

Anna breathed a sigh of relief and thanked Bev.

'If for whatever reason you don't need to come, then that's fine, I won't judge, or will try not to judge,' Bev laughed and Anna smiled a little. 'But on my way back from the airport I'll be swinging round to see you, OK? I'll call you when I land back in England and you can get the kettle on. Deal?'

'Sounds great.'

After they had said their goodbyes Anna stood, clutching the phone to her chest, feeling a mixed sense of relief and dread. She was going to get out and she had somewhere to go when she did. Looking over her shoulder, she was sure the broken and beaten door that covered the descending stairs into the basement was swaying slightly on its hinges.

Chapter 13

The kitchen was quiet aside from the ticking that came from the clock on the wall, the one shaped like a dog with the clockface on its belly. Its tail served as the pendulum, swinging from side to side. (A present from Graham, he liked to buy everyone a silly present for Christmas, '*just a bit of fun*' he would say). Truth was, she loved that clock. Even more than the *real* present he had got her, some ugly earrings that she knew cost more than she would ever pay. She had smiled though, and said they were lovely.

That was basically the summary of their marriage. Graham tried to please her, but it was the stuff he did naturally that brought her the most joy. The way he would do the majority of the night feeds when Mikey was a baby, just so she could get some 'well-earned sleep' as he used to say, smiling at her. He had always had a smile on his face; it didn't matter if it was straight after a hard day at work, or three o'clock in the morning feeding the baby. That smile was what had made her fall for him in the first place. The way he would make a stupid corny joke and laugh at it before he got to the punchline. She cracked up every time because of that cheeky smile. She didn't need diamonds or gold, or fancy designer handbags. Although she appreciated the effort, all she wanted was for everyone to be happy. They were happy, really happy, for a long time. Anna, sat looking down at Joy whilst she drank her bottle before bed, felt an extreme sadness as she thought of those happier times. A tear fell down her cheek, which she wiped away, and forced a smile so Joy wouldn't catch on to her depression. She tried to piece it all together, figure out when it had all started to turn from heaven into hell. She supposed it didn't matter now. There was no going back.

Joy finished the last ounce of milk and her eyes began to close after a short battle to keep them open. Anna put the bottle down on the side and took Joy upstairs ready for bed. Mikey was still playing on his Xbox; she could see his face lit up from the blue flashing lights coming from the TV screen. In Joy's room, Anna bent and placed Joy carefully in the cot and stepped backwards quietly.

She closed the door and when she heard the silent click of the latch catching, she let out a big breath of air she had been holding. She rested her forehead against the door and took a few deep breaths. This was it. Graham would be leaving to go to the shop soon. Get the last of the 'supplies' he needed. She could pack their bags, and if there was enough time, get them all out into the car and drive to Bev's. The adrenaline was already coursing through her. She felt excited and terrified all at the same time.

You try and leave me...I'll fucking kill you.

Graham's last words on the subject. She couldn't risk finding out if he truly meant it. She thought at the time he had meant it, and every time his pale, uncaring face had entered into the fore of her mind and replayed the memory, she believed it all over again. She didn't know what she would do if he hurt one of the children.

Stop it. Don't think about that!

She scolded herself. If she let herself think about the most horrible of scenarios, she'd never get out for fear of them becoming reality. She headed for the steps and stopped before being able to walk down them. Joy had started crying, the kind of cry that wouldn't stop after a minute or so. Anna walked back in and saw Joy, red-faced and flailing her arms like something was horribly wrong. Anna wondered if all the tension she was feeling was being projected on to Joy. Children are so perceptive.

'Hey sweetheart. Come on. Let's go back downstairs and get settled again.' Joy stopped crying as soon as she felt her mother's soft touch, and Anna lifted her out of the cot. She held her firmly and comfortingly against her chest and headed back downstairs. After she had made Joy a bit of extra milk, she sat on the sofa and rocked her. Graham would be up any minute to leave and go to the shop. If he had heard her on the phone talking to Bev earlier or not, his belief that something terrible was on the precipice would drive his need to get more supplies, stronger than the need to stay and stop Anna from leaving. This was it. Tonight was the night she set them all free.

Chapter 14

'What did you do?' Anna said.

Graham sat against the wall screaming, with his bloodied hands curled in front of his face. The blood which covered his visor must have blocked his vision, causing him to drive the truck erratically into the driveway. Where he had fallen back against the wall and slid to the floor, a streak of blood had smeared over the white paintwork. Blood from his clothes had dripped onto the tiled floor of the hallway, forming small puddles around him. He looked as though he had been in a massacre. He wouldn't stop screaming.

Anna looked towards the stairs when she heard Joy start crying. Barney came to the top of the stairs, yapping and barking as loud as he could. The cacophony was unbearable; it seemed to blur all of Anna's senses, leaving her on the verge of hysterics, not knowing what to do or who to help first. She looked at Graham and started walking towards him. His arms and vest were covered in big red handprints of blood.

'STAY AWAY!' He held out a hand, gesturing for her not to come any closer. 'It's happening... It's all over the news.' He was breathless, gasping for air in the middle of his sentences. 'The mutant strain...it's here.'

'Graham, you're scaring me.' Anna began to cry. 'What happened?'

'No time. I need to shower, get this disease off me. Stay in the kitchen, don't turn on the TV. And DO NOT go on your phone. Do you understand?' She could see his eyes through the visor of his mask. She knew many things about her husband; one was how she could tell when he was lying from the way his eyes looked over to the left when he spoke. He wasn't lying now. His eyes were dead straight and full of terror. Joy was still screaming upstairs.

'I won't. I'll get the bleach.' She didn't have time to think. How could she have been so nonchalant about this? She should have been wary as soon as she heard the Prime Minister warning about the mutant strain on the news.

'Dad?' Mikey shouted from the top of the stairs, seeing his dad covered in blood on the hallway floor. Mikey started to run towards him; his first thought was that his dad needed his help.

'Stay away son! Go back to your room! NOW!' Mikey stopped, and tears of confusion and fear welled in his eyes. He looked at his dad and then back to his mum. Anna nodded desperately.

Mikey ran back to his room. Barney ran down the stairs and started barking at Graham, his fur standing on end. His muzzle twisted in a snarl.

Graham kicked him away with his shoe. 'Get the fucking dog before it gets infected,' he said, getting to his feet. Anna pushed the dog into the living room.

'I need to get Joy first.' Without waiting for Graham's reply, she ran upstairs and got Joy from the cot. Her face was red and her tongue flapped wildly in her mouth as she screamed at the top of her lungs. When Anna came down, she ran into the kitchen with Joy, covering Joy's mouth with her hand and turning away from Graham, if that blood really was infected, she didn't want Joy getting anywhere near it.

After setting Joy down on the play mat in the living room, she walked back out into the hall and watched as Graham made his way up the stairs. She followed him, careful not to touch any of the blood that was smeared on the banister. Despite how chaotic and frantic Graham was, she noticed how he made every effort to keep from spreading the blood further up the stairs. He went through the hallway and into the shower.

Anna didn't want to look as though she was spying on him, so she stayed in the hallway and only peered around the door frame to watch him. He didn't know she was there; she thought, but she didn't know that for sure, but that was the impression she got. He was so manic, so...desperate. He threw all his clothes in the bin except his vest – that he threw into the bath and doused in soap and hot water. He jumped in the shower and turned to face the open door. Anna gasped and pulled herself out of sight. When she dared to look again, she saw that the visor on the gas mask had steamed up, so he wouldn't have been able to see a thing. He was frantically scrubbing his skin with an exfoliating sponge. He lathered it with soap and scrubbed every inch of his body. Hard.

The scrubbing stopped suddenly and he inspected the skin on his arm and chest as best he could, leaning in closely to be able to see through the condensation-covered mask. He'd got all the blood off his skin, but he looked unsure if it was enough. He jumped out of the shower, the water still running, and grabbed the bleach from the side of the toilet. He took the bottle into the shower and started pouring it all over himself. Anna covered her mouth with her hand, the smell was so strong. It took everything she had not to retch when Graham grabbed the exfoliator and scrubbed and scrubbed until his skin was red raw.

'Argh!' He stopped and flinched a hand to his left-hand side. When he pulled it back, Anna saw the red patch on his ribs where the skin had been scoured away.

He turned the knob on the shower, stopping the water. The gas mask came off, leaving marks on his face where the rubber seal had pressed tightly against his skin. He threw it into the bath tub with his vest and poured the remainder of the bleach into the water. He grabbed a towel, and dabbed it gently on his skin to dry the water off, Anna winced at the thought that more would peel off when he pulled back the towel.

Having seen enough, Anna walked back towards the stairs where she almost cried out when she saw Mikey standing right behind her, wearing a blue surgical mask.

'Mikey,' she said, trying to usher him back downstairs, 'you can't be up here.'

Mikey said nothing back. Judging by the paleness of his skin, she thought he was most likely in too much shock to form the words. Anna heard Graham step out of the bathroom behind her and run across the hall into the bedroom. He stopped in the threshold and looked towards her and Mikey.

'I need you both to go downstairs, now,' he said in a tone that made it sound more like an order than a request.

Anna nodded – now she was the one too frightened to speak. She turned Mikey around and gently nudged him to get him moving.

'Anna?' Graham called.

Anna looked back at him, he was putting on his baggy joggers and hoody, probably in the hope of keeping the fabric away from the open sore on his ribs.

'Yes, Graham?' She found her voice.

'I'm going to get the hall cleaned. Every last spec of that diseased blood needs to be gone. Keep everyone in the living room until I say.'

Anna nodded. 'Yes, Graham.'

Chapter 15

The blood was smeared on the tiled floor in the hallway, and splashed up the bottom half of the wall where Graham had slid down when he came in.

Graham, now with his gas mask back on and a full disposable suit (he had quite a collection of them in the basement) was scrubbing at the blood with a mixture of bleach, water and soap. Anna watched as he scrubbed relentlessly, trying to ensure he got every last molecule of virus eradicated. The emulsion on the wall scraped away on the coarse sponge, leaving patches of bare plaster that looked like ugly brown scabs.

This would normally concern Anna a great deal; as a very proud home- maker the thought of someone coming and seeing her home in such a state...well she would die of embarrassment.

When all the blood had been cleaned and anything that could be contaminated with the virus was scrubbed to death, they all sat in the living room. It was gloomy and hard to see in there; Graham had drawn the curtains, and refused to turn on the big light, only flicking the switch of the bear lamp in the corner. (Another funny Christmas present.)

Mikey sat close to his mother; he had an arm around her back, his other hand holding hers. She could feel the rapid beating of his heart as he pushed against her. He was petrified, which meant she had to not be, she had to protect him from what was going on as best she could. Joy was asleep in the Moses basket on the other side of Anna. She could have put her upstairs in her cot, but the thought of her being anywhere other than by Anna's side right now was inconceivable.

Graham sat opposite them all; his family were huddled together before him, waiting eagerly and patiently for his word on what to do next. Anna's eyes were fixed on him, she glanced away to look at Mikey and saw he was watching Graham with the same intent. Together, they watched as Graham stalked from one side of the room to the other, twitching at the sides of the curtains to check the outside was clear. The knees of his trousers were wet from scrubbing the floors. Then he sat, wringing his hands together. He looked as though he was developing the words in his head, figuring out a way to tell them what he had seen, what he knew. Suddenly his hands stopped still, his eyes opened wider. Anna's eyes met with his and when she saw the look in them, she held Mikey that little bit tighter.

Chapter 16

'It was...apocalyptic. The most terrifying thing I've ever seen.' He held his hands together in a praying gesture and held them exasperatedly to his face whilst he spoke, as if unable to believe that what he saw was true. 'People were screaming. Their voices...gargling on their own blood. Their eyes... God, their eyes. They were all screaming and crying, but the tears were red. Blood was falling from their eyes and ears, spewing from their mouths. They were scratching at their own faces so hard they were tearing bloody stripes, anything to get at what was causing the pain inside them. Some that were stronger had started going mad and attacking the others. I watched a man, a real big guy as wide as a door. His face was covered in blood and his eyes looked black from the congealed blood that stuck to his eyelids. He grabbed a woman who was running with her little kid, he threw her to the floor and pounded...' Graham bit his hand and held back the tears at the memory.

'You don't have to tell us,' Anna said sympathetically, seeing how hard it was for him and worrying it might be too much detail for Mikey's young ears...or hers.

'No, no. You have to know how serious this is. He pounded her face into the concrete. He wouldn't stop, he wouldn't stop until there was nothing left. Just...bits of skull and mushed brain. The kid in the pushchair was crying, crying for its mummy. I tried to save it, really, I did. But he got to it before I did. He lifted the little boy out of the pushchair with one hand. Lifted it up above his head and snapped him in half. Then his eyes grew wider from his own pain and his guts just...just, exploded from his stomach, like he was ripped open from the inside.

'Everyone was running and screaming, getting in their cars and driving home as fast as they could. No one was prepared though. Do you see? I was wearing my military-grade gas mask, so I know I'm safe. Everyone else was either wearing a blue paper one or nothing at all. Some just pulled the neck of their jumper over their mouth to show willing, but it's not enough. Not even close.' He jumped up, wiping his eyes. He grabbed a beer from the fridge and came back. He poured it down his throat. A trickle of beer spilt out of the side of his mouth. He wiped it with the back of his hand and stared at the floor for the longest time. Finally, he looked up at Anna. Her face had turned pale; she looked to have aged ten years in ten minutes.

'They were right?' Anna said to herself, staring into space, horrified by what she had just heard. This was too insane to believe, how could she have been watching the news one minute and this be happening the next?

They were saying this could happen though, in the paper, on the news...the look on the Prime Minister's face. Had he known what was coming? Anna argued in her head, trying to rationalise the madness of everything Graham had told her.

'Who?' Graham asked, responding to something Anna momentarily forgot she had said.

'What?' She said hazily.

'You said "they were right", who's they?'

'The people on the internet, the ones you were telling us about. They were right all along.' Anna started crying; she let go of Mikey's hand and covered her mouth, trying to stop herself from screaming.

Graham nodded. Mikey was gripping his mother's skirt, twisting it in his hands.

'Yeah. They were. I knew they were all along.' He stood and wiped his face. 'God, I wish you'd listened to me.' He shook his head and bit his lip, as if he were trying to hold back from laying into her.

There was no point in rubbing salt in the wound. What's done is done.

'I've been talking to my connections online,' he said.

'Your connections?' Anna interrupted, wiping at her eyes, swollen and red from tears.

'Yes, *MY* connections. I told you I was preparing. This is what I was preparing for. If it weren't for me, we'd be holed up in here without a scrap of food.' He stopped and took a deep breath, visibly counting backwards from five. Anna could see he was trying his best to keep calm. 'Let's move on. I've been talking with my contacts. They say the virus has mutated beyond anything we thought imaginable. Remember when the virus first came about, when I told you the theory of it being able to travel through the phone signals, 5G and all that that you dismissed as rubbish?'

'Don't tell me it's true?'

'Not only is it true, it's now been proved it can pass through *any* satellite signal. That means TV, that means phone reception, WIFI, telephone lines, all of it.'

'What are we going to do?'

Graham reached to his side and pulled out a box that had belonged to his father. They'd found it when they cleared out his house after he died. It was a dark wooden box, scuffed and chipped round the edges. Anna grew nervous at the sight of it, she thought it had been locked away somewhere so no one would ever get to it. It had originally belonged to Graham's grandfather. He had been a Sergeant in the Army during World War two. He hadn't made it back from the fighting, but his revolver had. Anna had begged Graham to throw it away, get rid of it, take it to the police station or a museum, something. He refused, told her not to be so ridiculous. It was an artefact from the war, a family heirloom. Besides, it was probably deactivated anyway.

Graham opened the box. Anna breathed out a sigh of relief when she saw it was empty.

'I want everyone's phones in here, switched off. I want the house phone unplugging, the WIFI router taken out, the TV aerial thrown away, the cable switched off, everything. Understood?' He put on a deep authoritative voice.

Anna and Mikey looked at each other and nodded. They both put their phones in the box and Graham checked them to make sure they were off. 'Good. You two sit tight here whilst I make sure everything else is done.' Before he got up, he smiled at them both, a smile that was reminiscent of the Graham that Anna had married. Caring and reassuring. Loving.

'We'll be OK, guys. I'll make sure we're all safe.'

He softly put his left hand on Mikey's cheek and brushed away a rogue tear that had spilled from the corner of his eye.

Graham got to work, pulling wires out from the walls, wrapping up the house phone, the cable box, WIFI. Everything on his list was placed into boxes and taken downstairs.

Anna took Joy upstairs, fed her a bottle (that she sterilised three times before giving it to her) and put her down for the night in the travel cot beside her bed. She shut the bedroom door quietly and started sobbing as soon as the door clicked shut. She cupped her hands around her mouth so that nobody would hear her, and desperately tried to calm herself down. Graham always said she had a tendency to get ahead of herself and this wasn't the time to panic and become hysterical.

As she reached the landing, she could hear Graham talking to Mikey downstairs. He was telling him how it was time to be a man. How there was going to be tough times ahead of them. But if they worked together, as a team, as a unit, they would get through it. He asked if Mikey could be his brave little soldier. Mikey said yes.

'That's my boy.'

Anna sat against the door and cried. How were her children going to be OK growing up in a world like this? How long would she be able to keep them safe? She felt like a fool for disregarding Graham for so long.

You're getting ahead of yourself, the voice in her head scolded again. *You don't know how bad it really is out there. It could all be sorted in a week.*

The look on the Prime Minister's face from his TV appearance told her otherwise, yet she had to hold onto some hope.

She sorted herself out, washed her face in the bathroom, in the hope it wouldn't look like she had been crying. She went downstairs and noticed Graham had locked all the doors and windows. The key they always kept in the front door was gone. Mikey had started moving the furniture around in the living room; the book shelves and sideboard units were moved to the window, as if forming a barricade.

Graham saw Anna and went to her. He grabbed the top of her arms and squeezed firmly, but with a gentleness that had been missing the last time he grabbed her like that. 'The world is going to be a crazy, dangerous place for a long time. People are going to be desperate, and desperate people do desperate things. We're lucky that we live out of town – hopefully there won't be too many stragglers that come by here. If we're going to survive this, we need to pull together. I need to know you're with me?' He looked into her eyes: she could see he was desperate for her to say yes.

'OK,' she said.

'That means the subject of 'us' has got to be put on hold. It's trivial, to be honest, in the grand scheme of things. Do you agree?'

'Yes. Yes of course.' She was feeling numb, so terrified at what could be outside that the idea of even wandering outside to see for herself was unthinkable.

He sighed in relief. 'Good, I can't tell you how happy I am that we're finally on the same way of thinking,' He smiled, and to Anna's surprise he did look happy. 'We need to make sure that no one can get in. Tomorrow, I'm going to make this house like Fort Knox.'

'How?' She said. She looked into his eyes and although he was smiling, she was afraid of the darkness she saw in them.

'Didn't I tell you? I've been preparing.'

Chapter 17

Lockdown. Day 1.

That night Anna had found sleep hard to come by. Graham, on the other hand, had fallen asleep as soon as his head hit the pillow. He had decided to come back to the marital bed, and although Anna initially felt uncomfortable, she thought it was probably for the best. Despite everything that had happened, she did feel safer when he was near. Graham was no SAS soldier, but he could handle himself.

Barney, who lay curled up on the floor at the end of the bed, seemed to have more trouble getting off to sleep than Graham did. She supposed Graham must be tired. What a thing to go through. His mind, as well as his body, must be exhausted. She didn't know how she would have coped seeing all that horror, seeing all those poor people die in that way.

Joy woke at 1 A.M. for her feed as usual. Anna had been awake, staring blankly into the darkness of the room when she stirred. She even got her out of the cot before she started crying, which came as a shock to Joy; her face looked disappointed, as if she *liked* screaming her demands in the dead of night and having people running around to bring her what she needed.

Anna made her a bottle and gave it to her in bed upstairs before putting her back into the cot. Joy went straight back to sleep, satisfied. Anna looked at Graham, watched as his chest rose high, and shuddered as it fell back down. Her eyes were growing heavy; the horror her mind had been going over and over in her head, like a terrifying nightmare, had floated away and disappeared like steam in the air.

Sleep took her.

She dreamed of an old memory, a time before lockdown, a time before Joy. They had taken Mikey down to the park to play on the swings. He had been five then and quite a handful. Always running away from them, too excited to start gathering his things to leave and go home.

In the dream, Graham's dad, Barry, was there. He wasn't there on the actual day but for some reason, her dream had put him there in the memory. Dreams play by their own rules. Barry was sitting on a park bench, watching them as they went about their day.

Smiling.

He never smiled. Anna didn't think she had ever seen him smile in the entire fifteen years she had known him. Yet there he was, sat on a park bench smiling at them. The closer she looked at him, the more she could see how little affection there was in that smile. It was a wicked smile, like some twisted movie villain.

It was a memory that had stuck with her all this time, because Mikey had had an accident. He had been on the swings, determined he was a big boy now and didn't need to go on the baby swings with the safety bars, he could manage the proper swings, with the big kids. Graham had told him it was fine if it was OK with Mummy. Anna had been reluctant, worried about his safety. Barry had shouted from the bench, *'Don't turn that boy into a sissy'.*

Which was so typical of that awful man; he had berated Graham all his life about being soft, telling him only puffs and women cry or get ordered around. Not that Graham had told her a lot about his childhood; he could only talk about it so much before clamming up, and Anna didn't like to pry if he wasn't comfortable.

Graham looked at Anna. Anna looked down at Mikey and said: 'Maybe next time.'

'That's it. Do what your wifey tells you. Way to be a man and take charge. You're going to turn that boy into a

fucking sissy, just like you! All we need, another faggot in the family.' Barry barked with laughter, slapping his thigh in hysterics. Graham shot Anna a look of contempt and pushed Mikey towards the swings. 'Of course, you can, boy.' In a voice that wasn't his own. Like he was putting it on.

Mikey was doing great; he was swinging so high and shouting *'mummy look at me, I can touch the sky.'*

Graham had put his arm around Anna as they both watched their first- born enjoying himself. Then Mikey tried to touch the sky, as if he could just grab at it and bring it down with him. He let go of the chain and reached a hand out, making the swing turn in on itself, sending him flying out of his seat and hitting the asphalt hard. He screamed in pain.

God, did he scream.

The others in the park watched on in horror as he lay there screeching. He had landed hard but nothing was broken. He had suffered a deep cut on his elbow. Graham ran to him faster than anyone in their late thirties should be able to run.

Graham had been trained in First Aid. Working on building sites, it was something he'd needed just in case someone cut their finger off with a bench saw or hammered a nail through their thumb. He knew exactly what to do. He was so calm and precise, it was like having a real doctor there. It looked as though Mikey instantly felt calm and safe in the hands of his dad.

Graham got him to the car, cleaned the wound and dressed it. Anna had been both amazed and impressed at how Graham had dealt with the situation. Mikey was screaming, scared stiff at the sight of blood. Graham spoke to him so gently and reassuringly, telling him: 'Everything's going to be OK, you'll be absolutely fine.' When Mikey looked in his dad's eyes Anna could see that he trusted him with his life. It was such a beautiful connection they shared. A bond between father and son that she'd hoped would only grow stronger over the years.

'*If he wants to scream like a sissy, I'll give him something to scream about.*'

Anna turned back, she watched as Barry edged closer to them, carrying a thick walking cane, laughing hysterically.

She wanted to scream but couldn't find her voice.

He was staggering towards them, dragging his feet as he walked; he had an intravenous drip coming from his arm and tubes coming from in between his legs. When alive, his eyes had been a dark brown, now his eyes were grey. The closer he got, the more dead he looked. The skin on his bald, liver-spotted head was rotting, peeling away from the bone. '*Time to man up boy*', he was yelling.

Anna tried to get to Graham but she couldn't turn away.

He got closer – his legs got tangled in the tube coming from between his legs, ripping his catheter out, and a bag full of his bright yellow piss poured out and soaked Anna's feet, that had somehow stuck to the ground.

Her dream had turned into a nightmare. Barry's face was now only inches away from hers, most of his teeth were missing, his gums were black; holes where his teeth had been, were now full of maggots, feasting on infected flesh.

He laughed in her face, his laugh sounded mechanical now, whirring, grinding.

She knew he was going to hurt her. Kill her. Eat her.

Closing her eyes tight, she told herself: *wake up, it's just a horrible nightmare.* The grinding laughter got louder and louder until she thought she could take no more.

It stopped.

Tentatively, she opened her eyes.

He'd gone.

She breathed a sigh of relief and turned to face Graham.

'*What's wrong Anna?*'

Graham's face started to decay and rot in front of her eyes. His hair fell out in lumps, his eyes went from green to grey, his skin aged a hundred years in seconds. His teeth turned black and fell to the floor; maggots poured out of his mouth. Anna realised she wasn't looking at her husband anymore, she was looking at Barry's rotting face again, where Graham's used to be.

She finally found her voice and screamed.

Anna woke to the sound of drilling, the clanging together of metal on metal. She bolted upright and swung her legs round so they dangled over the edge of the bed; her first thought was they were in danger, someone was trying to get in. She checked on Joy and saw she was sleeping. Anna sighed in relief and rubbed the sweat from her face. Her heart was still pounding from her nightmare. She'd hated having to put up with that misogynistic bully of a man whilst he was alive. Now he was dead, it seemed she had to suffer him in her dreams.

The clattering from downstairs was incessant. How Joy was sleeping through all that banging was a mystery to her. She looked back over to the bed, hoping to see Graham as alert as she was. Getting ready to see where the noise was coming from. The bed was empty. She placed her hand in the Graham- shaped dent in the mattress protector (that kept its shape longer than it used to) and found it was cold, which meant he'd been up a while.

I've been preparing.

She remembered his words. What it meant she didn't know exactly but now she was beginning to piece it all together. She had heard that sound before, the clash of metal on metal, the smell of ozone drifting up from the basement and filling the kitchen.

The bedside clock flashed 4:28AM.

How long has he been awake? she thought.

She checked on Joy again, cautiously peering in over the bars of the cot. After the news, and the fear Graham had put in her, she had decided to move the cot out of Joy's room and back into theirs. She needed to know she was safe and close. Joy was fine.

She got up, wrapped her silk dressing gown around herself and walked out into the hall, quietly closing the door behind her. She gently turned the door handle on Mikey's room and popped her head through the gap. Mikey was fine too, snoring softly.

Kids.

Those two would sleep through the Blitz. She made her way downstairs in her thin silk dressing gown, grabbed a cardigan and wrapped it round her. The house was cold, which made a pleasant change in comparison to the searing heat of the summer sun.

The living room door opened up into a metal workshop, there were nuts and bolts, steel sheets, drills and screw drivers. The smell was suffocating. Graham's face was covered with a black mask that had a window he could see through. It lit up in blue flashes as the welder in Graham's hands worked on the sheets of steel.

'Graham? What are you doing?' Anna said, trying not to raise her voice too loud.

Graham looked up, finally seeing his wife stood opposite him. 'Hey,' he said, lifting the mask up, revealing a grease-smeared, sweaty face. 'What are you doing up?'

'Well, I could hardly sleep with all the noise. What are you doing?'

'It's got to be done, and there's no point putting it off. These windows – ' He pointed to the windows that looked out onto the driveway – 'are leaving us exposed. People could walk straight up here, see what we've got, see we're in here, and get in. I've spent months collecting scrap sheets of steel from the scrap yard. Got the last few the other day, brought them in through the basement hatch outside. Just welding them into the right size. Then I'm fitting them into the window reveals. No one can see in, no one can get in.' He looked spectacularly pleased with himself.

She looked at a sheet of steel leant up against the wall, about the size of a door. 'What's that piece for?' she said, bewildered by all she was seeing and hearing.

Graham looked around; droplets of sweat flew off him as he did. 'Front door piece.'

'You're barricading the front door?' The thought of having no way out made her feel uneasy.

'Well yeah.' He laughed. 'No point doing the windows and leaving them a door to walk through.' He shook his head, still laughing at her confusion.

Anna opened her mouth to speak again and stopped. She had run out of words. None of this seemed real: Graham was so far from himself she just couldn't get her head around what he was saying. She wanted to question him but she knew how this new, controlling Graham would react. She felt like she was being forced to trust him. And she had to, didn't she? If what he said was true, they needed him to help keep them safe. She thought then that maybe it was her own failings that were the real problem here.

She remembered what Graham had said after telling them what had happened at the supermarket, how he had told her this was coming and she just hadn't listened to him. How close they would have come to death if she'd had her way. Maybe he was right about everything, she thought.

She walked out, shutting the door, hoping that would dull some of the noise. On her way back up to bed, she checked on Mikey again. He was still fast asleep. That was good, that meant he hadn't been up all night worrying about the state of the outside world. Why Graham had to tell him and put that pressure on him, she couldn't understand. He was a child, barely ten years old. He didn't need this worry. If it was up to her, she would have sheltered him from it for as long as she could get away with it.

It was good to see Graham in good spirits. If they were going to get through this, they had to get on better than they had been. She just wondered how long it would last.

Chapter 18

Anna managed another two hours before Joy woke her wanting breakfast. Joy had started crying but as soon as she saw her mum's face everything was OK. She giggled and flapped her arms in ecstatic fashion, grabbing Anna's lips and cheeks.

Anna put on some clothes, just some comfy home wear: baggy trousers and a loose t-shirt that she had referred to as 'lockdown attire', that she hoped she had seen the last of. Mikey was still sleeping when she checked on him. She felt she was in a constant state of anxiety since last night, wondering if it would ever fade. She tried to stop getting ahead of herself but that was not who she was. She wanted to know what was happening. What the government were doing about it, how long were they expected to survive like this? She had to calm down. They were probably already working on a vaccine.

How would we know?

If every form of communication and news broadcast was a port for infection, how would they ever know? Would they receive a letter?

Stupid. Like a postman is going to carry on working so I can receive my mail.

That would have been her only form of outside exercise, walking to the post box at the end of the drive. No need to go and check now.

When she walked into the living room, she gasped at what had become of it. The steel sheets covered every inch of the window, metal brackets had been put in place around the edges, a silver trail followed where the bracket and the steel shutter met, where it had been welded together. Not a single drop of natural light came in from the outside. Graham had cleared the living room of his tools, but neglected to sweep up any of the mess, or wipe the sides that were covered in greasy fingerprints and sharp metal shavings. The sound coming through the kitchen door suggested he had moved into there.

Anna walked in to see the kitchen windows and back door had been bordered over with the same steel sheets. Graham's face looked gaunt from fatigue, his cheeks and eyes were sunken, dark semi-circles shadowed under them.

'Graham. We can't live like this. There's no way of getting fresh air, sunshine. How can this be right?'

He grimaced with frustration. 'Don't question me!' he shouted, shocking her and Joy simultaneously. Graham threw a wrench on to the kitchen counter hard; it fell to the floor and cracked a floor tile into a hundred jagged pieces. He walked over to her, his eyes wild, like he had been possessed. 'I told you, you had to do what I said. I know what's happening out there, you don't. I tried to tell you this would happen, and you didn't listen. You *wouldn't* listen. Instead, you thought I was going crazy, having some kind of mental breakdown, instead of focusing on the real problem. Out there!'

Anna held Joy closer to her, stepping backwards. Her back hit the counter. He had completely changed from the man who was down here working two hours ago, different again from the man he was last night.

'I'm not the crazy one here. You are. The virus. Is airborne.' He laughed like a madman. 'And you're worried about fresh air? You dumb fucking BITCH.' He stepped up to her ferociously, putting his face into hers, close enough that she could smell his rank breath.

Anna saw the look in his eyes. It was something she had seen before, and didn't care to see again. He didn't notice or care that Joy was in her arms, he only saw the stupid bitch who questioned his actions, when all he was trying to do was protect them.

'Dad?' a quiet voice said from behind them.

Mikey.

Graham stepped back, his face filled with a smile that looked alien and out of place. 'Good morning son. What you doing up at this time? Wet the bed?'

Jokes? He's making fucking jokes? Anna felt maybe she *was* going crazy.

'What are you doing?' Mikey said, looking around at the boarded windows.

'We've got to keep ourselves protected, son. I was just telling your mother here, if the virus is airborne, we have to protect ourselves against it the best we can.'

Mikey nodded. Accepting the reasoning easy enough.

'I suppose if people are going crazy, it's probably better to cut off anywhere they could get in.'

Graham looked back at Anna, smiling and jamming a thumb in the direction of Mikey, an expression that said: *He gets it, why can't you?*

'That's my boy.' Graham moved over and ruffled Mikey's hair with his grease-stained fingers. 'Do you want some breakfast, son?'

'It's OK, I'll make us something.' Anna interrupted, moving over to the kitchen cupboards.

'No, you won't. *I'll* be making the food from now on. I know the ration portions.'

'Rations?'

Graham sighed again, as if fed up with her stupidity. 'Yes, Rations. We can't expect to last very long if we're having full meals like before. It's going to be tough but it's what we have to do to survive. How are you not getting this?' The vein in his forehead was throbbing, like a worm was burrowing under his skin.

'OK,' she said. Realising how Graham was wanting things to be. How he was wanting *life* to be. Maybe after some time things would calm down a little, she thought, in hope more than anything. She hated the idea of having no control, allowing Graham to make every decision. Again, that lingering doubt stuck in her mind that if she had believed him in the first place, maybe they would have been better prepared. She felt as though she was being led through a cave with a blindfold on, having to put all of her trust in the person guiding her, trusting they wouldn't let her fall. That thought was made all the more troubling, when the person leading her was Graham.

After making Joy's bottle, Anna sat at the table and fed her. Joy instantly calmed down and drank heartily, making desperate sucking noises as the milk flowed through the teat.

'OK, sit down Mikey.'

Mikey sat. 'We have a loaf of bread in, that is going to spoil the quickest so we'll eat that first. A slice each, with a touch of butter. Sound good?'

Mikey nodded his understanding. Anna lowered her head and looked back at Joy, wanting to avoid eye contact with Graham, worried she would only infuriate him further if he was to see the sadness in her eyes.

'I'm starving dad, could I get two slices?' Mikey asked, cheerily. Anna couldn't believe the good spirit Mikey was showing. *Did he not see how Graham was acting? Was he being blissfully ignorant or did he genuinely not know what was happening when he came in the room?*

'No Mikey you can't. We have to use what we have sparingly. In a few days, your body will adjust and get used to the smaller portions.'

Graham put three slices of bread in the toaster. He stood watching the element heat up until it glowed red hot, the white crumbs of bread turning slowly brown. The kitchen was silent apart from the sucking noises coming from Joy and the irregular drip of the tap in the kitchen sink. Graham's breathing was rasping, like it had been when he smoked thirty a day, a habit Anna had asked him (forced him, if you asked Graham) to give up for the good of his health and the family finances. Anna looked up at the clock on the wall, the dog's smiling face looking down on them with its tail wagging side to side as if everything was normal. Just another day.

The toast popped, restarting the noise in the kitchen, setting everyone into movement again. Graham spread a thin, transparent layer of butter on the toast, cut it into squares, and handed them out.

The first bite Anna took was like biting through cardboard. The toast was coarse in her mouth, absorbing any saliva she had, making her mouth dry.

Graham wolfed his down, spilling crumbs into his beard that had gained some length over the past few days. He brushed them off onto the floor without care. Their beautiful home was going to be turned into a shit-hole and Anna knew it.

Graham stood and put his plate in the sink. Mikey finished his and followed his father's lead and did the same.

'Wash them up when you've finished.' Graham said to Anna, gesturing towards the sink. 'Just because no one's coming round doesn't mean our standards have to slip. I have taken over the cooking duties, which means you can step up the cleaning.' He finished chewing the last bit of mushed-up dough and licked his lips. 'I think you can manage that. Can't you?'

His patronizing tone infuriated her. Never, in any time of their marriage, would she have let him talk to her like that. 'Yes,' she agreed. She knew it was for the best not to anger him any further. She was going to have to submit more than she was used to, to survive. Maybe some of those tips her mum had given her would come in handy after all. The obedient wife. *What a good little obedient wife I am.*

Chapter 19

The day passed slowly. Or so Anna thought. The light in the room didn't change, it was in a constant dim haze from the old halogen bulb in the bear lamp at the back of the room. The steel sheets seemed to absorb the sun's heat; they were warm to the touch on the back of the house. The front of the house, where the sun would beat down all day long, was hot. Really hot. The heat radiated from them. It was twelve o'clock, when the sun was highest in the sky, the temperature at its peak.

She was sweating profusely; she had stripped down to a pair of shorts and an undershirt to keep cool. Joy was playing on the floor, stripped of her baby grow and now just wearing a nappy. She didn't feel that hungry, even though she had only had a slice of dry toast all day. Her stomach felt full, like a heavy stone was sat in there, making her feel sick and nauseous.

Graham had retreated back to his basement. He'd said he had more work to do, the windows upstairs had to be covered as well. Luckily, he had more steel sheets down there to remedy that. Mikey had wanted to go down with him but Graham had refused. He'd told him he would be of more help if he was to clear anything and everything off the windowsills so they were clear to have a free run at when he brought the cut-to-size sheets up. Then, he could help him fit them. Hold them in place whilst he welded them shut.

Mikey's face had lit up like he'd just been told they were off to Disney land.

Anna knew that when Mikey looked at his dad, he didn't see a man who had let himself go or maybe had a few screws loose. He saw his hero, a man who could put his hand to anything, whether it be building a house, playing doctor, or welding their house together to keep them safe from the bad people outside. In his eyes, Graham could do no wrong.

Mikey came pelting down the stairs, making Anna's heart skip a beat. She was in a constant state of anxiety, jumping and gasping at any sudden noises. Barney could tell she was on edge; she guessed that was why he wouldn't leave her side. Wherever she sat, Barney was sat beside her, when she stood up to go to the toilet, he would go with her.

'Mum, I'm hungry. What's for dinner?'

'I don't know love. You best ask your dad.' Anna shrugged.

Mikey rolled his eyes. *Of course. Of course, I don't come to you anymore. I only need you to clean up after me.* Was what she saw in that expression?

Mikey walked out of the living room and into the kitchen. 'Dad, what's for dinner?' he shouted down the stairs. He knew not to go down there.

Anna could hear the thudding of Graham's heavy footsteps as he ran up to the kitchen.

'We can have a slice of bread and butter, a small wedge of cheese and a carrot,' he said, smiling.

'Ok Dad,' Mikey said, lacking the same enthusiasm he'd had in the morning.

Chapter 20

After lunch, yet another pathetic meal Anna struggled to choke down, Mikey and Graham headed upstairs to fit the rest of the steel sheets. The permanent barrier between them and the outside world. The thing that would protect them from danger, and sun and fresh air.

Graham's mood had changed. Whether he had taken a nap down there, Anna wasn't sure. But the look in his eyes had changed. He spoke to her again like she was his wife and not some insignificant burden that weighed him down and dismissed all of his ideas.

'Eat your food. I know you'll be feeling tense and nervous, but you need to keep eating. Keep your strength up. Be prepared that it will get worse before it gets better.'

Worse before it gets better.

It seemed unfathomable to Anna that things could in fact get worse. Worse than this? Then her mind ran away with her. Imagining how things could get worse. Eating portions this small was bound to have some effect on their bodies. Vitamin deficiency maybe? Weight loss certainly. Mental fatigue, depression? All possible. The lack of sunlight was a concern, she always felt a little down in the winter time. Some said it was a myth that people were more susceptible to blue moods during the changing of the seasons because of the lack of sunshine and vitamin D. She knew she suffered from it and grew scared at the thought of how low she could go without stepping outside and feeling the warmth of the sun's rays on her face and the breeze in her hair.

Poor Mikey would start struggling soon, he couldn't keep this up for much longer, not with a smile on his face and a skip in his step. All of his hobbies and interests were either outside or on the TV or PlayStation.

How long would they be locked up like this? Graham was acting as though it would be years. Would Joy grow up to believe this was her world? That this was all she had to know and learn? Anna supposed at least she wouldn't know what she was missing. That was some horrible comfort. Joy wouldn't grow up to know the colour of the sky or the feel of grass underneath her feet. Graham had enough provisions to keep them alive for over two years. If no news came on the radio, that's how long she suspected they would be down here, until starvation forced them out in search of food. What a state the world could be in, two-three years down the line. How many would die from it, would there be a cure, or natural immunity to it?

Her head hurt and her neck ached. She was dehydrated from sitting in that oven of a front room all day. She hadn't drunk enough, she put it down to that. Joy had been given a fresh bottle of water every hour, more if she made the right cues. Anna thought it funny that even when running on auto-pilot, the needs of her children were always met, even if she didn't look after herself all that well. Which of course was a noble but foolish way of going about it. As Anna's mother used to say, 'You've got to put your own gas mask on before helping the person next to you with theirs.'

The same applied here. If Anna didn't take care of herself then Joy would find there was no one to look after her and give her what she needed. Graham was useless when it came to Joy. He had been great when Mikey was a baby, hands-on, doing night feeds, changing nappies. Now though, he did sweet F A. It was as if he hadn't bonded with her at all. Anna had thought of forcing the issue, making him spend time with Joy, get to know the sweet little wonder that she was. Now, however, she thought it best to just leave him to it.

After lunch Anna cleaned the plates and the kitchen sides from the crumbs and used cutlery. Mopped the tiled floor, careful not to pull out any broken pieces where Graham had smashed the tile. He'd told her to leave it and he would fix it when he had a chance. He was busy at the moment, didn't you know? She hoovered the living room, Joy in her arms and Barney getting under her feet the entire time.

Graham and Mikey were finishing up boarding the last of the upstairs windows. Fully cutting them off from the outside world. Safe.

Anna took herself off to her craft room. She'd asked Graham if there was anything she could do to help. Like a child trying to get out of their parents' bad books. He had told her there was nothing he needed her for, just get the downstairs clean again. Feeling useless and, quite frankly, scared of what had become of the world, she needed to take her mind off it all. Just escape from her head for a little while. Joy stayed by her side, sleeping now in her Moses basket to the side of Anna's desk. Anna worked her length of red wool around the last side of the blanket she had been making. She'd have it finished in half an hour; she had hoped for longer. She laughed, realising that she actually had all the time in the world, she could make another blanket. Hell, by the time this was all over she'd probably have a blanket made for all of them, and the dog.

Barney let out a whimper. He was nestled safely under the desk, entwined in her feet. He was dreaming. His little leg was kicking and his eye- lids flickered. He needed the rest as much as she did. She wondered if he could tell what was going on? There was no doubt he had some idea *something* was happening. Normally he'd be wandering all over the house, sat with Mikey, begging to be let outside to go play. All he'd done since Graham came back was stay at her side, her loyal guard dog. She smiled at him, the adorable little mutt. As guard dogs went, he was about as much use as a chocolate fireguard. Brave, though. That was admirable. They had bought him during the first lock down when he was a puppy, as a way to bring the family together, give them something to take their minds off what was happening. Force them to go out for walks and get fresh air. He'd cost a fortune, the inflation on the cost of puppies and kittens was astronomical.

Supply and demand, the breeder had said. Turns out every one had the same idea. With everyone at home, they had time to give a puppy the attention it needed, train it so it didn't spend all night yapping at the bedroom door or shitting on the living room carpet. He was the best thing to come of that lockdown, she couldn't imagine not having him. She loved him and so did Mikey.

Before she knew it, the blanket was finished. She seemed to only blink and it was done. She checked the time and saw it had been half an hour. It was like a magician's trick, the threading of wool using hooks and loops. A hypnotist's watch, blanking her mind, giving it time to refocus and heal. She felt calmer, she saw things more clearly. The bigger picture, as Graham would say. She couldn't let herself dwell on having to be kept in, she had to knuckle down and bloody well get on with it.

This was for the good of the family, the good of the human race. She repeated this in her head, as if saying it again and again would give it more credibility. If it was as bad as they made out in the movies, this could be worldwide, destroying the world's population.

If other people were doing the same as them, then they would be able to rebuild society. Start afresh. A reboot for the world. Let nature take back what it had lost to the rich and the greedy. Then maybe it would let humans live here again free from disease and plagues.

Anna cut the wool and tied it to a neat finish. She held the blanket out in front of her, pleased with the final result. The even, symmetrical, multi-coloured pattern looked sharp, aesthetically pleasing. She put the new blanket on Joy and loved how it looked. It was too hot to keep it on, so she rolled it up and put it next to her. Joy shuffled against it, made a cute whinge and carried on sleeping. The study was cooler than the rest of the house; the window in her craft room was small, it couldn't have taken long for Graham to fit the steel on this one. She had liked the view from there though, she could see where the road trailed off over the hills, past the pine woods on the horizon. How she wished she had taken more opportunities to drive up there, go see the world. She hoped the world would still be out there, when she next got the chance.

Anna noticed in the bottom right corner, where the weld bonded the sheet and the steel bracket, a slight crack of light. Only thin, but maybe big enough to be able to catch a glimpse of the outside? Graham had rushed this room, a window so small he would have done it as quickly as possible, so that it was ticked off his list.

Was she to tell him?

The threat was real, she was almost sure of that, but would a slight crack in the welding be that big of a deal? There was glass behind it, surely the disease couldn't get through the glass and find its way through the tiny crack and into the room?

She decided against telling him. He wouldn't come in here again now; he never came in here. She leant forward, closing one eye to peer through. It had only been a day and already she was desperate for the outside. She stooped down, onto her knees, and looked.

The world was there and it was beautiful. She could see the trees on the horizon, gently blowing in the summer breeze. How nice that would be on her face. The green of the grass looked so vibrant; the individual blades moving independently from each other made it look like moving water, like an ocean of green. She felt as though she could actually smell it, the freshness, the pollen, the sweet pine smell that drifted down from the forest when the wind blew just right. She took in a deep breath and sat on the floor, with a smile on her face. This would be her escape. When things got too tough, she would come here to remember, remember there was still a world out there. To remember there was always hope.

Chapter 21

When Anna finally came downstairs, (she had drifted off after releasing her anxiety by seeing the outside world) she could hear laughing from the kitchen table. It was a warm laugh that filled the house. It brought back fond memories, like looking through a family photo album. She walked quickly, wanting to join in with them. Joy was wide awake and ready for her bottle, her eyes big and sparkling from the light in the living room. Barney followed her and curled up next to the sofa.

'What's funny, guys?' Anna said as she walked into the kitchen.

She noticed they were sat with two empty plates. They'd had their dinner without her. They had sat and eaten together, without her and Joy, on the first night of this awful lockdown. When they were all supposed to be sticking together. They had left her out. She couldn't but feel a little sick with disappointment.

'Have you had dinner?' she asked, trying to hide her feelings from being too obvious on her face.

'Yes, we have.' Graham stood and stroked her arms. 'Yours is in the oven, keeping warm. We were starving and you had fallen asleep so we decided to leave you to enjoy your rest.'

She covered her face shamefully. 'Sorry, I'm so sorry. I just thought you had both left me out.'

'Don't be silly, mum,' said Mikey. 'We just thought you looked too peaceful, that's all.'

'Well, thank you then. I did enjoy the rest. The stress of it all must have really taken it out of me.' She sat, joining them at the table. 'What's for dinner?'

'Beans, sausage and egg,' Graham said, retrieving the plate from the oven. His smile looked genuine for everyone to see, but something in his eyes was missing. His spark maybe? The spark that made him...him.

He put the plate in front of Anna, holding it with a tea-towel. 'Careful, the plate's hot,' he said, smiling that smile again.

Anna looked down at her food. 'I think you must have left the oven on full by mistake.' There was no hiding the look of repulsion on her face. He had given her a spoonful of baked beans, a slither of sausage and half an egg. The sauce from the baked beans had dried completely, the section of sausage had turned into a black crisp, and the half an egg was brown.

Graham leaned over her plate, inspecting it himself. 'Oh, well. Would you look at that. I must have. Sorry about that, *love*.' His brow furrowed. His face told Anna he wasn't sorry. She looked at Mikey, who seemed to be oblivious. The fact that Graham had kept his voice low and friendly, and used words like *love* and *sorry,* meant Mikey would think nothing was going on, that this was all façade.

'Can I have something else?'

Graham frowned. 'No love. You can't. We can't just throw away good food because it's a little over-done.'

She pushed the plate away gently. 'I'll go without. You can eat it if you're still hungry.'

'Oh no Anna. You will eat it.' Graham looked over at Mikey. 'Go to your room now, son.'

Mikey nodded and got up slowly from his chair. Before the kitchen door shut, he looked back at Anna, sat there uncomfortably. She hoped he wouldn't see the anxiety in her face. The last thing she wanted was for him to see his dad the way he had been with her.

'Put Joy down on the mat. And eat your food.'

'Can you take her whilst I eat?' Anna held Joy out towards Graham.

'Put her down on the fucking mat!' He slammed his fist on the table, making the plate and cutlery rattle. The noise had disturbed Barney, who now walked into the kitchen, his nails *click-clacking* on the tiled floor as he sat by Anna's side.

Anna put her down on her mat. Joy was visibly upset but didn't cry out. Anna sat with her shoulders hunched, her hands clasped together in-between her thighs. Graham's stare bore into her, aggressive and unforgiving. Anna looked at the plate of food in front of her, or the charcoal remains of what had once been food.

'Eat it,' Graham said, his voice low and harsh.

'I don't want to,' Anna said, choking back tears.

'You will eat that fucking food. You think we can just throw it away?' He paused. 'Eat it.' He pushed the plate closer to her.

Anna started crying. 'Why are you doing this to me?' she asked.

'Why? Whilst me and Mikey were working all day making sure this place is one-hundred percent safe, what are you doing? Huh!?' His voice turned into that embarrassing imitation of Anna he did when mocking her. 'Ooo, I know, I'll go do my crochet, then I'll take a little nap. I don't need to use any initiative and do something productive around the house.' He stopped and leaned over the table.

'I'm sorry,' she managed to blurt out in-between sobs. 'I thought you didn't need me to do anything.'

'*I* didn't need your help. You could have laid the table for dinner? Cleaned the oven out? Wiped down the inside of the fridge. Health is of upmost importance. If we get a bug or an infection, the kind that can be treated easily with antibiotics, we're fucked. 'Cos guess what Anna, there's no doctors to go get a prescription from anymore. Now eat your fucking food.'

Anna wiped away the snot and tears that were dripping down her face and picked up a fork. She scooped up

113

a few beans. Her hand was trembling so bad a few beans rolled off. She got the fork to her mouth and chewed. The beans tasted rank, like little crunchy pieces of grit with an aroma of tomato sauce. 'I can't eat any more.' She looked up at Graham in a 'please take pity on me' look she had. He wouldn't buy it this time.

Graham moved around the table, grabbed the cremated sausage in one hand, and gripped Anna's face with the other. He squeezed her cheeks so hard it made her lips pucker up as if she was comically asking for a kiss. He pushed the sausage into her mouth, she felt the burnt edges press painfully against her gums. She tried to push his hand away but he was gripping her with more force than she ever thought he was capable of.

Joy started screaming; her face turned red and her arms and legs flailed in the air as Anna struggled to free herself from Graham's grip. Barney stood over Joy protectively and started barking towards Graham.

He got the sausage past her teeth and then covered her mouth with his now free hand. His face was close in on hers, so close the bristles of his beard jabbed her smooth skin. The loud intolerable noises from Joy and Barney were piercing Anna's ears, making her heart hammer harder in her chest as panic rose in her throat.

'Don't forget this Anna: you need me, more than I need you. I can survive this virus; I can save Mikey too. You would already be dead without me! After all I've done this is the thanks I get!' He was screaming at her, sprays of thick spittle landing on Anna's cheeks. 'You will learn to do as I say. It's for your own good. We stick together, Anna. I don't like doing this but I will if it helps to get it through that thick, stubborn skull of yours. Do you understand?'

YES! She nodded, struggling to breathe with his hand pressed so firmly across her mouth.

He shoved her head backwards as he stood up to leave; she choked momentarily on the burnt sausage, bursting into a coughing fit. She spat it out onto the plate; the sound it made was like a pebble hitting porcelain. She coughed until she regained her breath. After she watched Graham go down stairs to the basement, she grabbed Joy and hugged her tight. She could feel Joy's delicate ribs convulsing as she sobbed and began to calm down, safe in her mother's arms.

Barney walked over to the basement door. He had stopped barking, instead he was growling deeply at the door.

Anna made Joy a bottle with all the rapidity of someone who had been making them all their lives, and ran upstairs. She got into the bedroom, Barney followed behind her, and she shut the door. Joy was crying again, her little face bright red and pursed up. She rocked her, shushing her, telling her everything was going to be OK. Trying to stop her own tears from making Joy more scared. Anna put the bottle near Joy's face; she took it and began to drink.

Anna relaxed as best she could in the silence. Her bedroom window being boarded up with steel meant the bedroom was almost pitch black, if not for the night light next to Joy's cot. Dozens of white stars covered the ceiling and spun in a slow orbit around the room.

She thought about flicking on the bedside lamp and decided against it. Her own sadness and fear of Graham had exhausted her. She lay on the bed and fed Joy, who fell asleep first, looking tiny in the double bed. Anna sobbed quietly, her tears soaking into her pillow. She prayed it to be over. Mikey would be OK; he was getting on well with Graham and would do whatever his dad asked him to do. He was good like that. Her main worry was that Mikey would see how Graham was treating her and think that it was OK. After what could have been hours of lying awake, she slept and didn't wake up until morning.

Chapter 22

Graham sat at his desk in the basement. His breathing was heavy and his heart pounded so hard he could feel it in his ears. The smell down there was damp and musty, patches of mould grew in the far corner, and the white paint on the block work was bubbling and peeling off in giant blisters. He upended a bottle to pour the last few drops of beer on his tongue before discarding that one and opening another. By his desk he had a stack of beer, six crates piled in a pyramid shape.

On the desk were a bunch of scattered papers, graphs and stats showing rates of infection for each county, nationwide and internationally, scribbled notes in writing that only Graham could read were scrawled in the margins.

He was calming down after what had happened with Anna. Why did she have to infuriate him like that? All he wanted to do was keep this family together. At all costs, that was what he wanted to do. He had put so much into preparing for this and yet she seemed to want to fight him every step of the way.

'Why are you doing this? Why are you doing that? My food's not very nice.'

She had no respect.

He couldn't remember the last time he had slept; he had been studying these graphs, day and night, figuring out the rate at which the virus could spread from person to person, the fatality percentages for each age group, the worst affected countries, the flights that were still coming in and out of the country, and the best and worst case scenarios of how many infected people could potentially have slipped through the net and managed to board the planes, despite on-the-door checks.

No, she had no idea what he would do. His dad was an arsehole, a low life scum bag who used to beat Graham and his mum on a regular basis, but he didn't deserve to die like that. Alone. Frightened.

Graham sucked down his beer; the trickles of sweat that had poured down his face from being stuck in the heat of the house had cooled in the basement that kept an almost constant temperature of ten degrees. Not low enough to be cold and not high enough to be hot.

He pushed the graphs to one side and fiddled with the radio he kept at the back of the desk. It was the same radio he'd had in his bedroom when he was a kid. Feeling the roughness of the dials in his fingers brought back memories of when he used to record the top 40 from the radio onto cassette tapes. His dad had told him records were too expensive, so this was the only way Graham could play the songs he liked whenever he wanted. He'd wait for the top 40 countdown to begin, and as soon as the DJ introduced the song, he'd hit the record button and sit there, completely still and silent. The radio had a built in Dictaphone that started recording whenever the record button was hit, so if he was to cough, sneeze or fart, it was likely to be heard on the tape when he played the song back.

He turned it on and fiddled with the dial that sent a small orange needle along a line of numbers. He found static and turned the volume up full.

The white noise calmed him, his heart began to slow and his breathing was easing. He pushed his chair back a couple of feet and opened the top drawer by his right-hand side. He pulled out a king-size chocolate bar, ripped the wrapper with his teeth, and bit off a big chunk that filled his mouth. He chomped, smacking his lips together loudly, enjoying the sweetness of it. His stomach had been cramping and growling at him all afternoon. He'd eat this one and probably have another. After all, he'd got several multi-packs of chocolate, crisps and sweets down there.

His eyes were still fixed on the open drawer. He swallowed the chocolate in his mouth and pushed aside the multi-pack that sat on top of something in the drawer.

It was his grandad's gun that he'd found when clearing his dad's house. It should have been disarmed. It wasn't. It hadn't been when he was a kid anyway, his dad used to show it to him with pride. Once, when they were down by the river, his dad had pulled it out and shot it into the water. It had scared the crap out of Graham; it was so loud, louder than he thought a gun would be in real life. It wasn't like the movies. His dad saw how much it scared Graham. That seemed to make him like it even more. Whenever Graham misbehaved and his dad didn't think a smack round the head or a lash from his belt would be enough, he'd threaten him that he would go get the gun from the box under the stairs. Graham would listen and do as he was told then.

He stroked the gun and that childlike fear that he felt all those decades ago came flooding back. He slammed the drawer shut and drank more beer.

CHAPTER 23

LOCKDOWN DAY 5

No word had reached them from the outside. Was Anna surprised? No. She had expected as much. Graham sat by the radio in the basement day and night; he told her it was imperative that he be there in case someone tried to broadcast any information. If they went to the trouble to record a message and send it out, then he was obligated to be patient and wait for it. There had to be survivors out there. If they could keep themselves safe then surely others could too. The days had got harder. Every day was the same. The steel shutters Graham had put up stopped any light from the outside coming in. They were all starting to lose any comprehension of what time of day it was; their body clocks were screwed up. On day three Joy had started to get so confused she fell into a deep night-time sleep when it could have only been the middle of the day. She was screaming the house down when Anna woke her. Graham had got so frustrated with the noise he'd slammed the door and gone back down to the cellar. Mikey's enthusiasm to embrace their situation and try and help Graham had faded from exuberant to almost non-existent.

They were starving. Five days of rations was already taking its toll. Anna had zero energy; she woke up feeling more tired than when she went to sleep. Mikey had black bags under his eyes all day long; he was sleeping for more than ten hours a night now and that wasn't like him. He always woke up at eight, ever since he started school. His rhythms were all off, and getting a smile out of him was like getting blood from a stone. Graham's mood swings had taken a toll on everyone.

Anna had been shocked by what he did with the food that first night. There hadn't been a repeat of anything like that since, but the tension in the house changed whenever he was in the room. Anna and Mikey just didn't know what sort of mood he would be in when he came up from his pit. He had taken to sleeping in there every night; he said it was better for their sanity to have a little space from each other.

Sanity. There was a laugh. She wasn't sure any of them were holding on to theirs and it hadn't even been a week. It was the shutters; they added an extra weight to the lockdown that it hadn't carried before. Taking away the view and the sun, being able to wander into the back garden and feel the wind in their faces. Take that away and you might as well be a prisoner.

That's what she was, she realised. In a prison full of her own possessions and memories, a prison of Graham's making.

Graham would come up on a morning, smiling, chatting, laughing. It would bring everyone up a little bit, a bit of positivity to an otherwise dingy, grey life whose only goal was to survive long enough that maybe, *maybe*, they could carry on the world afterwards. The idea that they could stay holed-up in here for nearly three years, to then open the doors and be killed instantly by rampaging maniacs infected with the most terrifying disease known to man, was too horrible to imagine.

Hope.

That was she needed. She got it from the tiny crack in the craft room window shutters where Graham had rushed welding it. She would sneak up there whenever she got a chance, (ensuring all chores and cleaning had been done first) and look out at the trees and the grass. She could fool herself that nothing out there was happening, that the world was actually just carrying on as normal, and what Graham had seen at the supermarket was a terrible accident, something unrelated. It was just a dream, though. The fantasy of a silly little woman who was struggling to face the grave reality of her situation.

The air in the house was growing thick. Like it was collecting all the dust that had no way of escaping the walls.

She wanted to tell Graham that they needed fresh air in here; surely he must realise that? But the thought of insulting his intelligence worried her. She didn't want to have food forced down her throat again until she choked. Better for him to realise it for himself, that way it could be his big idea, he could be the saviour who thought of a solution, and she could be the eternally grateful damsel in distress.

The smell of the dog shit had to be the worst. Because they couldn't leave the house, neither could Barney. He had to shit in a specific area of the house. Anna put a mat down and whenever he had pooed, she would bag it up and go flush it down the toilet. Then she would clean the whole area with bleach and air freshener. But once a dog has taken a shit, you can't just get rid of the smell like that, regardless of how quick you get it cleaned up and flushed down the toilet. He was a good dog, and even learnt to piss in an old plastic bowl they'd used for washing the pots once upon a time. That got flushed down the toilet and wiped out; thankfully it didn't smell half as bad.

Today was a day like every other day. Anna, Mikey and Joy were at the table, Joy drinking her bottle, while Mikey and Anna sat patiently waiting for their ration of breakfast to be plated up. Mikey's cheeks were looking sunken. Anna was worried. If it got much worse, she would have to get him more food. Graham would never go for it but if he was distracted upstairs, she could sneak some in her pockets and give it to Mikey in secret. He would be so pleased at the extra food; he'd take that secret to the grave.

Graham was serving up the last of the cereal. A handful of cornflakes each with a splash of milk. The last banana was split into three pieces, it was black and bruised all over but it was extra energy that they all needed. Graham passed the bowls round the table. Barney barked loudly, making everyone at the table jump in surprise.

'He's hungry. Do you have some more dog food?' Anna said, pushing her cornflakes around the bowl with her spoon.

'He can have a quarter of a can after we've finished. Then another quarter tonight.' Graham had come upstairs in a cheery mood again. Anna assumed it was because everybody was following the rules so far. So far, nothing had gone wrong, no one had whinged or stepped out of line. That was good. That meant no shouting, no abuse, no being choked on burnt sausages.

She watched as her husband sat opposite her. Eating like a civilised person. He even dabbed his mouth with a napkin when he spilled a little milk down his chin. He was like two different people these days. The other one was a monster, a dangerous unpredictable psychopath who she couldn't understand or reason with. As long as this Graham was around, the better everyone would be. The problem with that was, she found she was always on edge, walking on eggshells, desperate not to upset him. It didn't take a lot for the personality change to start turning. Any little frustration he suffered would change the lines in his face. It was as if he just couldn't handle stress anymore, not the good Graham anyway. The evil Graham (as she had now come to calling that half of him) handled it with aggression and anger. Anna had observed him for long enough in this prison to realise what was happening.

Witnessing what happened at the supermarket had triggered something in him. He had already been struggling mentally and that had been the last straw for his mental health.

She hoped that if they carried on, maybe the evil Graham would let go of its hold over him, let the real Graham take back control. Right now, just normal tired agitation could bring evil Graham to the fore. Thankfully he spent most of his time down in the basement, leaving Mikey and Anna to slowly starve into nothingness. She was feeling thinner already; five days in and she was already starting to notice. Her shirts didn't fit right, she'd lost some of her bosom and hips. Mikey was too; he had been filling out into a fine young man, finally catching up with his height. How he'd got to be so tall, Anna didn't know. Graham wasn't small, but at five-foot-ten he was hardly the tallest person in the world. Mikey was losing the weight he had been putting on, only a little, but still noticeable. The funny thing was that Graham didn't look any different. Maybe his body was holding on to it? Needing the energy, it was storing all the fat for as long as it could? He wouldn't be eating behind their backs, he was so obsessed with his rules and everyone following orders, he wouldn't dare break them himself out of pride.

They sat in relative silence; the only sounds were Barney whining, Joy drinking and the nerve-grating crunching coming from the chewing of cornflakes. A small blessing that came with the smaller portions was that the chewing noises didn't last very long. Chewing and chomping was one of Anna's pet peeves. If someone in a restaurant sat near her slurped at their soup appetiser it would destroy her appetite for the rest of the evening. A restaurant, something they used to take for granted, think of as mundane – now she'd give her right arm to go to one. Not literally of course, but she missed them all the same.

'OK, if everyone's finished,' Graham said, spreading his arms to the side and looking between them both, 'Anna, if you could wash the dishes and clean the kitchen, please. Mikey, I would like you to clean your bedroom. If you were to get ill simply from being too lazy to dust and anti-bac the surfaces in there, you'd feel mighty stupid.'

'Yes, Graham.'

'Yes Dad.'

'Good. Now before we all get back to our tasks. I just want to say thank you. I've got to admit, after the first day of this new life, I had my doubts that you would both get on board. You've proved me wrong... So far.' He smiled. 'You've both kept to your jobs diligently and without complaint. Together, we *will* survive this.' He held both of their hands and smiled softly.

Anna smiled back. Mikey looked to her for guidance and followed her lead in smiling too. He was young, but he wasn't stupid. He could tell his father wasn't right. Graham had changed so much since those days when he would take Mikey to the park and push him on the swings, clean and dress his wounds and make all the hurt go away. The days when he would spend all of his spare time exercising, doing things around the house to make it a nicer place to live.

'Of course, we will. Because we have you.' Anna placed her hand on top of his. She knew that comment would stroke his ego enough to keep him as normal Graham for the rest of the day.

He nodded his head, agreeing with her. She was right, after all.

Graham stood from the table; he grabbed a can of dog food from the bottom cupboard. He pulled on the ring-pull and poured it into Barney's bowl, thick chunks of foul-smelling meat floated in the gravy. Graham hesitated, looked at Barney's face; the dog's head leaned slightly to one side and his eyes were wide and wanting. Graham shook his head at his own weakness as he poured a few extra chunks into the bowl. Barney ate it rapidly, as if in fear someone would take it away any second.

Anna sensed her chance. He was in the best mood he had been in since they'd first discovered the new strain of the virus. She wondered if it had a name? Scientists had probably given it some name that was hard to pronounce or made no seemingly related sense.

'Isn't the air stifling in here now? It feels thick doesn't it, Mikey?' Anna said, fanning her hand in front of her face. She looked at Graham from the corner of her eyes and swore she could see his ears flick as she said it.

'Yeah, it is,' Mikey said.

'I wish there was some way to get fresh air safely. Oh well, never mind. Right, I'm going to get on with the cleaning. You start your room Mikey, like your father said.' She stroked his face and felt his cheekbones.

'OK mum. Come on, Barney.' Barney licked his bowl clean and followed Mikey upstairs. Barney was settling into this new routine and had begun to trust Graham again after that first night.

Anna put Joy down on her play mat and gathered the bowls and began filling the sink with water, adding a splash of washing-up liquid. She scrubbed the bowls clean and stacked them in the drainer next to the sink. Looking over her shoulder she saw that Graham was looking at the windows, trying to figure out a way to let air in without compromising their safety. A thought struck him, she could see it in his eyes; he ran down into the basement, closing the door behind him.

Anna smiled victoriously to herself. He was good at solving practical problems so she knew he'd figure something out. Even if it was just that he would allow the front door to be opened for an hour or so a day. She had noticed how the steel shutter on the front door hadn't been welded all the way around, only bolted on to the door itself, and a frankly overkill number of dead bolts and chains put all the way up the side of the door, from top to bottom. He'd even put on one of those swing latches at the foot of the door you get on stables so you can flick it with your foot to unlock it. The deadbolts were locked with padlocks that required a number passcode to open them. A code she wasn't privy to.

When the dishes were finished, she filled the mop bucket with fresh water and soap. The tiles were still sparkling from when she'd done them yesterday. Nobody was bringing any dirt in from outside anymore; still, little bits of dust and crumbs were in the hard-to-reach areas; the corners and in the cracks of grouting between the tiles. That broken tile was a source of annoyance for her, she would have had a go at fixing it herself but she'd only mess it up. She was useless when it came to things like that, the most practical thing she could do was change a lightbulb, and even then, only if it was a screw-in fitting, it was the bayonets she always seemed to struggle with.

It was another hot day which only exacerbated the thickness of the air, making it hard for her to catch her breath. With the chores downstairs finished, she went up and did the bedroom. There was no getting away from the dimness in each room. If there was an image to show the meaning of depression, this was it. The artificial light that filled the bedroom had a yellow tinge; everything looked the same at any time of day. Joy was happy, that was the only thing keeping Anna going, her little bundle of happiness, always happy to see her, no matter what she looked like. That girl would be the real saviour of this family.

Chapter 24

Anna and Mikey were upstairs, Mikey spent an hour in his room, ensuring every surface was clean and sprayed with anti-bacterial spray. Anna did the same to the bedroom, scrubbed the toilet, shower and bath. (As well as Joy's room, even though she wasn't using it any more).

Graham shouted up the stairs. 'You two come downstairs, please.'

Anna grabbed Joy and headed down. Mikey and Barney followed. Anna walked into the living room and saw Graham with a crazy-wide grin on his face, his fat cheeks pushed up so far that his eyes looked slanted. His beard had grown so wild his neck hair was joining with his chest hair at the collar of his shirt.

'What is it?' Anna looked cautious. Mikey stood slightly behind her, Barney between her legs.

'I've come up with a plan. I don't know if you've noticed, but the air in here is getting a little stale, especially since I blocked off the fireplace. There is no fresh air coming in. Obviously, we can't just open a window. If the virus... the virus *is* airborne so we can't afford to take that risk.'

'So, what can we do?'

'I've made an air-filtration unit.' He brought up a box fan with a thin layer of filter paper covering one side. 'I'm going to get my grinder, cut a hole in the shutter here,' he drew an invisible shape with his finger over the steel, 'cut through the glass in the window with my diamond-pointed glass cutter, and fit the fan in the gap. I'll plug it in and when it's on, the air from outside will be sucked in and blown into the house, any impurities will be caught in the filter paper and we can all breathe clean, fresh air.' He looked at them like an actor at the end of a play waiting for applause and a standing ovation.

'Will that actually work?' Anna said sceptically.

The smile slowly erased on Graham's face. The way he looked at her made her realise that this wasn't the reaction he had expected. She thought then that he probably wanted her to treat him like a hero, like he was the saviour she needed, that her and the children were saved by his ideas. It dawned on her, stronger than ever, that he wanted her to come to the realisation that without him, they would not survive.

'Of course, it will work. Were you not listening to my explanation? For fucks sake Anna!'

'Sorry darling. Yes of course, fantastic idea. I never would have thought of it.' She was backtracking, hoping he would come back down.

He took a deep breath, counted backwards from five. He was still pissed, but he had it under control. 'Right, you two need to go back upstairs. It won't be safe down here whilst the window is open. I've got my gas mask so I'll be safe. Don't come down until I'm done. OK?'

They both nodded. Anna looked down at Joy. Thinking about how he called for them *both* to come down, and *both* to go back upstairs. He was referring to her and Mikey. It was like Joy wasn't a real person to him. She tried to think of the last time Graham actually spoke to Joy, or held her in his arms, and she couldn't think of one, aside from the first two months of her life. She put it down to late grieving after his dad died, but he had never shown love for her.

They did as they were told and headed back upstairs. Graham plugged his radio in and put a tape in the tape deck.

Chapter 25

The Rolling Stones were blaring loudly from the radio's speakers.

Mick Jagger singing 'I can't get no...satisfaction!'

Graham hummed along; it was one his dad's old tapes. He (though shamefully would never admit it) didn't own a Rolling Stones record himself. He knew most of the chorus on some of the hits but the verses were new to him. He set up his grinder to cut through the steel; he wore his gas mask for protection from any shred of metal or microbe of virus that managed to get in. The disc spun, whirring and screaming,

He put the grinder blade to the steel and followed the black outline he drew on with marker pen for precision. He swung his hips left and right to the beat of the music; sweat poured down his face, soaking into his bushy facial hair. A thousand orange sparks flew up in the air and into his face. He squinted against the brightness of them and kept his hands steady. He'd forgotten to wear his gloves, and tiny red-hot pieces of steel landed on his skin, coming up in instant blisters. He ignored the pain. Then embraced it. It almost felt good, as if he was getting some satisfaction from it.

The twenty-by-twenty-inch square fell to the floor with a clatter.

'WoooWeee!' he hollered, holding the grinder up in the air, still spinning wildly.

He put the grinder down and picked up a piece of hardboard with suckers he had glued on one side, and a handle on other. He put it on the windowpane so it levelled up with the hole in the steel. He pulled a diamond-tipped glass cutter from his toolbox, and scored round the hardboard. He was patient, concentrating fully. The vein in his head was pulsing as he did, not wanting to make a mistake. Perfection, when he was at work – back when he had a job – was of the upmost importance.

'There is no greater advertisement then the word of mouth from people you've worked for.'

That's what he used to say to anyone he hired. Make every job you do perfect, and you'll never be short of work. People would pass your name around the street, on Facebook, Instagram, everywhere. Working at home was no different.

He was still sweating profusely; the mask increased the temperature, making his head like an oven. It stung in his eyes, making him blink. He was so close to the end. He took a breath, holding the cutter perfectly still; his arms were aching from the awkward angle he had to hold them at. He carried on and finished. He put the glass cutter back in his tool box, and, gripping the handle firmly with his left hand, he pulled the perfectly cut piece of glass out through the gap in the shutter, careful of his arms on the cut steel edges that were as sharp as razors.

'YES! That's how you fucking do it. Ugh!' He celebrated, punching the air. He turned the volume up on the radio. *'It's only Rock N' Roll'* was playing. He danced around the room, paying no heed to the massive hole in the window, letting the virus particles creep in and fill the room. He picked up the air filtration unit (desk fan and filter paper) and slotted it in. It fitted perfectly.

Of course, it did.

He plugged it in; the blades spun into action when he clicked on the power. The breeze flapped up his shirt, cooling him instantly with fresh, clean air. He removed his gas mask; his face looked sweaty and swollen. Red from the intensity he put into his work. He took a deep breath, filling his lungs with his achievement. 'Yeah! Whoo!' he yelled.

He opened the door to the hallway. 'Anna, Mikey. Come on down.'

He stood in the living room, grabbed his silicone gun and applied the finishing touches for when they came in. He put a bead of silicone round the edge to seal it in and make it secure.

Anna walked in with Mikey and Barney. Joy was napping upstairs.

'What do you think? Not bad Eh? Eh?' He nudged Mikey in the arm and danced around like a boxer in a sparring session. He wiped his blistered hand under his nose.

'Nice one, Dad. I can already tell the difference.' Mikey said.

'Yeah Graham. You've done a great job.'

He really had. Anna was genuinely impressed with what he had done, and the difference was immediately noticeable.

'Yeah well, you know. I do what I do.' He bent down to put his tools back in his tool box, Anna noticed his jeans had fallen down, revealing his flabby back and arse crack. It was yet another reminder of how much he had changed from the slim, muscular man he had been.

Graham lifted his toolbox and turned round to them. 'Right, I'm off down to the basement, I need to cool off and it's nice and cold down there.'

He pointed to the mess around the room, 'Tidy all this up love. You too Mikey.'

He walked out, stepping back and unplugging the radio to take with him on the way. He shut the door that led to the basement and wasn't seen again until dinner.   Anna and Mikey shared a look. Mikey looked sad, on the verge of tears.

'Hey love, what's wrong?' Anna placed an arm round his shoulders and led him to the sofa. 'Talk to me. You haven't said anything about what you're feeling. This must be so confusing for you, like it is for all of us. But we have to talk to each other if we are going to get through it.'

131

Mikey started crying. He was sobbing; tears ran down his cheeks, and big globs of snot fell from his nose. Anna rocked him as he cried, it was five minutes before he could speak. He had held it in for so long, once he let it go, he didn't know how to stop it.

'Go on, tell me how you're feeling.' Anna said, rubbing his back.

'I just don't understand it. Everyone's dead? Like, the whole world? What about Kirsty and Zoe? What about my friends at school, Zack and Ben? Are they all dead as well?' He looked at Anna with pleading eyes, wanting her to tell him a lie.

She wasn't sure how to answer him, they had all thought about it, that much was obvious. Anna had thought about Beverly every day since the whole thing started, hoping that Italy hadn't got it yet and that she was just locked in a five-star hotel watching the unfolding nightmare on the news.

'I don't know darling. I wish I had the answers for you, I really do.'

Mikey sniffed, and wiped his nose on the back of his hand. 'We managed to get ourselves safe. We're still here. They could be safe too.'

He was looking at her as if she hadn't just spoken. Anna could see in his eyes what he wanted to hear; he wanted her to tell him that everything was going to be OK, that he would see his friends again. He could find out the truth one day when they got out, when he was a bit older and maybe it would be a bit easier to take. She knew they were dead; they were all dead. If Graham hadn't become so obsessed, they would be dead too, most likely.

'Yes love. There is a chance they are fine. Just like we are. In fact, I'm sure they are.'

Mikey forced a smile. His blurry eyes stared at her, grateful for the lie.

They hugged for what felt like an hour; she stroked his hair like she used to when he was little, back when he would sit and snuggle with her in front of the TV to watch his cartoons. She was lost in a daze of happy memories, taken back to a time when the only thing they had to worry about was organizing play dates and what film they were going to rent on Friday nights. When the idea of the end of the world was just a fictional tale told by mediocre acting and simple writing.

Mikey's rumbling stomach snapped them both out of their embrace.

'I'm so hungry, mum. Dad hasn't even made us any lunch.'

'Me too, sweetheart.' She realised then that Graham would be preoccupied downstairs with whatever he was doing until dinner. He didn't spend much, if any, time with the family anymore. 'Tell you what. I'm going to go grab you something from the kitchen, you stay here.'

'But mum, what if dad finds out?' The look of fear in his eyes made her sadder than she ever thought possible. How could they both be in so much fear of taking something as simple as a pack of biscuits from the kitchen, worrying what Graham might say or do?

'Don't you worry about that, love. I'll make sure he won't notice.'

Anna kissed Mikey's head and walked into the kitchen, tiptoeing as best she could. Aware that any creaks in the floorboards would be heard louder in the basement below them.

She opened the bottom cupboard, found the tub with the cookies and crisps that were saved for Mikey's packed lunch. She grabbed him two chocolate cookies and a pack of salted crisps. When she stood and began to walk away, the floorboard in between the threshold of the door that separated the kitchen and living room screeched. Her heart jumped up her throat.

He heard that, he had to have heard that.

Panic caused her to start walking faster. She fumbled the contraband into Mikey's grateful arms and hurried him off up the stairs.

'Hide the wrappers,' she whispered.

Mikey nodded, and ran upstairs, two steps at a time.

Anna sat on the sofa, perched on the edge of the cushion. She was so tense she thought even if there was nothing underneath her, she would still be in the same position, as if sitting on an invisible chair. She stared at the door to the kitchen, waiting for Graham to come upstairs, like he knew what she was up to. What she had done. How she had defied him. What punishment would he hand out to her? What foul thing would he force down her throat this time?

After five-minutes, she started to relax. He wasn't coming. He didn't know what she had done. When her heart had returned to its resting rate, she went up to bring Joy down.

Chapter 26

Mikey shut his door and ran to his bed. He scoffed the first cookie in five seconds flat, the crumbs tumbling down from his mouth and landing on his jeans. A chocolate chip had melted on his finger and he sucked it clean, tasting the sweet, rich velvety coating that spread around his teeth and gums. It was heaven. How long it had been, or how long had it *felt* like it had been. Then he enjoyed the bag of crisps; the saltiness stung his lips, in a good way. He upended the bag, getting every last crumb. Then he split the foil down the seam and licked the inside, not knowing when his mum would be able to scurry away another one for him. To have flavour, actual flavour, in his mouth was amazing, euphoric. Dad was the worst cook, he took the flavour out of everything, cooking it to death in fear of food poisoning or something equally ridiculous. Once, Graham had done a barbecue and handed out under-cooked chicken legs; everyone who ate one had had diarrhoea for a week. Ever since then he never cooked chicken legs on the barbecue, and if he did, he would cook them until they were dry and black.

Mikey picked up the second cookie and lifted it to his mouth. He stopped just short of biting it and decided to save it for later. He brushed the crumbs from his lap into his cupped hand and poured them down the side of his bed that sat flush against the wall. Then he jammed the empty crisp packet down there with the crumbs and the left-over cookie. He stood and walked over to the door, knowing his dad never set foot in his room, if he ever wanted him, the doorway was the closest he would come.

He turned, looking at the bed from the perspective of anyone looking into his room from the door, checking to see if anything was visible. As far as he could see, there was nothing noticeable. He breathed a sigh of relief and sat back on his bed. His guitar stood in the corner. It had been covered in dust until he gave it a wipe and sprayed it with anti-bac earlier. He hadn't played it for over a week, he could already feel the callouses on the tips of his fingers softening.

He picked it up and pulled the plectrum out of the strings he weaved it through every time he finished. He was a pretty good guitarist for his age. His music teacher told him he would get even better as he grew older and his hands got bigger; they would find their way around the fret board much easier and wouldn't hit the small space in between the strings.

He hit a few of the strings and turned the tuning pegs at the top. It always fell out of tune when it hadn't been played for a while, like some childish ghost was playing a prank on him. He pulled a sheet of tablature out from his bedside drawer that his music teacher had given him to practice. Mr. Sharp had told him when he gave it to him,

'Your Dad will like this one.'

It wasn't that he *knew* his dad or anything, it was just a generalisation that any man in the world would like this song for its notoriety and well-known opening riff and chorus.

Highway to hell-ACDC.

He hit the first chord three times. His eyes moved to the next set. He played them through before rounding back to the first chord again. It was simple enough, his fingers found it hard to flow between them at first, but after the fiftieth time or whatever it was, he nailed it. The hope was that he could take his guitar downstairs and show his dad. Hoping his dad would be proud of him. It was his dad who hadn't wanted him to learn it, who never supported his idea of being a musician as a viable career choice. Maybe this would show him he was wrong. Over the past twelve months though, he hadn't said a single word about it, or shown an interest in anything he was learning. Maybe he was just sick of hearing 'Smoke On The Water'. This might make him more interested.

Mikey thought about plugging it in; playing an electric guitar unplugged was like watching a film with the sound off. You got an idea of what it was, but you didn't get the full effects until it was plugged in and the volume was up. He decided to practice a little more, make sure he got the song nailed down, then he'd plug it in.

Chapter 27

Anna had Joy on the mat in the living room. *This damn mat,* it was like a full-time babysitter, Anna thought shamefully. Whenever Anna had something else to do, put the baby on the mat, got to talk to Graham, put the baby on the mat. God forbid Graham might actually look after his daughter. That was woman's work, cleaning and child minding. Graham had far more important things to do in the basement. Trying to figure out a way to communicate to any survivors, or find a message on the air waves. It could be imperative to their survival.

She took the mat away and threw it to the side of the room. Barney lifted his head as it landed near him, almost in shock that Joy wasn't using it. Then he rested his head back down on his front paws and went back to sleep by the window, near to where the fan was plugged in.

Anna was on all-fours, hovering over Joy. Pulling funny faces and talking to her. '*Who's a pretty girl. You are, yes, you are,*' she said in her best baby talk. Joy loved it, flapping her arms in the air, making shapes with her mouth as she tried to imitate the noises and words her mum was making.

Anna moved back and sat on the floor. She started tickling Joy's feet, making each one kick like two pistons in a machine. Joy was laughing; Anna started laughing too. Anna put a toy on the floor to Joy's side in the hope she would reach for it.

As if hearing her mum's thoughts, Joy reached for the toy with her opposite arm. Bringing herself onto her side, she flipped all the way round so that she lay on her stomach.

Anna gasped in shock. Mikey had done that as early as three months, Joy was a late bloomer in that regard; six months old, going on seven, she still hadn't shown any intentions of wanting to roll over and try to crawl. She had everything she needed; the people she saw everyday attended to her every need no matter what, so why bother eh? Anna thought.

Now though, she was doing it.

'Well done! You clever girl!' Anna squeezed Joy's ribs, making her laugh. Joy rolled back on to her back, smiled at Anna, as if she was just checking Anna was still there, and rolled back on to her front to get the toy again. A little rubber ducky with a sun hat and glasses on. Anna grabbed the toy, this time placing it a few feet in front of Joy's face. Joy looked at it and stretched out an arm. So close, yet so far. She kicked with her legs, trying to propel herself forward, but only finding air. She grabbed the rug and pulled herself forward, managing to move about half an inch.

Anna was amazed at the steely determination in Joy's face. She wanted that toy duck and she was going to get it. She pulled on the rug again, still kicking her feet; this time she made contact with the floor and managed to get forward half a foot.

She giggled. It was the most wonderful sound Anna had ever heard; her baby was giggling and rolling over, trying to crawl. It was as if something had clicked and all of a sudden everything became clear as to what she was supposed to do.

Whether it was being constantly kept on the edge of emotional turmoil by Graham, or how tired and hungry she was, Anna didn't know, but she started crying. They weren't sad tears this time though, they were happy tears, the happiest tears she had cried in a long time.

She positioned Joy's legs so she could come up on to her knees, and lifted her arms so her palms were flat on the floor and her arms were straight. Joy looked at her, wobbling unsteadily as she turned her head and smiled at her Mum as if to say, *I've got this.*

She reached a hand out in front of her, wobbling violently from side to side like she was made of jelly. Then she tried to bring her leg forward, following the path of her arm and collapsed into the rug face first. She rolled back onto her back. She was still smiling, but clearly knackered from all that exertion.

'You did so well, you little star.' Anna held Joy close and hugged her. She was in a state of elation, like it was the greatest thing to ever happen in the history of the world. She wished Graham had seen it; she should maybe have shouted for him. She told herself he wouldn't have come up anyway, and he probably wouldn't have been that interested either. She decided to keep it to herself. Joy was making an O shape with her mouth and sticking her fingers in there. She was hungry. She had used up her energy and needed to replace it.

Anna stood up and headed to make Joy a bottle, feeling proud as punch at what Joy had just done, when something from upstairs vibrated through the walls.

It sounded like 'Highway to Hell.'

Chapter 28

Mikey, now having nailed the intro to 'Highway to Hell', plugged his guitar into his amp. Standing in his room, facing a poster of Jimi Hendrix rocking out at Woodstock, he put the guitar strap over his head. He hit the distortion button in the amp and filled the gain up to 10.

The A-chord hummed around his bedroom, reverberating from the steel shutters and back into his ears. He closed his eyes and imagined the crowd, the thousands of people there to watch him shred the guitar like no one else in the world. He could hear them scream his name, '*Mikey! Mikey! Mikey!*'

He had the crowd in the palm of his hand, they were waiting for him to drop the riff, hit them hard with it, melt their faces with a trilling masterpiece guitar solo. Here it came.

'Highway to Hell.'

He opened strong, hitting all the right strings, his fingers flowed with the precision of a guitar player three times his years. The crowd were dancing, rocking out, throwing him the devil horns, saluting their new God.

He sang along, it came so naturally to him. This was what he was meant to be. He was meant to survive this pandemic to do exactly this, change the world with his music like so many before him.

His mum and dad would be proud, standing at the side of the stage, being all old and feeling out of place but clapping along anyway. Joy could be part of the band; he could teach her how to play rhythm. A family rock n' roll band.

He was lost in his imaginary world of dreams and possibilities. It hadn't dawned on him that with the disease so out of control, there might not be thousands of people left to attend gigs anymore. In the world he had made in his head, there was no disease, people were free to live how they wanted, sticking the finger to the man and not caring who saw 'em. This was his world and no-one would take it from him.

'*I'm on a Highway to...*'

His bedroom door burst open; he jumped towards his bed, his room filling with the deafening squeal of feedback from the amp. His dad stood at the door, looking sweaty and out of breath. His face dark and full of rage.

Chapter 29

Graham was sat in the basement. High off of his own achievements, blissfully unaware of what his daughter was going to achieve in the room above him, or what his son was working so hard to accomplish another floor higher. Graham was only concerned with what he was doing, as long as everyone else was doing as they were told and sticking to the rules, that was.

So far so good in that regard.

It was just that inkling of lack of trust from Anna that had been the only blemish on the day, but he had managed to control his temper. Which was good, that was a good sign.

He flipped off the cap from a bottle of beer and swigged it. A beer after a good day's work was simply divine. There was no greater feeling than going to the pub after work, especially on a Friday when he could afford to have two or three with the lads. John and Dave would be a right laugh on a Friday, getting into all kinds of shit after a few pints, chatting up the barmaid in front of her boyfriend, or spiking each other's drinks with vodka shots when the other wasn't looking. Even Tig would show up every now and then, the little pen pusher as they all used to call him, in reference to the fact that he made his living sat at a desk instead of grafting with his hands.

Graham was smiling as he thought of them; the memories he had with his friends were some he held as some of the greatest times of his life, certainly the happiest times of his life. A far cry from where he was now. Now he was fucking miserable; the sweet-tasting memory quickly turned to bitterness, like ashes in his mouth. He didn't have them anymore, they were too busy to check in on their old pal Graham. As soon as the business went under, they didn't want to hear how his day was going. Oh no, if the money and the work wasn't coming in, he could just fuck off. Well, they could too. 'Fuck off!' he said to the empty space in front of him. He drank his beer and opened a fresh one.

They didn't want anything else to do with him. Fine. So be it. It was Tig that he couldn't understand. They had been friends since they were Mikey's age. He should have been in touch. Just because he had got married and had a new baby didn't mean he couldn't call his oldest friend for a chat, did it? Fuck him and fuck the others too.

Graham smiled sadistically at the thought of his so called 'friends' catching the virus, their insides exploding out of their stomachs, watching their loved ones die in front of their eyes. If they'd have kept in touch with him better, he could have warned them. They deserved everything they got.

He pulled a pack of Marlboros out of his desk drawer, and walked over to the basement doors that led to the garden, emerging from the side, out of sight from the front of the house. He sat on the steps and sparked his lighter. His eyes crossed as he watched the flame engulf the tip of the cigarette. He sucked and breathed deeply, blowing the smoke out of the cracks in the door, relaxing with the feeling of satisfaction. The beam of sunlight that shone through illuminated the dancing plumes of smoke that hung in the air. Anna had tried to take one of his small pleasures from him; fucking bitch. Who was she to question him? Make decisions for him? He was the man of the house, the *head* of the house. For too long he had let her make all the decisions, let her take charge. The words of his father rang in his head:

'*The woman of the house should know her place, she stands behind the man, trusts in everything he does and accepts his decisions as final.*'

His dad had never liked Anna; he thought she had ideas above her station. Graham was beginning to realise that now. She was trying to emasculate him at every turn. Laughing about him behind his back with her friends. He'd heard her talking to Beverly fucking Cage about how he'd put on weight, stopped looking after himself. She didn't find him physically attractive anymore, well that was fine with him. After all this was over, she'd be begging him to stay around. She had wanted to leave him, and take the kids. Break up *his* family? Part of him wished he'd have just let her go straight away. Watch as she came running back when the virus hit because she didn't have the first idea how to survive it.

'Good luck surviving with two kids and no husband!'

He laughed, his breath pushing the smoke in the basement in all different directions. He imagined the scene, leaving the house after being cooped up for so long, telling her she was on her own. It was a dog-eat-dog world now, more so than before and he wasn't going to get dragged down by her and those little versions of herself that were supposedly his.

He started methodically popping the tiny blisters on his hands and forearms, watching as the clear fluid spilled from each burn.

He'd seen the way she eyed up other men, even his friends when they used to come round, laughing with him and sharing jokes. Laughing *at* him most likely. Well, he'd be the one laughing when they were all dead and gone, and he was free to live how he wanted to live.

The final nail in the coffin was when she'd refused him to go see his father during the lockdown, saying, 'But we're vulnerable'. Fuck off. She just didn't like him and wanted him to die, old and alone.

'He wasn't even a good dad to you! From what you've told me he was a bastard to you and your mum when you were growing up,' she had said, like she even knew a fucking thing about him. After his dad had done the test and it came back positive, he had the virus, she'd firmly said no. And he was too weak to argue with her, and she knew it. She'd used the power that she held over him and now it was his turn. After

everything, after showing him how weak and pathetic he was all of their married life, she was going to leave him. *Well now the tables have turned,* he thought, *now she can't fucking leave.* If he continued to show her how strong he could be, no, how strong he *was,* how she couldn't possibly survive without him when the worst happened, then she would realise her mistake and stay.

Graham could never forgive her for not letting him visit his dad, and she would pay. Even though the other half of him knew that if he had been to see his dad, he could have brought the virus back and killed the kid in his wife's stomach. That half of Graham was fading every day; the parasites in his head were slowly gnawing away at it, relieving him of it, so he could be free.

He threw the cigarette down on the floor and crushed it out with the toe of his shoe. Walking back to his desk, through the boxes of food and supplies, he reached into a box that was marked in big black letters that said: 'DAD'S STUFF'. He pulled out the Rolling Stones vest and held it up. 'I'm never taking you off again,' he said to it. He flung the shirt he was wearing over his head and threw it behind him; it landed on a pile of boxes. He pulled on the vest. It got stuck just after his chest; he pulled it down over his stomach, the material stretching further than it was designed to. He sat down and his belly hung out above his belt. He could smell his armpits, dank and musty with old sweat.

He shut his eyes and thought of his dad.

Barry had become frail in his old age. He had survived a bout of cancer, doctors had managed to catch it early. The chemo had taken it out of him and he'd never fully recovered. His limbs had been skin and bone and his hair had grown back, but only in random tufts at the side of his head.

Cancer of the bladder. Not the most common of cancers. They'd had to cut the tumour out, forcing him to have a catheter fitted for the remainder of his life.

Barry had hated that. Carrying a bag of piss everywhere he went.

He never would have believed that Graham was man enough to do what he was doing now. Yet here he was. Doing it. His dad would realise that Graham had learnt from all those *lessons*. Yet Anna still showed signs that she harboured questions and doubts about what he was doing. She needed a reminder, a jolt.

Graham reached out and turned the volume control on the radio, leaned back in his chair and squeezed his eyes shut, focusing on the static. He drifted a while, though he didn't feel like he had slept, more that he just blacked out, like trying to remember what happened the night before after a skin-full down at the pub.

A voice came over the air-waves. It sounded far away, yet clear as a bell as if it had been transmitted from the same room. He pushed himself forward hastily; he turned the volume knob all the way round and listened to the man's voice. It was panicky and breathless.

'If anyone is out there...if anyone has survived. The virus has mutated, the streets are filled with bodies of the dead. They are being picked apart by scavengers. There is a small group of us, we've managed to hold up in the old radio station. Don't try to find us...if you're somewhere safe, stay there. It's crazy outside, we haven't seen a living person for nearly a week. The only ones we have seen roaming around are...this sounds insane...there are some that don't die from the disease, they just turn...zombies, is the only way I know how to describe it...Their eyes glow red with blood, they bleed from everywhere, eyes, mouth, ears, nose. Their skin is ravaged with boils and sores, oozing with puss. They are devoid of all human characteristics. We saw one bite the head off a bird and drink its insides. They are attracted to noise, so stay quiet and for God's sake avoid breathing the air outside at all costs. It travels in the vapour molecules in the air and can live for...I don't

know. There is no government left...no law and order...this is the end, Armageddon. May God bless you all, pray we can get through this. I'll try send another report out, but if you don't hear from me again...Fear the worst.'

Before the message clicked off and went back to static, Graham heard the sounds of crying coming from the message. He hit the side of the radio with the flat of his hand, he fiddled with the long chrome antenna, trying to find a signal again.

'Come on! COME ON!!'

He leaned back in his chair. He rubbed a hand through his hair and scratched at the beard that grew wildly down his neck. The vein in his neck throbbed as his heart started pounding hard against the inside of his ribcage.

A small fluttering of dust fell from above him; there was a faint sound of rock music, distorted guitar vibrating through the house. His eyes spread wide in fear, remembering the message,

'They are attracted to noise...'

Mikey was playing his guitar, that fucking guitar! Graham bolted up the stairs like a bat out of hell. Anna was stood in the kitchen, feeding Joy and smiling like a drugged-up moron. He pushed passed her, nearly spilling Joy from her arms.

'Graham?! What are you doing?!' she shouted at him.

Raised her fucking voice at him!

He ignored her for now, charging up the stairs to Mikey's room. The dog started barking at him; it stood at the bottom of the stairs, yapping after him. He'd kill that fucking dog before this was over. The guitar was getting louder, how could he be so stupid? Graham kicked the door, sending it smashing into the wall. Mikey spun to look at him and fell back on to the bed. He looked at him, knowing he was doing something he shouldn't.

Graham moved into the room towards the amplifier and hit the off button. He ripped the leads out of the front and disconnected the mains power lead from the back. He lifted the amp up and took it out of the room. He didn't speak, such was his fury. He'd been scared at first; now, looking at his son's stupid, ignorant face, he was just plain mad. He threw the amp down the stairs; it hit two walls, bouncing like a bowling ball down an alley with the barriers up, and smashed on the hallway floor at the bottom. Barney jumped to the side, narrowly avoiding being killed by the impact.

He turned back towards Mikey's room and saw him cowering on the bed, holding his guitar over his body like a shield. 'Get downstairs now.'

Chapter 30

Graham gathered them all in the dining area. Mikey sat next to Anna; he had shuffled his chair along the table to be nearer to her, and further from his dad. Barney lay between Anna's feet, quietly growling with every breath. Graham sat at the head of the table, the rest of his family opposite him, huddled together. He sat silently, just looking at them. Anna found she couldn't make eye contact with him; he was just watching them watch him. She tried to look at him again but couldn't last longer than a couple of seconds. He had them where he wanted them, she knew. Waiting for him to speak, not knowing what he was going to say or what he was going to do. She could Mikey's heartbeat as he pressed closer to her.

Joy started crying, Anna put a dummy in her mouth, which soothed her; the gentle rocking of Anna's arms sent her to sleep quickly.

'There's been a message.' Graham's voice, although low and deep, cut the silence like an axe and sent shivers up Anna's spine. The air felt thick despite the fan constantly blowing in the background.

'What kind of message?' Anna was ashamed at how shaky her voice was, and how afraid she was of the unpredictability of her husband.

'On the radio. It came through over the static. It came from a survivor, there's a group of them out at the old radio station, 'Wymere sounds.' They confirmed my worst fears. The country has fallen, the *world* has fallen. There is no government, no law and order. The scariest part of it is that what I saw was only the start.' He paused, letting the information sink in.

'The virus kills most people instantly, which if what I've heard is true, then it's a blessing in disguise. Those that don't die instantly, carry on walking around, mindless and violent, like some kind of mutant zombies.'

Anna gasped and held Mikey and Joy tighter to her. Her lip was trembling like her hands.

'The air is compromised. If we had breathed the fresh air, we would be destined to suffer the same fate. The monsters are wandering the land, attracted by noise. From here on out, we have to remain as quiet as we can.' He shot a look at Mikey, 'That means no more guitar, no more power tools or music played too loud. It's for our own sake.'

'Graham, how long are we expected to live like this? What you're talking about isn't possible. Trapped in here with no light, one source of fresh clean air, living off rations that are frankly starving us, now we can't make a noise?'

Graham turned his head away from her, like the sound coming from her was offensive to his ears. Questioning him, now of all times.

He flashed his eyes back at her; they were wild and crazy. The expression of fury gave way and a smile spread across his face that was wicked and chilling.

'I'll tell you what, Anna. If you want to risk it, I'll open the front door for you right now. You can go and take your chances on the outside. One less mouth for me to have to feed.' He smiled at her still, wanting her to accept. She only shook her head and lowered her chin to her chest, planting a kiss on Mikey's and Joy's cheeks.

'Didn't think so.' He stood and placed his hands on the table. He leaned over them and they recoiled from him instinctively. 'I need to think. We may have to survive in here longer than I first thought. You two can go upstairs, out of my sight. I don't want to hear any footsteps on this floor whilst I'm in the basement. Is that clear?'

They nodded. Barney growled.

Graham looked down at the dog on the floor. Its teeth were revealed to him, little white fangs over black and pink gums. 'And if that dog starts barking at me again. I'll rip its fucking head off.' He looked at Anna so she knew he was serious.

She knew.

He went back down to the basement without saying another word.

Anna squeezed Mikey and they both started to cry. Mikey's heart was fluttering like a hummingbird's. Anna could feel it through his ribs, ribs that were now more prominent than a week ago.

She breathed deeply and put a finger under his chin, lifting his face to hers. She smiled at him. 'Chin up, Mikey. We've got each other, we'll get through this together.'

Mikey nodded and wiped his eyes.

'Come on then, let's go upstairs and play a game in the craft room. Joy will be asleep for the next couple of hours.'

Chapter 31

Anna and Mikey played a game of Snakes and Ladders. Mikey won, as he often did. Snakes and Ladders was more a game of chance; the only reason they hadn't played something more sophisticated, like chess, was because Anna was useless at it and it took the fun out of it for Mikey. Anna had taken an early lead, rolling a six and landing at the bottom of a ladder that took her from a square on the bottom row all the way to the third row from the top.

'Ahh, look at that,' she said quietly, but still able to express her delight at getting ahead so early in the game. 'I'm gonna win.' She chanted like a kid in the school playground

'Don't count your chickenth Mother.' Mikey said in his favourite impression of his school teacher Mr. Silence with the unfortunate lisp.

They both laughed, relieving some of the tense anxiety they both felt in the pit of their stomachs. Anna got all the way to the square that was only four steps away from the finish line, only to roll a one and fall down a snake. She then followed it up with a two and hit another snake, falling down to the bottom row again. Mikey smelt blood and finished the game in his next two throws of the dice.

'Well Played Misith Willow.'

He held out a hand and shook it comically.

They played again and then Mikey said Anna could do some of her craft work. He knew how much she enjoyed it and wanted her to have a bit of time to herself before Joy woke up. She'd had an hour but was still sleeping soundly in the next room, so Anna decided to leave her; she was probably needing the rest after her physical exertions earlier in the day. She wondered if Joy was dreaming about it, putting one hand in front of the other, figuring out where she'd gone wrong the first time. Next time she would probably manage it and then that would be it, she'd be into everything. They'd have to baby-proof all of the cupboards, especially in the kitchen where they kept the bleach and cleaning products.

'Thank you, Mikey. Yes, I will.' Anna said, amazed at his maturity.

'OK. I'll read my comics. Do you mind if I sit in here with you, though? I won't make any noise.'

'Of course, love. You go pick one.'

Mikey smiled and ran off to his bedroom to pick a comic. He was a big fan of the Marvel franchise; his favourite comic was Spider-Man, reading which foes Peter Parker would encounter in each one. The ones he liked to read the most were the ones that had lots of fight scenes between Spidey and Venom, the alien Symbiote from outer space who had a great big smile full of dagger-like teeth.

He came back in with his comic and sat in the corner near the door, cross-legged and utterly engrossed.

Anna looked at him lovingly and started a new project. Every time she'd had the chance to come in this room lately, she hadn't felt like crafting, instead favouring looking out the crack in the steel shutters, seeing the world outside, how peaceful it all looked. After her afternoon with Mikey though, she was feeling more relaxed, so got her wool and crochet hooks out. She was going to make beanie hats for Joy, each one a different colour. The first one, though, was going to be a rainbow pattern. How cute she thought it would look, Joy wearing a rainbow hat with matching rainbow blanket.

They both sat quietly for another hour. Mikey's stomach kept rumbling like rolling thunder in the corner of the room. Anna's stomach was doing the same. She had been starving but didn't want to steal any more food than she thought she could get away with. Stealing for Mikey was risky enough; if she was to start as well, Graham was sure to find out.

154

'Do you think it's dinner time yet?' Mikey said, breaking the blissful silence they had created.

Anna shrugged, 'I'm not sure, darling. It could be.' She looked over at the window, wrestling with the idea of showing Mikey where they could look out of the window and see the outside. It would cheer him up, of that she was certain. She decided to do it. On the promise that he wouldn't accidentally mention it when Graham was in earshot.

'Come here.' She nodded her head in the direction of the window. Mikey looked at her, confused, but did what she said. He walked over to the steel shutter and stood there looking at her.

'See that bottom corner.'

'Yeah, what about it?'

'Kneel down and look closely.'

He pulled a face that said, 'meh' and got down on his knees. He saw instantly when he got eye-level with it. 'We can see outside,' he said, his face full of amazement.

Anna nodded, smiling emphatically. Mikey pressed his face up against the shutter, careful not to bang into it and send the metal rattling. 'Oh my God. It looks amazing, and so peaceful out there.'

'You wouldn't know the world was falling apart, would you?' Anna sighed.

'It all looks the same. I can see the road, I can see the trees, birds are flying in the sky. It's amazing.'

'It is. But listen Mikey, we can't let on about this, if your Dad knows he missed a bit...'

'He'll be straight up and fix it,' Mikey finished.

'That's right.'

'I'll keep quiet. Don't worry.'

Anna held out her pinky finger, wanting Mikey to take it like they used to do when he was little, when he'd make promises about eating all of his dinner or getting his pyjamas on like a good boy. Mikey shook his head, rolling his eyes like it was SOOO babyish. He wrapped his pinky finger in hers and shook.

     'Pinky promise?' she said.

     'Pinky promise.'

Chapter 32

Graham called them down for dinner. It had been about an hour since they had done the pinky promise ritual. Anna had got Joy up and they all played together in the craft room. Joy was desperately trying to show her big brother that she could crawl now. Mikey showed as much excitement as Anna had when he first saw her do it. Willing her on, like he was her very own cheerleader.

'She's doing it! Mum, she's really doing it!'

They all went down together. Barney stayed upstairs as if trying to give Graham space. They sat round the table and waited for their food. It smelt awful; a scent of smoke and burning filled the kitchen. Joy drank from a bottle Graham had made; he had made it two ounces smaller than Anna normally did, saying that she needed to drink less to let their supplies stretch further, adding that a decent mother would have started weaning her onto solid food by now.

That had stung Anna hard. Like a dagger in the heart. She knew she was mollycoddling Joy a little, but it was her baby girl, her last baby. There was no way she was going to have another. Who could blame her for wanting to keep Joy a baby for as long as she could? Before she knew it, Joy would be grown up and wouldn't need her that much anymore. Before eventually not needing her at all and able to do everything herself.

Anna watched as Graham pulled a tray out of the oven; a plume of smoke hit him in the face as the door swung open. He put the tray down on the side. 'Argh!' he exclaimed, and shook his hand in the air, then sucked on the end of his fingers where the tray had burnt him through the over glove.

'Fucking thing,' he said under his breath. He picked the food out of the tray with the same fingers he'd just sucked on and put it all onto one plate. The amount of food he had pulled out looked less than an average meal for one person, never mind three.

He cut through the pieces furiously. Whatever meat it was, it looked as tough as leather. Sweat was dripping from his forehead; the summer heat wasn't letting up, the house constantly felt like an oven. The only reprieve came from the fan in the living room, that actually managed to do a more than adequate job of keeping that room cool.

He divided the food over three plates and brought them over to the table.

'Eat up guys, you'll need your strength.' He went back to get his own plate. He sat and started digging in straight away.

Anna and Mikey shared a look and lifted their knife and forks solemnly. Anna felt as though she could cry; she'd been so desperate for food all day and this is what she'd got. Two small chunks of chicken breast, a blackened roast potato and a palm full of peas. She put a chunk of chicken in her mouth; the meat was dry and lacking in any flavour. She could have been putting a piece of cardboard in her mouth for all her taste buds knew. She choked it down. It was hard to swallow; even after it had dropped down her gullet, she still felt that something was there in the back of her throat.

The only sounds in the kitchen were those of cutlery on plates, and Graham's grotesque mouth-breathing as he ate. Wolfing down his food.

He stopped in-between chews. His eyes darted back and forth between Mikey and Anna.

Mikey ate his food quickly; he had the ability to eat anything when he was hungry, which served him well in their current situation. He looked round at everyone, saw the tension in everyone's faces, and was desperate for them to all get along again like they used to.

'That wath loverly. Pleeth sir, can I have thum more?' he said, combining a classic part of Oliver Twist with his teacher Mr. Silence.

Anna snorted a laugh and flung a hand up to her face to stifle her laughter, remembering the new rule of having to remain quiet. Mikey's impressions never failed to crack her up, no matter the situation. She always told him never to try do that at a funeral to cheer her up; she was likely to break out in a fit of giggles in front of the mourners.

Mikey laughed at Anna's reaction; they shared a couple of playful nudges whilst Graham watched on.

His jaw ground the meat in his teeth. It swung excessively from side to side as he chewed. Watching. As they laughed.

'Mikey,' Anna tapped him on the shoulder playfully. 'I hope your teacher never hears you doing that impression.'

Mikey pulled a face that made Anna laugh again. This kid is non-stop, she thought, and couldn't help feeling a surge of pride in him.

Graham slammed his fist on the table. Joy screamed in shock, Anna jolted in her seat and Mikey sat up straight, his smile long forgotten.

Graham breathed heavily, panting almost. 'Something funny about the food, Mikey?'

Mikey looked at Anna in shock, then back to Graham. 'No. Its fine, Dad.'

Graham looked over at Anna. 'You think it's funny, to encourage a boy to *laugh* at his father?'

'W-What? No, of course not. We were just laughing. Mikey does this impression of his teacher. It's so funny. You have to hear it.' Anna looked at Mikey, imploring him to do his bit.

'You think, *now*, is a good time for jokes? Do you think what's happening outside is a joke? You think what all those people out there are going through, who don't have someone

159

in the know like me, is a joke?' He looked at them both, disgusted.

They both looked down at their plates. Anna was holding Joy tight, scared that if Graham did anything suddenly, she might drop her.

'Well, Mikey? You think it's funny? You want to mock the food that sits in front of you every night? When others have nothing?'

'No...Sir.'

'Graham, leave him. He didn't mean anything by it.'

'You make me sick.' His eyes shifted towards Anna; he wiped some spittle that had gathered in the corner of his mouth. 'My father always warned me about you. He had your number the first day he met you. He told me, every chance he got, that you would control me. I wouldn't listen. He said when you were done with me, you'd leave and take everything I had. That's what you're doing isn't it? You're putting a wedge between me and Mikey, and the first chance you get, you're going to be off. It's been your plan from the start, hasn't it?'

'No! I loved you! If there's a wedge between you and Mikey, you've done it yourself.' Deep down she'd found some of her old self and as a surprise to herself as much as everyone else at the table, she'd bitten back.

Graham looked furious. 'You never loved me. That's why you flirted with the lads when they came round to watch the game, isn't it? You were always looking for the next one.'

'You're not making any sense. Flirting with your friends? They were your friends; I would hardly say two words to them.'

'I've never been man enough for you. That's what my father always told me. I wouldn't be man enough to control you, keep you in check.'

160

'Your dad was an awful man, Graham. His views were twisted. A wife isn't someone you're supposed to 'keep in check".'

'Don't you speak about him! You don't have the right!'

'I know he was a terrible husband. Your mother must have been scared her entire life. Death was probably a release for her.' Anna could feel herself bordering on angry.

'She respected him! Like a wife should, she would never have got between me and him, she would never have looked in the direction of another man. Unlike you!'

'She didn't respect him, she feared him!'

'I'll teach you some fucking respect!'

Graham stood up and raised his hand. Anna cowered away, covering Joy's face with her hands. She could see the hate in his eyes. She thought she could see his father in them. Not the father she had met, but the one that had visited her nightmares.

'Stop!' Mikey jumped up and grabbed Graham's arm.

Graham looked down at his son and saw the fear and desperation in his tear-filled eyes. 'Don't hurt my Mum!' Mikey shouted and tried to pull his dad away from the table.

'Mikey!' Anna screamed.

Graham looked at Mikey and then back to Anna. His lip curled at one side.

'This might teach you both some respect.' Graham pushed Mikey away from him. He stumbled and fell over the chairs. Anna rushed over to help him up.

'Mikey, go upstairs. Go into my room and lock the door!' Anna cried.

Graham searched in the cupboards and brought out a can of dog food. He slammed it on the kitchen counter and pulled the ring to take the lid off.

'Come up with me. Please Mum, let's go. Come on!' Mikey pleaded.

'You want to laugh at the food I give you? You want to make jokes at your old man behind my back?'

Mikey stood shaking his head, clinging on to his mum's arm.

'If the food is so awful Mikey,' Graham continued, 'how about you swap with the dog?'

Anna turned to Mikey, 'Mikey, go upstairs now. Lock yourself in my bedroom,' she shouted. 'Go, now!' She pushed him towards the door. Joy, in her other arm, was crying louder now. Barney barked and darted between them all.

Mikey darted for the door; he opened it and was about to open his legs, build up some speed, when he felt a hand grab the back of his collar. He was yanked back with such force all the air left his lungs as he hit the floor, the neckline of his t-shirt dug into his throat and chafed his skin, creating a sore red line.

'Stop it!' Anna stood, screaming at Graham. Joy was looking from side to side, her lip protruding and tears falling from her eyes.

Graham ignored her. 'Do you even know how much I've done for this family? You wouldn't have a clue 'cos you're so fucking self-obsessed!'

He dragged Mikey across the floor, choking him with his t-shirt. 'You want to take the piss out of my food boy, here you go, you can have your fill.'

'Graham stop it, please!'

Graham emptied the can of dog food over Mikey's face.

Chunks of meat clung in his hair, gravy crept into his mouth when he tried to scream; as soon as the taste hit his tongue, he shut his mouth to keep it out, but the gravy filled his nostrils and he breathed it in. He coughed against it, making him vomit from the disgusting taste and smell.

Anna put Joy on the floor at the other side of the room, Barney backed away from Graham, barking and yapping, then he ran straight to Joy and stood over her, snarling and growling in the direction of Graham. Anna ran over and tried to pull Graham off.

'Get off him! Get off him!' she screamed in his ear.

He was so strong; she was pulling on his arms with all of her might and he didn't move an inch. She dug her nails into his chubby flesh, trying to scratch and claw at him, hoping that would force him to release Mikey but it didn't.

'Is that better, boy?' Graham rubbed the gravy and meaty chunks into his son's face, smearing it all over so his skin was a muddy brown, with pink, mushed-up meat stuck in his eyebrows and hair.

He put his mouth next to Mikey's ear; through gritted teeth he said: 'Don't ever take the piss out of me, you piece of shit, or this will be the least of your worries. Now get out of my sight!' He pushed Mikey to the floor.

He was coughing and gagging; his hand rubbed at his throat. He was trying to scream, cry and catch his breath all at the same time. Struggling to get to his feet, slipping in the spilled gravy on the floor, he got his footing and ran through the living room and up the stairs.

Graham turned to look at Anna. She stopped clawing at him and stared into his eyes. Her husband had gone. It hadn't taken much to push him over the edge, but he had gone now. Her fury at what she had just witnessed now outweighed her fear. She swung a hand at him. The slap connected with his cheek, making a loud clapping noise that echoed around the steel shutters on the windows. It was the hardest slap she had ever given; her hand instantly stung and her wrist screamed in pain.

Graham's face hardly twitched.

He stood facing her; he licked at the corner of his lips where a cut had opened up and blood began to seep out of it.

His right hand came up from nowhere; the back of his hand connected with her eye-socket and sent her crashing into the kitchen worktop, spilling the tray that had come from the oven clattering to the floor.

She lay there, looking up at this man who used to be her loving, attentive husband. Her hand clutched to her face that was now a fury of fiery pain that spread all the way across her face and down the tendons in her neck. Joy was crying at the other side of the room; Barney was growling and yapping. Graham ignored their cries and bent down to her, his hideous gut hanging out from the awful vest that was too small for him, his teeth full of bits from his dinner. His breath was foul as he moved closer to her. She wondered if this would be the end, the last thing she would see, if her children would be left to survive with this monster of a man.

'All you have to do Anna, is get in line, learn that nothing is breaking this family apart. The more you struggle, the more you rebel, the harder things will be.'

Anna lifted herself up on her elbows and began dragging herself backwards towards Joy. Her hand landed on something sharp. She looked down and saw the broken tile under her splayed fingers.

Graham turned to look at Joy and Barney.

Anna quickly peeled out the longest shard of tile she could find: it was three inches at most, but big enough to stop him if he tried to kill her.

'Will you fall in line, Anna? Or will this situation get worse for you?'

Graham bent down low and grabbed her face in his gravy-covered fingers. He began squeezing, she tried to pull away but his grip was too strong. If he didn't stop soon, she was sure he'd break her jawbone. She twirled the piece of tile in her hand, making sure she was holding it the right way, and swung it towards his leg. She felt the sharp end go in, only a little, but it was enough to make him let go of her face and yell out in pain.

She started scurrying away from him.

164

'You fucking bitch!' He screamed and pulled the piece of tile from his leg and threw it across the room. He stomped forward and grabbed her by the throat.

Anna tried to speak but all that came out was choking sounds.

'Take, that screaming brat, and that yappy fucking dog, and fuck off upstairs.' He let go of her throat. Anna rubbed at her neck and as she took in frantic breaths of air. It felt as though her throat was burning.

'Who are you?' Anna managed to say, between sobs.

'I'm the man I always should have been.' He smiled and began to laugh. He stood and headed into the basement.

Anna, not wanting to hang around, jumped up and grabbed a bottle and made it in preparation for Joy's next feed, grabbed an empty bottle of coke from the cupboard, and filled that with water for her and Mikey, knowing neither of them would want to be heading downstairs for as long as they could possibly avoid it. She ran and picked Joy up from the floor, 'It's OK sweetheart. Mummy's got you.' She kissed Joy's head, trying to calm her.

Anna's face was throbbing, but she ignored it for now. She got upstairs as quickly as she could. She knocked on her bedroom door and Mikey let her in when he knew it was her. She sat on the bed; Mikey looked either side of the corridor.

'I'll be back in a minute,' he said, and darted out.

'No Mikey!' she said, reaching a hand out for him, but missing his arm.

She held Joy and watched the doorway nervously, waiting for Mikey to come back so that they could lock the door and hide away from Graham.

'Please come back, come on Mikey,' she whispered to herself repeatedly.

Mikey ran in and shut the door; he turned the key in the lock and sat beside Anna. He wrapped his arms around her and hugged her as tight as he could.

He stank of dog food. The gravy was soaked into his clothes and hair. They let go after a while, sniffing and wiping away the last of their tears.

'Had to get my cookie.' He showed her the cookie she had stolen for him earlier, the one he had saved for later. He snapped it in half and they shared it, enjoying every bite, knowing they would probably be skipping breakfast in the morning.

Barney was whimpering patiently on the floor, sat waiting for his bit of food. Mikey giggled at the look on Barney's face and held out a bite of cookie. Barney avoided the cookie and licked the remnants of dog food gravy from his hand.

Chapter 33

Graham was furious. He ran down into the basement, adrenaline pumping through his veins, making him shake. He slammed the door and slid the bolt across. He charged over to the desk, almost falling into it as he reached to grab a beer from the crates stacked to the side. He put the lid on the edge of the desk and smacked his hand down, knocking the bottle cap off and taking a chunk of the wood from the table top with it. Graham drank the beer in one, the cool fizzy liquid cooling him down from the inside. The heat upstairs only exacerbated his rage when she did things like that.

Though it wasn't just her now, it was Mikey too.

He winced at the pain radiating from his leg. He would get that cleaned up before infection had a chance to set in, get it good and bandaged. Thankfully it was only a little nick.

His hands were shaking still. He dropped the bottle to the floor. It clunked as it bounced on the cold concrete floor but somehow it didn't smash. He pulled out another beer; this one he opened by using the bottle-opener he laid on the desk. He sat in his chair and sipped at the bottle. His breathing was slowing and he was beginning to calm down. His hands were shaking less and he could feel the muscles knotting in his shoulders.

Reflecting on what had just happened up there, he felt saddened. Not because of what he had done; he believed that was the only way to get them to listen. He was doing what his dad had showed him.

He opened the desk drawer, the sliding mechanism stiff from the damp coldness of the basement. He pulled out a pack of Marlboros that sat next to grandpa's World War two gun. He lit his cigarette and sucked it deeply, watching the glowing tip burn away down the white shaft. The radio was on the desk. He plugged it in to the wall and hit the play button on the tape player. The Rolling Stones started playing. He turned the volume low, but loud enough to drown out his thoughts.

'Paint It Black' played. He nodded his head along with the drums, the tune of the guitar filtering through his soul, making him feel closer to his dad. He would be proud of him now. He wished he was still around to see how he had changed himself. He was a different man now, he saw where he had gone wrong all of his life, had seen why his dad had to teach him all those lessons when he was a child. His dad hadn't been hurting him, he was trying to show him the way, the way to be a real man, the kind of man that doesn't get turned down in the bedroom, or the kind of man who doesn't spend all of his life working towards building a life for his family, only to have the whole thing ripped out from under his fucking feet!

The beers were taking effect; the excessive smoke inhalation filling his bloodstream with nicotine and a thousand other chemicals made his head swim. He went back in time, to when he heard this song for the first time. He had long associated this song with pain and misery; the lyrics of the song reflected his feelings when he was young, younger than Mikey was now.

He flung his hand to his back where the bruises and lacerations had once been, where he still felt them every time he had submitted to his wife; they seemed to burn like freshly-opened wounds whenever he felt emasculated, but was too much of a fucking pussy to do anything about it. They had long since faded, the scars were barely visible, but they were there...He knew they were there.

Chapter 34

When Graham was eight years old, he had been down at the park, playing football with his friends. He had just been given a new ball for Christmas. They'd had no money back then; his mum was a housewife, she'd wanted to go back to work but his father had forbidden it. He had work in a bottle factory; it was his job to check all finished products for any damages to labels or chipped glass, until his knee went and he was let go. If he couldn't stand by the production line all day, he was no good to them.

So, when Christmas morning had come round and there was a present under the tree, Graham had been shocked to the point where he believed there might actually be a Santa Claus. It was a football, and not a cheap plastic one that would go anywhere except where you were trying to kick it, it was a proper one that the professionals played with on a weekend.

The other kids were jealous when he turned up at the park. It was a freezing cold day, the dew on the grass had turned to frost, the blades were white, and the mud was solid. But they had a football, a proper football, and they were going to play.

Jamie had gone in for a slide tackle and cut his knee on the ground; they thought he would have needed stitches but, Jamie being Jamie, just wiped the blood with his hand and cracked on. He was a 'tough little fucker', Graham's dad used to say whenever Jamie had been round.

'Takes after his dad, that one. He was a tough bastard when he was younger an'all.'

Tig was there, Tig was a lanky streak back then. He filled out as he got older but the impression of him never changed. Graham always saw him as the lanky kid who wouldn't say boo to a goose. Tig played in goal; his knees were cut and grazed after diving to make saves, or at least trying to.

The three of them had been playing for well over an hour, their skin was sensitive from the cold, their cheeks rosy and as hot as fire against the cold wind.

Then the bigger boys came, the ones who were already in the second year of high school. The one who appointed himself as their leader was Vince Armstrong. Flanked by his two goons, Terry Reed and Butch Price.

'Hey dickheads. Can we play?' His smile told them he wasn't actually asking.

He got his kicks from making their lives a misery, there wasn't much to do in Wymere back then, not like there is now, so kids had to make their own amusement. Graham and his pals were content enough playing football or making dens in the woods near the lake, but that wasn't enough for Vince and his goons, they needed to assert their authority.

Jamie, even though he was four years younger than Vince, was the only one of them who stood a chance against him because of his freakish size, but three on one meant he had no chance, and he knew it. Jamie wasn't scared of anything, but when Vince and the goons showed up, he always chose to walk away.

'No, sorry. We're just going now,' Graham said, picking up his ball and heading for the road.

'C'mon. Don't be an arsehole,' Vince said as he moved towards them.

Graham looked over his shoulder and Tig was already gone. He never professed to be a hero and stuck by it. 'Run away, and live to fight another day.' That was his motto. Although 'another day' would never come, because Tig would never fight.

Jamie and Graham started heading for the road, the fleeing footsteps of Tig still visible in the crushed grass. Jamie turned when he heard the footsteps of Vince and the goons getting closer.

They only had one extra man, but they still managed to surround Graham and Jamie, so it felt they had nowhere left to run.

'Leave us alone, man.' Jamie said, talking directly to Vince.

'We just wanna play. I don't know why you're being bitches about it.'

'It's Graham's ball and he doesn't want to play anymore, so we're off home.'

Vince turned to Graham and eyed the ball in awe, as if he was holding the Holy Grail.

'Nice ball. Who'd you steal it from?' He laughed, and looked back to his friends to make sure they were laughing too.

'I got it for Christmas. It was a present. I didn't steal it.'

'Oh yeah? Is that right?' Vince touched a ponderous finger to his chin. 'Although I heard your dead-beat dad couldn't even keep hold of a job at the factory. You know, where the women and retards get sent to work 'cos there's nowhere else to put them.' He laughed again. Butch and Terry joined in harmoniously. 'There's no such thing as Santa, y'know, it's just whatever your mummy and daddy can afford.'

Graham remembered what he thought when he saw the present under the tree that morning, that there might actually be a real Santa. He suddenly felt very small and very stupid for thinking it.

'Everyone's been talking about it down at the pub. What a loser Barry Willow is, and his little dweeby son Graham. And that poor wife of his. What is your mum's name again, Graham? Debbie, is it? Well, they all talk about her too. Wondering what a fine piece of ass like that is doing with such a loser, when she could be getting cock from anyone else in town.' He covered one side of his mouth with his hand, as if to whisper a secret, 'Although, from what I've heard, she's already had most of the cock on offer, now that your dad's, you know, useless in the downstairs department.'

Graham carried on looking at the floor. He wanted to hit him, he wanted to punch Vince's face in until it was unrecognisable, a mess of blood and bone. He also knew that if he tried it, he would be laughed at and then beaten up anyway. His muscles were frozen stiff, not from the cold, but from fear and shame.

'Got nothin' to say? You little son of a whore?' Vince poked him in the shoulder.

Jamie grabbed Vince's hand with lightning reflexes for someone so big. 'Leave him alone Vince, you've had your fun.'

Vince pushed Jamie to the floor and kicked him in the stomach. Butch added one for good measure, knocking the wind from him, so he was curled into a useless ball on the floor.

'Why don't you just give me that ball, Graham? Huh? We both know you don't have the bollocks to stop me. Sure, I'd love for you to *make* me take it from you, but it would be a lot easier if you just gave me *my* ball back.' Vince held out a hand, waiting for Graham to pass him it.

Graham held that ball so tight his knuckles had turned white. He was waiting for the punch to come; the thought of it hurt more than an actual punch. He opened one eye and saw Vince was still giving him the chance to hand it over peacefully.

Graham started to cry; he'd used all of his strength holding onto the ball, and had none left to hold back the tears.

'Last chance, arsehole.'

Graham handed the ball over, and started sobbing as he walked away. He stopped when all of the air in his lungs was forced out of him at once. Vince had swung a leg up and

172

kicked him in the side of the ribs with his steel toe- caps. Graham fell to the floor beside Jamie who was now on all fours catching his breath.

Vince knelt down next to Graham and said, 'You best run home to your retard daddy and your whore mummy, little boy, before I beat you harder than your dad beats your mum.'

Then he started laughing wildly.

'Good one Vince,' Butch said, or it could have been Terry. They never spoke much, just stood looking like a couple of dumb security guards at a supermarket.

'C'mon guys. Let's play with my new ball.'

Jamie and Graham went their separate ways at the crossroads, Jamie heading past the pub on the corner and Graham heading to the council estate down on Appleby way.

The fear of what Vince had put him through had been swapped with fear of what his dad would do when he found out he had let someone take his ball from him.

He walked in and tried to head straight upstairs to his room, shutting the front door as quietly as he could, but the latch always made a massive '*CLUNK*' when it shut.

'You there, boy?' his dad shouted from the living room. The air was full of smoke, the kind that came from self-made cigarettes with no filter, that turned his dad's fingertips an orange-yellow colour. He had his record player on and was sat in his armchair by the unlit fire. The song was 'Paint it Black.' Graham remembered it, not because of the quality of the song, or because of how big the Rolling Stones were back then. It was because of what happened whilst it was on.

Graham walked into the living room, desperately trying to keep his head held high, Barry always told him a man should walk with his chin up and squared shoulders. Instead, he looked more like someone suffering from scoliosis of the spine then a man brimming with confidence.

'Did your friends like your new ball?' he asked.

'Yes, Sir.'

'Well don't be leaving it outside, you idiot. Someone will be off with it. It wasn't cheap, that.' He gestured a flinging arm in the direction of the front door.

Just then Debbie, Graham's mum, walked in through the kitchen door, sporting a new black eye her husband had honoured her with for asking when he was going to go back to work full-time.

Graham's hand whipped to his side where his ribs were already beginning to bruise from Vince's kick. He tried not to wince but did, subconsciously hoping his mum would notice and take pity on him, distract from the conversation about the ball, and take him into the bathroom to get cleaned up and maybe have a hot bath.

She noticed. Instead of helping out her son, she placed a cup of tea down on the side table next to Barry and left the room, flashing an apologetic look at Graham as the door closed, leaving him alone with his dad. Graham guessed she'd had enough of dealing with Barry for one day, opting instead to let Graham shoulder some of the punishment.

'Go get it then,' Barry said. His voice had changed to an accusatory tone.

'I can't,' Graham muttered.

'Speak up boy, I can't hear you!' Barry shouted at him. He grabbed for his walking stick and pushed himself up from the chair, his face creasing with pain.

'I can't,' Graham said a little louder, his voice breaking slightly, hoping his dad wouldn't notice. He knew how he felt about boys acting like little girls.

'You can't? What d' ya 'mean, you can't? Where is it?' Barry hobbled towards Graham. Graham noticed that as the anger built up in his dad, the hobbling got easier.

'A boy took it.'

'What boy was this then?' Barry's face was flushed with anger, his cheeks were reddening and spittle was gathering at the corners of his dry, cracked lips.

'Vince. Vince Armstrong.' Graham started to sob; he tried to stop it but instead ended up making a noise like *A-Heek, A-Heek.*

'So, not only are you not man enough to keep your own possessions, but you're also that much of a nancy, you're snitching on people as well. Is that it?'

Graham nodded.

'Did he beat you up for it?'

Graham shook his head.

'Did he snatch it from you and run away? Take it when you weren't looking?'

Graham shook his head again.

'Jesus Fucking Christ boy. What's left? Did he ask you to give it to him? And you just said, "Aye, 'ere you go mate."'

The fact that Barry thought Graham might call Vince mate showed how much he knew about the bully and bullied relationship Vince and Graham shared.

Graham nodded and wept pitifully. Barry bent to get on Graham's eye level. His breath stank of cigarettes and old tea. When he spoke, Graham could see the yellow fur on his tongue.

'You're telling me, this boy came up, told you to give him what was yours, and you just...gave it to him. Is that about right, Graham?'

'Yes sir.' Graham couldn't muster up the words to explain what happened fully, and didn't expect his dad to listen or care if he did.

Barry chewed his lip, staring at Graham's face, red from the cold. He stood straight and walked back to the fireplace. He didn't speak. That made Graham feel worse; he was expecting a slap. Expecting a barrage of screams and hurtful words, sent to his room without food, the things he had come to expect when disappointing his father or acting weak.

Barry put a match to the balled-up newspaper in the hearth, the edges of the paper curled in the flames. As the flames grew higher, they started eating at the kindling stacked on top, making spitting noises as the pine started to burn. Barry watched the flames intensely. When the kindling had taken hold, he put on a shovel of coal from the bucket beside his chair.

The flames dulled a little, then started to work away on the lumps of coal.

'I'm going to teach you a lesson the same way my dad taught me. The only way that makes sure you're going to remember.'

Graham was crying, scared and cold. His skin was covered in goose- bumps. He was shivering uncontrollably.

'The lesson is respect. The way a family works, is that everyone in that family has to respect each other, and each family has a head, that would be me. As the man and the provider of this family, I deserve respect. If any one of my family disrespects me, then it is my obligation to teach them so they will learn. Do you understand?'

'I'm sorry dad, I will get the ball back, I promise.' Graham meant it. The way his dad was toying with the fire poker gave him the incentive to fight with anyone in the world if it meant his dad wouldn't hurt him.

'It's too late for that, son. If you had a shred of respect for me, you wouldn't have been so thoughtless and disrespectful in the first place.'

'Dad please, I'm really sorry.'

'Sorry? Fucking sorry? Your own mother has got more balls than you.'

Graham noticed his dad's need for the cane he carried was non-existent now. Like he had been putting it on all this time. Vince's words rang in his ears, about how everyone was laughing at his dad, saying cruel, untrue things about his mum. How they had no money. Something grew inside, like the fire that was growing in the hearth. He felt angry, not at Vince but at his dad. He lifted his head up for the first time and stared at his dad.

'At least I'm not the one that everyone's laughing at. The whole town know you're lying about your leg, just because you're too lazy to work.'

Graham instantly regretted it; his dad's face blurred from fury to hurt, then to rage.

'You son of a bitch,' Barry said, sounding like he was struck with disbelief, like he'd seen something crash through the sky from outer space. 'How dare you speak to me this way! I am the man of this house, and you will show me some goddamn respect.'

Barry reached out, his cane dropping to the floor. He grabbed Graham by the scruff of his shirt and threw him to the floor face down. Barry ripped Graham's shirt off his back. Graham writhed in terror on the floor, desperately trying to cling to the strips of fabric left on him. He wanted to yell for his dad to stop but couldn't form words between the screams.

Barry stood and started to remove the belt from his trousers. 'I'll teach you a lesson you won't forget, boy.' He was breathing heavily; this was the most energy Graham had seen his dad use in months.

Graham looked at the kitchen door, knowing his mum was behind there, hoping and praying that she would come in and save him, burst through the doors and pick him up from the floor and take him away from here.

She didn't.

She was as scared, or more scared of Barry than Graham was. She had suffered, not suffered, Graham thought, learnt was the right term. She had learnt from Barry a lot longer than he had. Graham just had to catch up.

Barry lifted his belt high above his head; he brought it down with all his might and whipped Graham's lower back. Graham squealed in agony. The crack seemed to echo around the room. Barry hit again, and again. Graham screamed louder after every hit. Barry's face was red with rage, spit flew from his mouth with every whip, his cracked lips started bleeding when he stretched them, grimacing as he put all of his strength into his movements.

After whipping him a dozen times, he stopped. Graham was weeping into the carpet; he crept a hand to his back and flinched at the instant sting, it felt hot and wet. He was about to get up when Barry put his foot on his back and pressed down on the lashes in his skin. Barry tutted. A glob of spit fell onto Graham's head.

Barry turned the belt around so the buckle was at the business end. He swung it around and around so it made a woosh sound in the air, he brought it down on to Graham's back, when the metal buckle connected with the skin, it tore a piece of flesh from Graham's back. One final blow to really show him what it meant to disrespect his father. The cut was so deep and so bloody, it seemed to shock Barry out of his rage. He dropped the belt and stepped back. Graham screeched and screeched. The sound was so horrifying it sounded like a pig being tortured.

'Debbie, get this faggot cleaned up, and tell him to cut his whining,' Barry shouted towards the kitchen. He fell back into his chair.

Debbie came running in, helped Graham to his feet, and ran him to the bathroom to bathe his wounds. Graham sobbed and sobbed; the will to get away from his father was the only thing that gave his legs strength enough to carry him out of there.

Barry picked up his cup of tea and sipped. He sucked his teeth and peeled his lips back. 'Still hot,' he said, and smacked his lips together.

In the bathroom, Debbie was panicking. Graham had started sweating profusely, and blood was pouring from his back. She was trying to stem the flow with wash-cloths.

Debbie ripped the clothes from him so he was naked. 'My poor boy. I'm so sorry. My poor, poor boy.' Debbie was crying with her son; she sat him in the bath and started bathing the wounds. The water turned red almost instantly.

Graham screamed at the pain. 'No dad, please stop.' Darkness was taking him; the pain was too much. His eye lids grew heavy; he didn't know where he was or who was with him. His head rolled to the side, he muttered incoherently into the green tiled wall as everything grew dark. 'Please stop dad. Stop, please... Please... Dad...'

Chapter 35

'STOP!! '

Graham jolted out of his chair. The cigarette in his hand had burnt down to the filter, burning his fingers, bringing the pain in the dream into reality. Stood in the basement, his hands were shaking; he stuck the burnt fingers in his mouth and sucked, not realising the tears that were streaming down his face. The horrible memory of his father, how he beat him so mercilessly, was the first of many as he grew older, and he learnt more lessons from doing things to upset him. He learnt how to keep his emotions hidden, buried away deep inside. Barry would beat him, whip him, burn him with cigarettes, lock him in cupboards, in the hope it would turn him into a man. Graham thought that was probably what his Grandad had put his dad through, that was why he was like this. Copying his own childhood - if it had worked for him then it would work again. Only it didn't work on Graham. Graham just didn't have it in him to be aggressive and confrontational. He wouldn't have considered himself a sissy, he liked football and smoking and drinking beer down at the park with Jamie and Tig. But in his father's eyes, a man had to be dominant, controlling and ruthless. There wasn't room for gentleness in a man. That was for the role of the woman.

Debbie had died before Graham met Anna; a brain aneurism was written in the autopsy report. Back then the cops weren't so thorough when it looked like an accident. They didn't ask about the bruises to the side of her head or marks around her neck. If they had, they might have learnt how Barry had thrown her down the stairs just a few hours before the bleed on the brain ended her life.

Debbie would have liked Anna; she was everything she had wanted to be but didn't have the strength. Anna was

180

confident and self-assured, was independent and happy by herself. She didn't need anyone in her life; that was why Graham knew that when she hung around, she really did love him. They moved in together quick; her job as an accountant brought in more money than Graham's, even though she was ten years his junior. Barry loved that, he laughed at Graham whenever he got a chance. 'How does it feel knowing a woman earns more than you? You should give her them trousers, she's clearly the man of the house.'

Graham knew how lonely Barry was. He never had many friends, and when Debbie died, he had no one. No one to care for him, so Graham had to organise a nurse to go round and make sure he had everything he needed. Graham wasn't brave enough to face his dad every day.

Graham sat back in the chair and sobbed; he stopped the music. He looked at his hands, sticky with dog food and beer, spots where the small blisters were healing and a fresh burn on his fingertips. He was a mess, falling apart. Anna's face came into his mind, the look she gave him when he towered over her. Like she was looking at a stranger. It was the same look his mother would give his father when he rained down on her with fists of fury.

Graham reached in the desk drawer and pulled out the revolver. Stuck the barrel in his mouth.

He told himself it was his only way out, the only guarantee he wouldn't hurt them anymore. Mikey would never forgive him. His chest was racking as he sobbed, snot pouring from his nose. Every shudder from his chest made the metal barrel of the gun rattle against his teeth, sending unbearable vibrations through his ears.

Another part of him was wrapping its invisible fingers around the gun and trying to pull it from his mouth. The work was far from over. If he wanted to prove himself as a man, finally, after all these years, he would have to get them through this pandemic and out the other side to salvation.

He put the gun back in the drawer, and breathed out heavily, trying to control his sobbing. He drank another beer, taking away the taste of metal from his mouth. He lay in his chair, and closed his eyes.

Things will be better tomorrow, he promised himself. Things will be better tomorrow.

Chapter 36

Lockdown day 14.

Water cascaded over Anna's head, washing away the dirt and slick sweaty film that had covered her skin for days. The water felt nice on her face, where the swelling around her eye from the backhander Graham had dealt her had been. Now the only thing left of her injury was a yellow tinge with a touch of purple circling her eye like cheap eyeshadow.

The mental scars ran much deeper; she doubted they would fade for quite some time. Mikey had been a mess the first few days, he hadn't left the bedroom. When he needed the bathroom, he would need Anna to walk him there and stand guard at the door. He was getting better now. After *'The Talk'*.

He wasn't back to the old Mikey, that would be impossible with everything they were going through, and the lack of nutrients and entertainment. The boredom was forcing them to get lost in their own heads. Mikey was torturing himself over images of his friends dying, all his guitar heroes gone. With films and TV shows they had on nowadays, it wasn't hard for Mikey to conjure up a realistically gory image of what infected humans, losing their guts through rotting flesh, would look like. Anna was sure he had a pretty accurate picture of it in his head. An image that he saw every night before he went to sleep, just to scare him that little bit more every day. She knew he did because she did. If the images in Mikey's head were half as bad as the ones in hers, God knew how he managed to get to sleep at all.

A chirping sound came from a small digital alarm clock that sat on the bathroom windowsill. It was the alarm

Graham had used every day for getting up for work. The alarm hadn't been set for quite a while now. It had a setting where you could programme the alarm to go off every five, ten or fifteen minutes at any given time. In 'The Talk', Graham had made a plan about water and electric usage. There would come a point when their supply would run out. There wasn't going to be people at the other end sorting out who got what energy, (of course that also meant, in theory, that they might never get cut off). But they couldn't take that risk. Graham decided that the shower could be used every four days. For ten minutes at a time. It was the middle of summer. Anna had to bite her tongue from telling him this like he didn't already know. Since the dog food incident, she had learnt that biting your tongue was the best thing to do around Graham.

The heat in the house was incredible. There had to be a break in the temperature soon, they hadn't heard a single drop of rain for weeks. They sat around sweating in their own filth. The house was stinking; the best place to sit was the living room with the fan. Graham allowed that to stay on 24/7, as it was a necessity to keep fresh air flowing in.

Anna stepped out the shower and wrapped a towel around her, folding it in at the top so it would stay on her without needing to be held. She hit the button on top of the alarm clock to stop the chirps. The sound drove her crazy; before it had been the sound that forced them out of bed, now it was the sound of limiting their freedom to wash.

Steam had covered the large mirror that filled the back wall; only the bottom third wasn't covered. That was a nice stone tile to match the floor and shower walls. She wiped her hand over the mirror and studied the stranger's face that stared back at her. The stranger that looked a lot like her, only not the strong, confident woman she used to be. Now she was just a skeletal wreck of a woman, a woman that didn't dare stand up to the man she supposedly loved and had shared a life with, a woman who was so weak she didn't know how much longer she could go on doing this.

The tears ran out of her sunken eyes like juice spilling out of rotten fruit.

Pull yourself together. You're better than this.

She wiped her hair back and away from her face. Her cheekbones were so prominent she thought she looked like a bad plastic surgery job.

Her towel fell to the floor in a heap around her ankles. She instinctively grabbed for it and missed, resulting in only hugging herself protectively, trying to cover herself up as if someone else was there. This was who she had become, she realised. Someone who was so constantly on edge, she was scared of being naked in her own bathroom because it made her feel vulnerable. It was the first time she'd had a chance to look at her body in the mirror, something she used to do every few days to ensure she was keeping on top of her figure.

She had been a size ten, an eight if she starved herself for a week. Well, she had been starving for two weeks now, literally starving. Also, in 'The Talk' Graham had decided it best to cut their rations again, as it could go on for longer than he thought. Now she was a bit lower than a size six.

It wouldn't be long before she had the kind of figure owned by a woman that Netflix make documentaries about, 'The woman who eats air' or something equally dumb. The caption at the end of the two-hour show would always read, (after sucking you in and getting you emotionally involved with this woman) *Casey died shortly after the making of this documentary.*

Anna moved her hands across her body, examining everything as though looking at it for the first time. She counted her ribs; each one was almost fully visible, her stomach had shrunk away, and her hips and pelvic bones were beginning to stick out like daggers under her skin. Her collarbones looked angled and wrong. She started crying again and when she put her hand over her mouth to stifle the noise, she realised how thin her hands had got. Now they were just tendons and bones wrapped in skin.

Again, she told herself to pull it together, she couldn't break. There were two kids in the room next door, they needed her, now more than they ever had or ever would. She doubted Joy would make it longer than a few days if Graham was looking after her. He hadn't paid any attention to his daughter; not once had he watched her crawl or roll over. He didn't try make her laugh or feed her. It was as if she didn't exist to him. Until she cried, in which case he would give Anna the option, 'Either you shut her up. Or I will.'

Anna didn't dare ask what he meant by that, so she just took Joy away and soothed her by singing softly. The 'Things' or 'Monsters', as they were now referred to, that roamed outside, were attracted to noise, so keeping quiet was imperative. Especially at night. Graham explained how sound travels further at night because the world is quieter. They had to be quiet. That was fine by Anna, she could barely keep her eyes open most of the time, so if she got the opportunity to go to sleep and be quiet, she took it.

Joy was being just as her name suggested. She had seen some awful things, when Graham lost his mind and did what he did to Mikey, rubbing dog food in his face and choking him with his t-shirt, then hitting Anna and threatening her. Joy had been so scared. Thankfully, she wouldn't remember any of it. A child psychologist would tell her that actually it *would* have an effect on her development, but Anna didn't know any child psychologists. Maybe she'd need one when all this was over.

Anna grabbed the towel from the floor; bending and lifting it back up over her shrunken breasts was a monumental task. Her whole body ached as it moved. After drying herself off she got dressed into a clean 'floaty' skirt and vest top. A few weeks ago, the vest had been a tight fit, enhancing her curves, pushing her breasts together, like two moons caught in a net.

Now it hung from her like a rag on a stick.

When she got back into her bedroom, she was heartened by the sight of Mikey playing with Joy, giving her so much attention. Pretending to chase her on the floor while she crawled away in fits of giggles, all the while being cautious of danger, her bumping her head on the corner of the dresser or putting her hand down on a lost earring.

Mike was losing weight as fast as she was; any energy he had left in him he gave to Joy. He hadn't let his fear get in the way of pretending everything was perfect for her. As far as Joy knew, they were all having the time of their lives. She didn't want to go to sleep in case she missed something.

The burn on Mikey's neck from where his t-shirt had been pulled tight round his throat, and then he'd been dragged over the kitchen floor, had almost disappeared now. Which was such a relief. Anna had heard somewhere that if the body lacks nutrition it would struggle to heal itself when injured, putting it at risk of infections. They just had to keep on keeping on.

Mikey and Joy were the hope, they were the ones that were going to get Anna through this. Just then, watching Mikey crawl around the floor after Joy, she thought for the first time, that they *were* going to get through this. Graham could do whatever he wanted, make whatever rules he concocted on a night, but they were going to get through this despite him.

Or *in spite* of him.

Chapter 37

The days had all merged into one, Anna couldn't be confident of the exact date anymore, she was thankful she was able to have a look out of the window in her craft room. That way she was able to keep a handle on what time of day it was. The chores round the house still needed to be done. Anna and Mikey weren't about to risk the wrath of Graham over a few dusting and cleaning jobs, so they did each job perfectly to keep him content. As long as he felt like some sergeant-major watching over his cadets, he was happy.

It occurred to Anna that Graham had become more obsessed with the need for control than the fear of what was outside. He could go on and on about how he wanted things done in the house, coming out with statements like '*God, where would we be without me eh?*', waiting for one of them to answer, to tell him; '*We'd all be dead without you, hun. You're our saviour.*' The desperate need for him to have his place at the head of the family, to be the man in charge so he could play this hero figure that had saved his helpless little family from certain doom, was getting tiring. Still, she played along and so did Mikey.

Anna was still managing to steal the odd scrap of food for Mikey whenever she got the chance. The rations had gone to nothing more than a mouthful of food for every meal. Graham hadn't noticed so far. Anna thought maybe there was someone up there watching over them. She had never been a believer in religion, more of a follower of science and coincidence. If you want something, go out and get it, work for it and it will come. Sat on your knees asking someone to give it to you was a big fat waste of time. This was the first time, ever in her life, that she had hoped she was wrong. A little guidance from someone who knew what to do would be gratefully received. Of course, if she was to ask Graham, he would see that the one who knew what to do was him.

Chapter 38

Graham was downstairs in the basement, no doubt sat in that dank office chair smoking and listening to his dad's old cassette tapes, or 'waiting for another radio broadcast'.

Anna was scrubbing the kitchen sides, cleaning the oven (which required a metal scraper to get the charcoal residue from the bottom that kept burning and smoking every time the oven was on). Then she scrubbed the floors; she had to do it on her hands and knees now. Graham had grown paranoid that maybe his air filter would be letting the tiniest of microbes in, so the daily cleaning regime had to be thorough.

Joy was in the living room with Barney and Mikey. Mikey had done his bedroom, now he played the role of brilliant babysitter whilst Anna finished the rest of the jobs.

The smell of bleach stung Anna's nostrils, the chemicals were over- powering, causing her eyes to sting and her vision to blur. She scrubbed back and forth with a stiff-bristled hand scrubber, dipping back into the bucket filled with red-hot water, bleach and soap. She scrubbed in the cracks; Graham would know if she missed them. He inspected them thoroughly before and after every clean. Everything had been satisfactory so far.

Her arm felt like a dead weight; every push and pull against the tiles hurt, her back screamed in pain, her shoulders and neck had started cracking with every swift movement. She felt as if her body was shutting down. If it wasn't for the drinking water being in plentiful supply, she knew she would have been dead by now.

When finished, she poured the remaining water down the sink, and watched as the last of the bubbles swirled in a whirlpool before disappearing down the plughole. The rubber gloves snapped off her hands with an elastic *thwack* noise. She hung them over the tap and wiped any water splashes from the kitchen worktops with a kitchen towel. She rubbed her eyes with the back of her hands, hands that still smelt like bleach despite the use of gloves. Her eyes stung like she'd been up all night, like they used to when they had been younger. When the music and wine flowed just right and they would spend all night talking and laughing, dancing and making love.

She smiled at the flash of memory before it disappeared again, replaced by the nightmare reality.

Anna walked into the living room and saw her three children (Barney was an honorary child), circling around the room like a train, Joy leading, with Mikey just behind and Barney taking the rear. Joy was in a fit of giggles as Mikey tapped at her toes making her crawl away faster. There was no stopping her now, it wouldn't be long before she learnt how to pull herself up and then she'd figure out she could walk faster than she could crawl. Funny, she thought, how one minute you think they'll be babies forever, that you can't remember a time when you didn't have a baby to look after, then five minutes later they're getting around by themselves, eating and drinking by themselves, potty-trained, off to school, *poof*. Gone.

'Is dad downstairs?' Mikey asked.

Anna nodded.

God, am I too tired to use words? she thought despairingly.

Joy had rolled back over on to her back and was hitting the frills of the hem of the sofa, watching and laughing as they swung above her. Barney was by the window; he had taken to chewing on the cord of the fan, and Anna had to make sure she stopped him before Graham noticed and did something awful to punish him.

Mikey stood and approached Anna, his footsteps were light and assured. 'Can I get some more food? I'm starving.' He held his stomach for clarity.

'I'll try later, darling.' Anna rubbed her face with her hands; she was ready to drop.

'But Muuuum, I'm really hungry.'

'I know-'

'I need some more food, mum. Please please please get me some.'

'ALRIGHT! I know you're hungry, we're all fucking hungry Mikey. I'm running a risk doing it as much as I do anyway.' She snapped at him, he recoiled from her quickly and went back down to the floor. Making her instantly feel like shit. As if he didn't have enough to deal with, now his mother was shouting at him for saying he was hungry.

'I'm sorry Mikey. I didn't mean to lose my temper. I'm just really whacked.'

'I know.' Mikey was upset. Anna could tell. He wasn't going to cry, even though he wanted to. He would just be quiet for a while now, a little less responsive. Maybe take himself off to his room to play his guitar (without an amp) or read a comic book. Anna hoped that he would, she could do with a break. She'd had all three of them wrapped round her since the beginning of all of this, and it was beginning to grate on her.

'I'm going to my room,' Mikey said. His bottom lip quivered as he said it.

'Don't be upset Mikey...Hang on.' She sighed, and her head flopped down a little, like that of someone defeated.

She returned to the kitchen and looked at the basement door. It was closed tight. That was good. She opened the cupboard with the crisps and snacks. They had depleted quite noticeably now. Thankfully Graham had never gone for them. He said sweet treats would come much further down the line. No matter how shit we felt now, 'there was a long road ahead' he would warn them.

Anna grabbed a pack of crisps, careful not to rustle the foil bag. She was going to leave it at that but grabbed the last cookie from the pack too. There was something about grabbing the last cookie that felt more dangerous, like there was more chance of it being noticed.

She walked quickly back into the living room and handed the stuff over to Mikey.

'Go quickly, and hide the rubbish.'

'I know, mum. We've been doing it every day,' he said, now smiling. They had been doing it every day, and in doing so Mikey seemed to have grown cocky in the thought that they would never be caught.

Mikey, so pleased with his haul he was almost licking his lips as he headed for the stairs. As he got a foot on the bottom step, there was a knock on the front door.

Chapter 39

A sound that would normally be met with nothing more than faint intrigue was now met with petrifying fear. Mikey stood motionless on the stairs; one hand gripped the handrail and the other clung to his food, almost crushing the biscuit between his fingers. Anna was stood in the threshold between the living room and the hall; her first reaction was to grab Joy and hold her tight to her chest. She did this and shot mad eyes at Mikey to carry on upstairs quietly.

The knock came again, louder and harder this time. Anna's heart jumped up her throat. Everything she did suddenly felt as though it was being amplified through a set of speakers. Every time she shifted her weight from one foot to the other and the floor boards creaked, every breath felt as loud as a scream. She covered her mouth with her free hand, her eyes darting between Mikey and the front door.

She wished Graham was here.

The man she feared more than ever. Whether he had beaten her down enough to make her feel he was her only chance of survival, or because deep down she did still love him, either way, she felt he would know what to do better than she did.

Mikey started climbing the stairs, one slow, quiet foot at a time. He had a double worry, the thing on the outside discovering there were people in the house and not stopping until it found its way in, or something equally terrifying – his dad finding him with an arm full of stolen confectionary.

The thing outside hit the door again, harder than the previous two times. Why wouldn't it go, why was it still there? Anna remembered how Graham had told them that the infected were attracted by noise. Maybe her shouting at Mikey had attracted it to the house? What if its banging was attracting more infected to them?

Her lip quivered, she looked around for inspiration. Joy was smiling nervously, wanting her mum to react in a happy way, letting her know everything was fine. Anna couldn't do it.

Barney stood guard at the door; he was growling low. Anna tapped his hind leg. When he turned to look at her, she held out a 'don't you dare' finger to his muzzle. He understood the message and backed off away from the door.

'Get upstairs.' The voice that came from behind Anna was whispered yet clear and assertive. Graham had heard the banging on the front door after all. Anna was amazed how a man so big could glide up those old rickety basement steps without making a sound. His new-found personality had given him ninja-like attributes, it seemed.

'Get upstairs with Mikey and Joy. I'm going to go out the basement doors to the side of the house and distract him. Try and make him go someplace else.'

'But what about the air?' Anna asked.

'I've got my mask.' He smiled in a way that was supposed to convey confidence and reassurance but only unmasked his fear and nerves.

What if it sees you? Graham, I don't think going outside is safe.'

'I'll deal with it. It's not your job to figure these things out. Your job is to look after the kids,' The front door banged again, followed by a couple of slaps on the front window.

Graham leaned in, getting face to face with Anna. Just then, she saw how scared he really was. That scared her more than the thing outside.

'Go. Now.' He shoved her towards the stairs. She climbed as quickly as she could. Barney went with her, his place was by her side and he wouldn't leave her.

Chapter 40

Graham ran down the basement stairs. His heart was thumping in his chest. The gas mask was hung on a nail embedded in the wooden beam that ran along the ceiling. It smelt of rubber and stale cigarette smoke as he pulled it over his face. His hands were shaking as he opened the desk drawer and removed his grandfather's gun. He checked to make sure it was loaded. Then headed for the basement doors to the outside.

Chapter 41

Anna rounded the top of the stairs when she heard a faint but clear: 'Hello? Is anyone in there?'

A hundred ideas swam through her head. Was it a survivor? Her initial reaction was that it had to be an infected, but why couldn't it be a survivor? What if it wasn't as bad as they thought? There had to be a chance they had overestimated how bad it had become?

On the other hand, even if it was a survivor, they could still be infected. Have some delayed response to the infection. Anna could have let them in and a couple of hours later they could all be sat dead in a circle of their own guts. Graham would know what to do. She had to look after her family, that was all she could do.

Anna and Mikey sat with Joy and Barney in the craft room. They huddled together quietly. Mikey was shaking, although his eyes were focused and ready; he was trying to overpower the fear that grew inside him. Anna wished she could be so brave.

Mikey turned and looked out of the crack in the shutter. The day was filled with bright sun, the sky was a crystal blue without a cloud to be seen. The trees were tall and as strong as ever. Mikey looked back to Anna. 'What do you think dad's doing out there?'

'I don't know,' Anna said, shrugging her aching shoulders. 'We have to trust him.'

'Trust him? He's losing his head. It's not even like it's dad anymore.'

'Mikey, stop. He's still your father. As he said, if it weren't for him, we wouldn't even be here right now.' She realised then that all the doubt she had was gone. She had known it from the debilitating way her heart jumped up into her throat when the knocking started on the door.

Mikey sulked, folding his arms over his bent knees and lowering his head. He said something under his breath that Anna didn't quite catch.

'What was that?' she said. She was getting frustrated, which didn't take much. She was getting frustrated at herself as much as Mikey. She couldn't believe her words. Almost protecting the man that had done awful things to her own children. The primary human instinct was to survive, to protect their children. She knew now her best chance for survival for her and her family was Graham. He had made that perfectly clear and she had seen it.

'Nothing.'

'No, go on. What did you say?'

'I said, how do we know he's even telling the truth? We've not heard the radio broadcast that he heard. We've not seen anything on the news or anything. This is the first person to come to our house in two weeks. If it was that bad, surely other survivors or infected people would be here slamming on the door?'

'Mikey, we live out in the country, off any major roads. The radio broadcast isn't played constantly, it's random, to try and reach people whenever it can. We can't watch the news or go on our phones because they transmit the virus.'

'How does that even work? Have you heard the words coming out of your mouth?'

'Don't you talk to me like that. I am your mother.'

Joy started to shuffle and cry uncomfortably. The smell that filled the small craft room told Anna that Joy needed changing. Anna sniffed and pulled a disgusted face.

'I don't want any more of that talk. If your father hears, you know what he'll do. I'm going to change Joy's bum and then I'll be back. Stay here and be quiet. OK?'

'Fine,' Mikey snapped back and turned to look out of the window once again.

Barney sat by his side, with his ears up. As if readying for something.

A huge gunshot came from outside. Mikey was staring out the crack at the outside when it happened. He saw a flock of birds fly from the trees; the way the sound echoed over the hills was spectacular.

Anna froze in fear out in the hall. She looked back at Mikey; Mikey looked at her.

They both wondered the same thing. Who had fired the shot?

Chapter 42

Graham lifted the latch on the out-swinging basement doors to the outside and carefully pushed them open, keeping hold of them until they were opened fully without making a noise. The gas mask was stifling as the sun battered down on him. It had been so long since he'd been outside, he swore he could actually feel the sun's rays working on his skin.

He was tense and nervous, his palms greasy with sweat. He kept on loosening his grip on the gun and grasping it again, trying to keep a sure grip on it. As he stepped on to the grass, the slight summer breeze felt like silk on his neck. Every fibre in his body wanted him to rest, take in and enjoy the outside.

'Hello? Is anyone in there?'

Graham felt a surge of panic go through him so hard he thought his knees were going to give way and drop him to the floor. Summoning the courage to keep going forward, he shimmied along the wall of the house. His breath was threatening to steam up his visor, which would compromise his ability to aim. He calmed his breathing down and the mask returned clear.

He stopped at the corner and rested his back against the wall, holding the gun in both hands, preparing to try and look around the corner without being seen.

Sweat was beginning to pour down Graham's face and sting in his eyes; he blinked rapidly to fight against it. He took a deep breath, counted backwards from five, and leaned out.

The overgrown clematis that grew up the front of the house helped give him cover; through the thin wiry vines he could see a man looking up at the windows, hand on hips.

Graham shifted to get a more comfortable stance. The gravel around his feet shifted noisily.

Graham almost cursed out loud; the man put a hand to his brow, trying to shade the glare of the sun as he looked towards the noise. He moved towards Graham, the gravel crunching under every footstep.

The gun felt heavy and right in his hands. He loosened his grip and gripped it tight again. He lifted it up, held it out in front of him. Closing one eye, he looked down the sight. Lined up with the man walking towards him.

'Eat shit and die. Mother fucker.' Graham pulled the trigger. He gasped as he watched the top of the man's head fly through the air. The man's eyes rolled into the back of his head before filling with blood. He collapsed into a heap on the gravel. Blood spewed out from where his brain was now visible, and flowed through the gravel in small red rivers.

Graham sighed in blessed relief. He relaxed his arm that still held the gun up in the air. His shoulder and wrist had a slight twinge of pain from the recoil. That was the first time he'd ever fired a gun, a real gun that fired bullets instead of water. They make it look so easy in the movies, but in reality the power made it kick like a bitch. He shoved the gun into the back of his jeans and moved over to the man lying dead in his drive.

He was cautious – he was ninety-nine percent sure a shot to the head would kill it, but there was still a one percent doubt. He kicked at the man with the toe of his boot. As he did, a little extra blood came out of the head wound.

He was dead.

That much was clear. Graham's first thought was to leave him there, let him rot in his driveway. Save him the trouble of getting rid of the corpse. He looked around, taking in everything he had taken for granted all his life. He saw the peaking rooftop of his neighbour's house, half a mile or so away. The tip of the chimney was visible in amidst the sea of trees.

The gunshot was hellish loud.

He was chewing his lip to the point of bleeding as he thought of every different scenario. Anyone could have heard that shot. Doubtful, but possible.

He ran back to the basement; boxes thumped to the ground as he pushed them out of the way to get to the rack on the back wall. He found an old tow rope he had used once for his neighbour Reese.

Reese had tried to go to the supermarket in the middle of a snow-storm, in a shitty Nissan Micra of all things, and got stuck. Graham had had to go and drag him out with his truck.

He went back outside with the tow-rope and wrapped it around the man's neck. He fed it through the gap between the floor and the man's throat, careful not to touch any infected blood, wrapped it round and fed it through again. He pulled it tight and hoisted it over his shoulder. He dragged the body over to the trap door, leaving behind a trail in the gravel, along with blood and chunks of brain.

He dumped the body in a shady patch. It wouldn't help with the smell and the rot, but he didn't have time to dig a hole and he couldn't bring it down into the basement.

The man fell over to one side, spilling more blood from the crater in his head. The look on his face was vacant and cold. Graham thought the face looked… familiar.

He looked over at his driveway, and back to the man slumped in the shade against his house. 'Fuck it,' he said, and shot into the basement. He came back with a shovel.

He dug a hole in the giant flower bed that separated his house from his lawn; he chopped and smashed through rose bushes and crocosmias. Flinging them to the side as he dug, he was going as fast as a man half his age.

He had to.

He'd managed to dig two feet down when he couldn't take being outside in the open any longer. The entire time, airborne versions of the virus were landing on his clothes, his

202

skin, searching for a way to get inside him. Crawling along every part of him, wanting to take him over.

Graham threw the shovel on the floor and ran over to the man with the hole in his head. He grabbed the rope and dragged the body over the flower-bed wall. He rolled him into the hole he had dug and covered him over as best he could, leaving a hand and a trainer sticking out of the soil. Time was getting away with him. He was panicking with every second that went past.

'Fuck it, that'll do,' he said and ran back for the safety of the basement. He did one last check of the horizon before descending back into where he felt most protected.

Chapter 43

Graham slammed the basement doors shut, followed by the deadbolt and latch. He took off his gas mask and breathed deeply. He put it back on to the nail on the crossbeam and began to strip. He took off all of his clothing and put it all in a plastic bag. The trousers, the pants, the socks, they could all go straight in the bin, he didn't care. The vest though, he couldn't get rid of that.

It was cooler in the basement than upstairs, much cooler. He enjoyed how cool it felt on his skin, how freeing it was to be naked in the cool air. The image of the man's head exploding as he shot it, first time, one hit. The first time he had ever shot a gun; he'd dealt with the kick-back perfectly, like he'd done it all his life. He knew where he was aiming and he got it.

'No spray and pray here,' he laughed into the empty basement. Looking around, he saw every lurking shadow, every corner that held potential hiding spots.

His smile faded. His eyes fixed on the dark corners, staring into the blackness.

He grabbed a shovel, keeping his grip on the handle firm and his muscles tense, ready to swing at anyone who jumped out at him.

'Hello? If someone's there, you better show your face.' He moved towards the back of the basement, cardboard boxes piled high either side of the room. He moved between them, his eyes moving from side to side, looking for any signs of movement.

He heard a scratch behind him; he swung round and shouted in fright. The end of the shovel hit the lightbulb that dangled from the ceiling, sending the entire room into darkness.

'I know you're there! Get out here!' he shouted, swinging back and forth with the shovel, hitting boxes and sending the contents spilling onto the floor.

He grunted and groaned as he felt his arms beginning to tire, still he swung the shovel in the darkness at any threat that came for him.

Graham.

A voice whispered.

He stopped. 'Hello?' he whispered back. The sweat dripping down his face turned cold and his skin prickled with goosepimples.

You can still make me proud.

'Dad?' Graham's voice broke as he said it. It was his dad's voice, not the voice he'd had when he was younger, but the croaky, hoarse voice when he lay in bed dying.

'Why did you have to die?' Graham said when no reply came. 'It was easy when you were alive. When all I had to do was hate you.'

Graham. The voice echoed again.

'You were awful to me,' Graham spoke through sobs. 'You made my life miserable!'

I taught you how to be a man.

'Now I don't know any other way!' Graham cried into the darkness. 'When you were alive, I could block it all out with hate, then you had to go and die and let everything out. Pushed away memories of the beatings, the scalding's, the lashings- all came back.' Graham wiped the dripping snot from his nose with the back of his hand. 'Everything started slipping away after you died. I was losing everything and I didn't know how to stop from losing it all. I only know what you taught me, and sometimes, it doesn't feel right. When I look at her, she looks at me with those eyes and I think of mum. Am I doing the right thing?'

Yessss, the voice said, and Graham sobbed uncontrollably.

Graham hunched over and rubbed his eyes with the heel of his palms. 'I always wanted you to be proud of me. That's all I ever wanted.'

There's still time.

'What can I do, dad? She wants to leave. I'm trying to be stronger but she won't listen, now they hardly speak to me.'

You know what you have to do to be together. The same thing I would have done.

Graham sobbed. 'I know. It's just so hard.'

But you will do it, you know it is the only way.

Graham nodded. 'Not yet. They might change, they might learn to love me again.'

They will never change! You are too weak to be loved, too pathetic, too soft. The only way to be together forever is in your grasp.

Without realising, Graham was now holding the gun. Stroking his finger over the trigger. 'I will. When all else fails. I will kill us all.'

Chapter 44

Anna and Mikey had stayed in the craft room for as long as they could. Anna had hoped that Graham would have been up to tell them everything was OK by now. It had been ten minutes since the gunshot had scared the living shit out of her and now she was getting worried.

How and when did Graham get a gun, was the first thing on her mind. The thought of him having a gun scared her to death. The only other thing that scared her more was the thought that it wasn't *Graham* who had the gun. It was the intruder, the one at the door banging, maybe a desperate man searching for safety and food. She could only imagine how hard it was out there. The thing could have been a violent thug escaped from prison, a murderer or a rapist. If he'd shot Graham, he could be heading up here now.

The tap in the kitchen sink turned on; water splashing and the sound of scrubbing and heavy breathing made its way through the hall and up the stairs.

That was Graham's breathing. She knew that sound anywhere.

So, it was him with the gun. She remembered the box that he had made her put her phone into when this all started. Where he had put it, she never knew. Somewhere in the basement no doubt, but that basement was massive and she'd had hardly spent five minutes in there since they moved in. She wasn't a fan of spiders and things that lurk in dark, damp corners.

It was the gun he had promised was deactivated, the one they couldn't possibly get rid of because it was a family heirloom.

'C'mon Mikey. Let's go down and see your father.'

'He killed someone, mum,' Mikey said. His face was pale and his long hair had flopped down in front of his eyes.

'He saved us. That's what matters.' She gestured for him to come with her. Reluctantly, he obliged.

Walking through the living room, Anna was careful not to make any noise, looking sharply back at Mikey if he was stepping heavily on the floor. As they walked into the kitchen, Anna almost screamed as she whirled away and covered Mikey's eyes.

Graham was stood at the kitchen sink, scrubbing at his Rolling Stones vest with bleach. He was stark naked, his folds of fat flapping as he scrubbed. His skin was covered in spots and patches of black curly hair. He turned to face them; his penis hid behind an overgrown bush.

'Graham, what are you doing?'

'I got the virus on my clothes. I'm scrubbing them and me clean. Stay away, don't come any closer.' He started scrubbing his skin raw with the dish sponge.

'What was out there? What did it...look like?' Anna asked, unsure if she really wanted to know.

Graham seemed to hesitate for a second, as if thinking it over before telling her. 'It was one of them. It was awful Anna. Like looking at the face of death.' The image in his head was the man's head after he had shot him, that was what had stuck with him. 'Its face was covered in blood; its eyes were red and vacant. I used my grandfather's gun, so we have nothing to worry about...for now. If any more of them heard the shot, they'll be back. We all need to remain quiet. You go back upstairs, give me a chance to get cleaned up. When I'm done, I'll sort us some food.' He sighed and barked a quiet shot of laughter. 'I tell you what, Anna. If it weren't for me, you guys would be fucked. Absolutely screwed. That thing would have got in here and ripped you lot to pieces.'

'Graham, stop. You're scaring Mikey.'

He smiled as if this pleased him.

Foaming bleach covered his speckled skin, thick red lines of stretch marks were drawn all over his stomach and arms.

Anna pictured the image of her own body in the mirror this morning. How sad and scared it made her feel to see how thin she was, she could almost see every bone in her body. If she sucked in, she could see the outline of her major organs.

Mikey was the same, even the dog was losing a bit. Graham though, stood before them, wobbling and naked like he hadn't even lost an ounce. If anything, he looked fatter than before.

'How do we know he's even telling the truth?'

Mikey had said that. Insinuating Graham had made all of this up wasn't right. But he was hiding something.

Chapter 45

Later, at dinner, Graham pulled his chair closer to the table, his belly nudging and knocking the glasses of water, causing Anna's to spill slightly before she caught it and kept it upright. He was breathing heavily, not the kind of heavy panting you get from physical exertion, but that of someone struggling to breathe from weight on their chest, an unhealthy breathing. He kept coughing into his hand. He stank of stale cigarettes and beer. Anna thought she had smelled cigarette smoke when she had walked into the kitchen a few days ago, but had put it down to her brain not firing on all cylinders like it used to.

Graham had eaten his food grotesquely quickly, chomping and slopping like a pig eating gruel from a trough. She had noticed, in that fraction of a second when his plate still had food on it, that his portions were getting bigger. They were certainly a lot bigger than hers and Mikey's.

Tonight's was a packet of powdered mash, shared between the three of them, with a cup of gravy and a handful of frozen vegetables. Not too bad, she had thought, but when her plate was put in front of her, she was able to count the peas, there were so few of them.

Five peas.

The kicker was, she didn't like peas. Graham knew that, once upon a time, back when Graham was still Graham and not this obese, crazy stranger who fired guns at trespassers and buried them in the back yard. This Graham who had become estranged from a dumbbell and his bicycle. He hadn't given it a second thought; he was giving them enough so they could physically survive, like he was trying to break them down so they literally had to rely on him to spoon-feed them when they didn't have the strength to lift the food

210

up to their mouths. He would notice Mikey had more energy than he should have soon. He'd catch on that she was giving him extras when Graham's back was turned. Then she'd be for it. She hoped Mikey would escape punishment. It was all down to her, it was her idea, after all.

Graham had all the carrots, Anna noticed.

Twelve. She had time to count them before he shovelled them down his throat. Twelve cubes of carrots to her five peas. Hardly fair. He had a couple of rogue peas on his plate, a little easier with his own portion control, his mash pile was at least five scoops, compared to her one. He put the spoon into the bowl, scooped out a bit of mash and slopped the spoon and mash on to her plate and handed it to her.

Bon appetit.

That mother-fucker knew carrots were her favourite. *Was it crazy to think he had done it on purpose? Another show of his control? His superiority?*

She brushed the thought aside as crazy paranoia. He wasn't that smart. His depth wasn't that deep. Sure, he could be cruel, she'd seen that. But smart enough to plug away at her slowly? No. He wasn't that sharp. He was all or nothing. Always had been. Getting blind drunk or sober as a judge. Now he had no control over himself, he drank all day every day. If he thought she didn't know about his drinking, he was wrong. She could smell it on him, that thick odour of stale beer seemed to ooze out of him. Now he was a crazed drunk who scared his family and lashed out over the slightest thing. He was his dad. He had turned into the one thing he hated; he had kept visiting him after his mother died out of some sick sense of duty that had been beaten into him as a kid. Something he couldn't change without the help of many hours of therapy. Like that would ever happen. His dad had had a hold over him to the end. When it was over, and his dad had passed, maybe Barry's soul simply floated out of its useless, lifeless body, and found its way to the next best thing. Evil will always find a way, it's the good in people that dies forever.

Chapter 46

The night was hot, the summer had hit its peak. By Anna's estimation it had to be July 30th? Something close to that.

She'd seen a programme during the first lockdown about the war. It had all this footage that had been re-mastered into colour. The picture quality was outstanding, the images though, were horrendous. The poor children. She had wanted to turn away whilst it was on but couldn't, she had thought it not fair on them. They'd had to endure so much, the least she could do was catch a glimpse of what they had been through, to even try and comprehend how bad it had been. Nazis poking and prodding, choosing on a whim who would live or die. Mothers being torn away from children, husbands and fathers shot dead on the spot for refusing to leave their children. How they were kept in dank holes with no food or sanitation, boils and sores that wouldn't heal. Wondering if they'd ever see daylight again. She was beginning to feel something like that now. Wandering if she'd ever feel the cool grass beneath her feet, the water of the sea lapping against her bare ankles when they ventured out for a jaunt at the beach.

Eating food in a restaurant, drinking with friends in the pub. Going shopping, putting weight back on and filling out nice dresses and having a cleavage and curves, feeling sexy again.

Her dreams of what the outside world could hold for her brought a smile to her face; she marvelled at how quickly she could flow from one mood to the next, from utter despair to dreaming joy.

She was unravelling, she thought. She also thought, so fucking what? She could unravel if she wanted to; one night she could sit and think about a million different things with a million different emotions. She was holding it all together as best she could for the kids but she needed a minute to sit and let her mind drift wherever it wanted to go. If she wanted to sit down here and cry, she would. If she wanted to get mad and hit something, she would. If she wanted to laugh hysterically like some mental patient, she fucking would.

The bedroom was too hot for her to get comfy. Joy had fallen asleep naked, bar her nappy. Anna couldn't, that's how she'd ended up downstairs. Graham was down in the basement, as he always was. Drinking, smoking, whacking off.

Anna was wearing a vest and not much else. She had a pair of old running shorts on that had string through the waistband. She found if she pulled the string tight and tied it in a bow that it stayed on her hips. It required the occasional tug upwards every now and then, but it was fine.

30th of July. It must have only been two weeks or so. *Was that right?* It seemed it should have been at least a month, at least. Two weeks sounded pitiful, but it had to be right. Her mind wasn't that out of it yet. If it was right, it was her wedding anniversary soon. 4thth of August. It would be sixteen years. She'd only been eighteen when they met. They'd got married when she turned twenty and he was thirty, then she'd had Mikey at twenty-six.

What a smooth romantic Graham had been back then. Even for the first few years of marriage. It had trailed off a little after Mikey came along, that was OK, Anna was a realist. Adulting was hard, having a kid was harder.

The bear lamp was on at the back of the living room; that bloody thing had been sat there for years, since they bought the place. The shadows it projected on the wall beside the fireplace brought back a memory. She was drifting off to sleep as she remembered their first anniversary in this house.

It was the year before she got pregnant with Mikey, their last anniversary of it being just the two of them.

'Why don't you go have a nice soak in the tub, read a book, unwind for a bit?' he'd said, after telling her how excited he was to watch the England match that night.

'Hmmm, well played sir,' she'd said, smirking.

She'd gone upstairs to the bathroom, ignoring the fact that he must have forgotten it was their five-year anniversary.

She'd opened the bathroom door and found the whole room lit with candles. The bath was filled with inviting bubbles; rose petals were scattered on the floor and in the tub. A single rose sat in a vase on a wooden plank that sat across the bath. The rose was accompanied by a glass of champagne and a note.

For My Anna X.

She'd unfolded the paper, her hands trembling with shock and surprise.

Happy five-year anniversary, my love. Relax and enjoy this bath your fantastic husband has drawn for you, then come downstairs for part two.

P.S, there's something on the bed for you.

She'd smiled so wide her cheeks hurt.

In the bedroom she found a purple box, wrapped with a silk red ribbon. She pulled on the bow and the ribbon fell. She lifted the lid and saw a negligee, black and revealing. She slipped herself into it, the material was soft and it fit her like a second skin. Graham's attention to detail never ceased to amaze her. She clipped on the suspenders, *nice touch*, she thought, and covered herself up with her fluffy red dressing gown.

Downstairs, she opened the living room door. The room had been transformed like the bathroom had, filled with candles and flowers, rose petals scattered on the sofa. The fire was lit; thankfully it was a cooler July evening. He had opened the windows to ensure they wouldn't melt.

215

'What's this, Mr. Willow? Are you trying to seduce me?' She smiled at him, holding the opening of her dressing gown closed, threatening to drop it at any moment.

'Is it working? Mrs. Willow?'

'Might be. What else have you got planned?' she asked.

He pointed to the floor where he had set out soft blankets and pillows, a wicker picnic basket sat in the middle, along with a bottle of champagne nestled in an ice bucket.

'Graham, you're so sweet.' She kissed him gently on the lips and sat down.

She picked up a strawberry from the basket as he popped the cork from the champagne, it shot out and hit the ceiling making Anna shout out and then giggle. Foam spilled out over his fingers before he poured it into glasses.

'Cheers,' he said, holding up his glass.

She clinked hers with his. 'What did I do to deserve you?' she asked, tilting her head and biting her lip seductively.

'I don't know.' He smiled. 'But I'm glad you did it.'

She kissed him; his smooth, freshly shaved face pressed against hers made her tingle between her thighs. Their kissing grew intense, passionate. He put one hand on the back of her head, caressing and playing with her hair. Her hand slipped down his silk shirt; the buttons already undone most of the way. He slipped her dressing gown off her shoulders; despite the warmth of the air in the room she felt a tingling chill flash over her skin. Nerves. Why was she nervous? She had no idea, tonight felt special, they felt together, as corny as two becoming one.

He laid her down on the blanket; the picnic basket lay on its side forgotten, fruit and deli snacks tumbled to the floor. He stopped kissing her soft lips, just long enough to look down and breathe her in. He moved a hand up the warm, soft flesh on the inside of her thigh. He put himself inside her, they both groaned in pleasure, unparalleled by anything they had ever felt before.

The flickering light from the candles made their shadows dance along the wall, like poetry across a page. She watched their shadows entwine, become one shape, one person, one soul.

Chapter 47

Graham sat in the basement, wearing his Rolling Stones vest and a pair of boxer shorts. Whether there was something in the air that night or it was just a coincidence, Graham was also having flashbacks of times spent with Anna.

He had his hand in his pants; he was pulling relentlessly on his member, grunting and groaning.

The memory he had dredged up wasn't the same as Anna's. Not the moment of pure love that was laid out on a beautifully romantic setting. A night where they celebrated their love for each other.

No.

He was remembering a different night. A night when they had been a few years younger than that night. They had been to the bar in town, had had far too much drink with friends. He liked getting Anna this drunk.

Her inhibitions were lowered, more easily persuaded. They got home; he helped her upstairs in to bed. They fucked like porn stars. She was so drunk she let him do things to her, things that would never be on the table again.

He'd been so drunk he had let his normal self go, treated her like a piece of meat for his pleasure.

He remembered the touch of her skin, the way her breasts bounced as he rammed her forcefully and clumsily.

He was beginning to sweat; he was nearly there. Sat at his desk pulling on his cock like it was a newly discovered toy, when he stopped. A voice, in the back of his mind spoke to him. Mocking him.

Look at you. Sat down in a dark damp basement, pulling on your cock at the memory of a time when you were a man for once in your pitiful life. Man enough to take what you wanted. Man enough to satisfy the urges that you had suppressed for so long. Is that your wife upstairs? Or someone else's?

'Mine,' he said to the voice.

Go to her.

Chapter 48

Anna came round on the sofa. She had been dreaming so vividly she swore she could feel Graham inside her. She felt hazy, like she was stuck in a fever dream. She shuffled on the spot, feeling sweaty and uncomfortable. She felt a stab of pain, coming from between her legs. She opened her eyes, her lids felt heavy.

Struggling, she managed to open them enough to see the room. Her two hands were resting on her thighs. Her eyes closed before they could focus again.

She was distracted by the breath on her face and the awful stench that lingered on it.

She forced her eyes open again, her heart rate started to rise; she knew something was wrong. Her eyes opened, her eyelids not as heavy as before; the pain and discomfort between her legs was increasing, the breath on her face got faster and louder. She looked, and between her thighs was another hand. A fat hand in comparison to her own hands, her hands that sat limply on her thighs. The hand moved faster, slamming up inside her forcefully. She gasped against the pain, she tried to move away from it and felt another hand push down on her shoulder. The realisation of what was happening triggered a flood of adrenaline. Immediately she was wide awake.

Graham was there, forcing his hand inside her. He was panting in her ear; she froze momentarily in fear, not knowing what to do.

'Graham stop,' she said, her voice trembling and weak.

He didn't hear her. Or chose to ignore her.

'Graham, please. Stop.' She tried grabbing his hand and pulling it away from in-between her legs. He was too strong. He laughed and nibbled on her ear.

'Remember when we used to do it in here? We used to fuck all over this house, didn't we? What happened babe?' he said coarsely.

'Get off me!' Her voice was getting louder.

'Don't shout, babe. You don't want to attract anything from outside, do you? What if Mikey hears you, and comes down to check, huh? You don't want him to see this do you? His own mum acting like a whore while he sleeps?'

Anna started to cry; panic flushed her face. She bit her lips to stop from screaming and started slapping at Graham frantically, pushing him, trying to create a distance so she could get away.

'Now, now, dear. Didn't know you liked it rough. Is that why you've not fucked me for months? Huh? You been getting it somewhere else? One of my friends, which one was it? Dave? John? Not Tig, that wet blanket could have his cock in you, he still wouldn't have the bollocks to fuck.'

'Graham stop it. You're being crazy! There is no one else.'

'What did I say, about raising...your...voice!' His forehead connected hard with the bridge of her nose. Blood ran down her lips and chin, splattering on her chest.

Graham spun her round, bent her over the arm of the sofa. The middle of her back was bent low, her head and neck craned up on the hard armrest.

'Don't you fucking lie to me. Bitch. I am your husband; you will fuck me when I want it.'

Yanking her shorts down, he slammed into her, making her yell out. He placed a hand over her face, keeping her lips closed. His face came over her shoulder so she could see the sneer on his mouth; the gunk of tartar built up on his teeth looked like porridge pasted in the cracks.

'Please... Stop,' she managed to whimper.

He didn't hear her, he was gone; mentally he wasn't there anymore. Her body jolted as he slammed into her like she was nothing, some plaything that didn't feel. She cried as best she could; the tears struggled to come, the sounds she made were nothing more than quiet whimpering. She watched the shadows projected on to the wall by the light of the bear lamp. One shadow violating the other. Clearly not two becoming one as they had been that night, a thousand years ago. Now they were merely shadows of who they had once been.

Chapter 49

LOCKDOWN DAY 22

Mikey loved his guitar, he thought he'd never tire from playing it. He could sit and play that thing for hours. The thing that kept him so entranced by it was learning, wanting to know how to play a song, studying the music, playing it, messing up, starting over. Doing it again and again until he nailed it. The satisfaction he felt when he would play something and whoever was listening knew instantly what he was playing.

That's what it was all about, learning, testing yourself, playing for the crowds, the dream of playing. His Dad had always tried to squash his dreams. Told him to focus on getting his grades and then learning a trade like him, something useful.

His Mum told him to keep dreaming, reach for the stars: *'You can be whatever you want to be.'*

He believed her too. Why shouldn't he, someone had to do it? Someone had to write the songs that would change the world, go down in history as one of the greatest acts to grace the world. The Beatles did it. David Bowie. ACDC. There were countless musicians who had done something, and they'd all probably had a dad who told them not to bother. They all probably had *worse* fathers than he had. Or had used to have. He doubted many were worse than what his father had become now.

The guitar sat in the corner, staring back at him. All inspiration had floated away like a lost balloon. No one was going to hear what he had to play. He didn't even have an amp any more. What good was an electric guitar without an amp? It was like a crocodile without teeth.

He picked it up and sighed. He played the opening riff for 'Smoke On The Water' by Deep Purple. The first thing he'd ever learnt. The tune that would drive his mum and dad crazy.

He played it on a loop, staring into space. He was thinking about how worried he was about his mum. How her nose was slightly out of joint, and her vest was covered in dried blood.

She told him she fell in the dark and hit her nose on the floor because she couldn't get her hands up in time. She had no conviction in the lie which was what gave her away. His Dad had done it. He knew that. Everything bad that happened in that house stemmed from him. Mikey wished he would just fuck off and leave them to survive by themselves.

Mikey shuffled himself back on the bed. There was a loud rustle as he disturbed the ever-growing pile of empty packets of crisps and cookies his mum had continued to steal for him, despite her obviously broken nose and fear she carried around for her husband. She couldn't hide it any longer; she quivered and shook whenever his dad walked past her. Whereas his dad had started strutting, actually strutting around the house like a man who had just found his mojo.

Still, as always, his dad spent most of his time down in the basement. Rolling Stones played softly through the house, cigarette smoke floated up through the door and into the kitchen. His mum had stopped feeding Joy in there, she'd never even take her in if she could help it. Passive smoke was bad, especially for infants.

Mikey wanted it all to be over. How could they go on like this?

He put the guitar down. Bored. Fed up. Depressed. He headed for the only thing that gave him any slight pleasure any more. That was the craft room.

Chapter 50

Anna sat in the craft room, with Joy crawling round on the floor and checking out all the balls of wool. Anna had done a thorough safety check of the room to ensure there was nothing Joy could get to that she shouldn't. Anna was working on the hats; she had done five, with matching gloves. Now she was doing a red set. Then she'd move on to the next project. Probably another blanket. Something she could do whilst switching her mind off, taking her away from this hell.

Hell was the right word for it. Graham had seen to that. There was no other way to describe it. She had been such a confident woman all her life, even in their marriage. She had never felt like she had to be an obedient wife, someone that lived in fear of their husband, and now that was exactly what she was. She thought she could probably write a book about this when it was over.

Graham would laugh at her. Of course he would. Like he laughed at Mikey dreaming about being a rock star. *Things like that don't happen to regular people like us,* that's what he'd say. That's what he had been taught.

Not that there would be anyone to read the book. Not with the whole world destroyed or murdered or shot and buried in her back garden.

'Hi mum.'

'Jee-sus Mikey. You gave me a heart attack.' Anna clutched at her chest. It didn't take much for her heart to go racing these days. It had to work a lot harder than it used to.

'I'm just coming to look outside.'

'OK love. It's still there. I checked.' She smiled at him. Her face looked wrong, purpled and blackened around her eyes. Her nose had a new crook where the cartilage meets the bone.

Under any other circumstances she'd have gone to the hospital and had the thing reset, pushed back into place. The thought made her toes curl but it would be worth it to have a straight nose. Now she'd have to live with a crooked nose for the rest of her life.

Mikey sat by the window, looking through the crack with one eye. Anna couldn't tell by his expression if he was smiling or crying.

She turned back to her hat; Joy was slobbering over a roll of wool in the corner, examining everything with her mouth, as babies do.

She pulled and hooked the wool in the repetitive pattern, working her way round.

When winter comes, she would be really glad she'd made these. She imagined the house would get pretty cold in winter. The heating would have been switched off by then, no gas for the cooker or the radiators. Or hot water. Hopefully the electric would still be working so she could have a shower.

After Graham had raped her, (it took her a few days to come to terms with the fact that she had been raped) he refused to let her shower for the following three days. The inside of her thighs was covered in spots of semen, her face spotted with dried flakes of blood from her busted nose. He told her that maybe walking around looking like a mouthy whore might teach her to satisfy her husband properly in future.

When she was finally able to shower, she stayed longer than the radio alarm clock demanded she have. She carried on scrubbing, getting every last bit of him from her.

She was terrified of him, more terrified than she had ever been by anyone or anything. That didn't mean she was going to stand for that shit anymore. She was going to feel safe in her own home, no matter what it took.

After her shower, when she started to feel a little more like herself, she went into the kitchen. Graham was asleep in the basement. He had taken to sleeping most of the day and coming out at night. She heard him in the living room while she lay in bed awake. He was dancing to music, eating and drinking. She came down one morning to find cigarette butts all over the carpet. Where their daughter crawled was littered with ash and fag ends. The TV screen and the wall of the fireplace were streaked in something she could only assume was semen. She felt sick; he stood there every night and whacked off on to the wall and TV. The thought of him doing that, touching himself whilst no doubt thinking about what he'd done to her, made her sick with rage. She thought of taking a pair of scissors between his legs, well and truly making sure he'd never touch her like that again. He had completely lost his mind; it seemed obvious now and she couldn't believe she hadn't come to this conclusion earlier. She had suspected, but now, she was sure.

She didn't want to clean it up, but if she didn't, it would still be there. Every morning, before bringing Joy down, she would clean up all the fag ends, sweep up the ash, wash and dry the carpet and anti-bac the TV. The one positive from the lack of food was that Barney wasn't shitting even half as often, meaning the lingering smell of dog shit in the air was now only faint.

Enough was enough. She crept into the kitchen, careful of the creaky floorboards, and grabbed a kitchen knife they never used. It wasn't the biggest but it was sharp. And if she stabbed his throat, it wouldn't matter how big it was. He would bleed out regardless and then they would be safe. She taped it to the underside of the desk in her craft room, so it was always there within reach. If he came for her again, she wouldn't let him take her easily; she'd rather she was torn limb from limb by the monsters outside than raped in her home, just a floor away from where her children slept. If he came for her again, he would fucking die.

'Mum!' Mikey was shaking her by the shoulder. Anna flinched; her hand flung to the knife she kept taped under the desk.

'Mikey, you keep making me jump. What is it?' She could see from his face it was serious.

'A car.'

Chapter 51

'What do you mean, a car?' Anna said, struggling to comprehend what it would mean if there was a car.

'A car! A car just drove down the lane. Look, Look!' Mikey grabbed her arm, pushing against the bruises that were already there, making her wince.

She went over to the window and looked; her back creaked as she bent down. She saw a red car, just a glimpse before it went over the other side of the hill and to the unreachable horizon, but there was no mistaking it. It was a car.

'Mikey? I...What does it mean?'

'Maybe not everyone's dead? What if it's a survivor? They've found a car and are out looking for other survivors? Wouldn't it be better to find a group of others?' He looked over his shoulder cautiously and leant closer to Anna. 'Wouldn't it be better if we got away from him? That is, of course, if the virus is even real.'

Anna could hardly bear it; the thought of getting away and being safe was torture. Hope, she found, was the thing that tortured her the most.

'I know he did this to you, mum. I'm not stupid. He got mad at something, and hit you. Didn't he?' Mikey raised an eyebrow, a mature look often seen on the face of a parent saying *'You can't hide anything from me.'*

Anna nodded, smiling through her tears.

'Let's see if we can get out. It's about midday now, he'll be asleep. Let's find a way to escape. Yeah?'

Mikey's expression looked like when he tried to convince Anna to buy them tickets for Disney Land. 'How?' she asked, already sounding defeated.

'I don't know yet. Do you have any idea what the codes for the chains on the door could be?'

'No idea.'

Mikey paced around the room, stroking his chin, Anna thought he had the look of someone desperately trying to think of a solution. Joy watched him walk back and forth; she looked like she was watching a tennis match in slow motion.

'There's got to be a way?'

'You did all the shutters with him. Where do you think's best?' Anna asked.

'The only one he didn't do properly is this one. But I still don't see how we could pry this open.'

Just then the door to the craft room opened. They both drew in a breath. Anna's hand shot to the knife taped under her desk.

Barney's head popped round, he had something in his mouth. It was long and thin like a wire. He trotted in and dropped it at Anna's feet.

'What is it, boy?' Mikey said, squatting down and ruffling Barney's fur.

Barney nudged the thing on the floor towards Anna. She picked it up and studied it.

Her eyes widened. 'Mikey. Let's go downstairs.'

Chapter 52

Anna, holding Joy in her arms, made her way down the stairs quietly. Mikey followed closely behind with Barney taking the rear. Barney, in his excitement, ran past them all and darted into the living room.

'Barney!' Anna hissed. As if Barney should know to be quieter.

They opened the living room door and walked in. The floor was covered in cigarette butts and ash again; the familiar streaks down the TV and chimney breast were present. Anna looked away in disgust.

'What are we doing in here, mum? What's your idea?'

Anna held up the wire Barney had brought her. 'This. Barney's been chewing on this damn thing for weeks, finally he's snapped it. Look.' Anna pointed to the air filter Graham had put in the window.

Mikey pushed on it; the silicone had come loose from Barney pulling on the cord, and the whole unit was ready to drop out.

'We can't fit through there,' Mikey said.

'No, we can't, but Barney can. We write a note and stuff it in his collar, put him through there and tell him to run. Someone will find him and read the note, then they'll come and get us, and take us to where the other survivors are.' Anna was smiling, genuinely excited and optimistic the plan would work.

'Right...and what if one of the infected things gets him?'

'I think they'd struggle. Barney's a smart dog, he'd know to run away from one of those things.'

'What about the air? Isn't it polluted? Dad said it would take seconds to get infected by it?' Mikey was shaking, Anna could see he wanted it to be true, he wanted to know it would work. He had been told too many things by Graham, he didn't know what was true and what wasn't.

'I don't think it's as bad as that. Think about it, our air filter is a fan with some fucking filter paper on it, Mikey.'

'Language.'

Anna smirked, 'If someone is out there driving around, it can't be that dangerous to breathe the air, because they'd be holed up somewhere like we are. If Barney does get ill, then we'll know. But we have to try. We have to.'

'OK, let's do it.'

Mikey, being the stronger of the two now that Anna was nothing but skin and bone, lifted the fan out of its hole. He had put on a paper mask for at least some protection. Anna had gone upstairs to put Joy down for a nap. She came down wearing a mask of her own.

The fan wasn't heavy and came away from the window easier than either of them had expected. They put it down on the floor, slowly and gently, careful not to make a sound.

Anna wrote a note that had their names and address on, an S.O.S and a brief plea asking for help from any survivors. She taped it to Barney's collar and put it back round his neck.

'OK, it's ready,' Mikey said. He took a deep breath and nodded at Anna.

Anna nodded back at him. She checked once more over her shoulder. In her mind she kept imagining Graham stood in the doorway watching them, swinging his gun around his finger.

He wasn't there. The coast was clear.

'Go get help, boy.' She kissed Barney on the head and stroked under his chin.

Mikey bent down and stroked him too. Mikey started to cry, then Anna started.

They hugged each other and Barney; his tail was wagging furiously. He could smell the outside through the hole they'd made and was desperate to get out of there.

'He'll be OK, won't he mum?'

Anna nodded. 'He'll be fine, love. He's going to get us help.'

Anna picked Barney up, kissed him one last time, and started to post him through the hole in the window. The cut edges of the steel shutter were razor- sharp; miraculously, she managed to post him through without cutting herself. His legs started flapping, eager to get on the ground and run around freely.

She put him through, she had to drop him two feet to the floor. He landed on the gravel with a soft thud.

Mikey put an arm around Anna and they both watched as Barney ran round the drive. He was chasing wasps and flies, he chewed on the long grass by the hedge rows, cocking his leg and sending out a yellow stream of urine against Graham's truck.

They watched him run free for ten minutes, then they started trying to usher him away.

'Go on Barney, go get help,' Anna said.

'Barney, go!' Mikey was getting nervous and impatient. Graham could come up any minute.

Barney ran back to the window; he was jumping up trying to get back in.

'No Barney, you have to go. Please, Barney. Go!' Anna was trying to push him away, careful of touching the sharp metal edges of the shutter.

Barney started yapping loudly, snarling and barking at the window.

Anna snapped her neck back to look at the kitchen door. It was still closed, but Graham would hear Barney and wonder what was happening.

'Go on, Barney!' Mikey snapped.

Barney carried on barking and jumping at the window.

'We're going to have to get him back in,' Anna said, panicked.

'But we've come this far.'

'We'll try again another time, but it's too risky. Graham will hear us.' She checked again and saw the kitchen door was still closed.

'Fine.' Mikey shook his head, clearly annoyed, and put his arms through the hole in the shutter. 'Come on, boy.' he said. Barney was trying to jump into his arms. 'Come on, that's it.'

Anna watched, gnawing at her fingernails through her mask. Her hair was falling over her face, stuck to it with sweat.

'Come on boy. That's it.' Barney jumped and barked. Every time he jumped and missed, he barked as if getting mad at himself, trying to cheer himself on.

This time Barney. This time Barney! Anna willed to herself.

He jumped again; this time Mikey caught him, grateful to feel the wiry fur of his pet dog. Mikey realised then how scared he'd been that he could have lost him out there for good.

Anna watched on with relief; she was so consumed with the fear that Mikey wouldn't be able to get him back in, she didn't hear the footsteps coming up behind her, or the slam of the kitchen door.

Graham shoved her against the shutters. Mikey jumped in shock, lacerating his arm on the jagged cut in the steel. He managed to keep hold of Barney and pull him in before dropping him to the floor.

Barney, covered in a gush of blood from Mikey's arm, started barking crazily at Graham. Graham pushed Mikey to the floor. A pool of blood was forming around him, soaking into the ash-covered carpet.

'You fucking idiots! You think this is a joke! Are you trying to kill us all?' Graham was screaming His face had turned bright red with rage.

Barney snapped at Graham's ankles. Graham grabbed him by the scruff of the neck and lifted him in the air. Barney was yelping in pain from Graham's grip.

Graham was about to hit him when he saw the note taped to Barney's collar. His face faded from red back to normal. He peeled off the tape and held the note out in his free hand. He read it, his lips moving, saying the words soundlessly.

'You were trying to escape... You think you'd be safer with strangers than with me?' His eyes filled with tears. 'After all I've done for you!'

He grabbed Barney by the neck with both hands and whipped him up and down. The crack was dense and sickening as his neck snapped. Barney let out a helpless yelp of pain before flopping in Graham's hands. It was clear Barney was dead but he snapped his neck again, this time over his knee; the crack was louder this time. He looked at Mikey and Anna as they huddled together on the floor, holding each other and crying, trying to scurry away from him. He threw Barney against the wall above their heads; he sprung back and fell limply between Anna's legs.

'After all I've done, you're still trying to leave me! We're a family! You need me!' He began sobbing and screaming, banging on the shutters so they let out a deafening sound. When he finally stopped screaming and banging, he looked at them both pitifully.

Chapter 53

Graham paced the room, his fingers laced together on top of his head.

'What did you think you would do?' he said.

'We need to get out, Graham. We need to find the other survivors!' Anna shouted at him.

'I will keep you safe. Me! We don't need anyone else.'

Anna looked at Mikey, he looked faint. He was struggling to keep his eyes open. 'Mikey?' She shook his shoulders. Mikey's head lolled back against the floor.

'Graham, we need to get him help!' Blood was still pouring out of Mikey's arm; the cut had gone through a vein.

Graham still paced the room. Scratching the hair on the underside of his chin like a dog with fleas.

'Graham!! We need a doctor!' Anna screamed, snapping Graham from his trance.

'I'm thinking!' He walked over to Mikey and crouched down. 'He needs stitches. You have a needle and thread upstairs, yes?'

Anna nodded.

Help me get him upstairs.'

They dragged Mikey up the stairs; he was looking paler with every passing second. Graham laid him down on the floor in the craft room. He looked around and found an old bed sheet that Anna was going to cut up for something. He wrapped it round the cut.

'Put pressure on it, we need to stop the bleeding.'

Anna put both of her hands on it, using whatever strength remained in her to try and stop the bleeding.

Graham searched the desk, knocking everything to the floor. 'Where's the fucking needles?!'

'In the plastic box on the side, there should be thread in there with it.'

He knocked a box of crochet hooks onto the floor and picked up the plastic box. He took out a roll of black thread and a pack of needles.

'Move.'

He pushed Anna aside, and put his own hand over the cut, applying pressure.

Anna curled up in the corner, her hands were covered in blood. She looked at them, struggling to believe what was happening. She held her hands out in front of her, turning them over. She began crying hysterically.

'Shut the fuck up!' Graham snapped.

He lifted the sheet away; the blood had slowed but it was still coming. He took his belt off and wrapped it around Mikey's bicep, just above the cut. He pulled it tight, the skin creased around it.

Then he put the sheet back over and applied pressure on it.

'If he dies, I'll kill you.' Anna said. There was no fear in her voice when she said it.

Graham looked over at her and then back at Mikey.

He lifted the sheet off; the bleeding had slowed some more. 'Come here, I need you to hold this.'

Anna crawled over quickly. 'Hold what? Tell me what to do.'

'Here, pinch the wound shut so I can start stitching.'

Any squeamishness she might have had before didn't apply here. She grabbed where the cut was and pushed the two sides together.

Graham sucked the end of the thread and put it through the eye of the needle first time. He pushed one of her hands out of the way and replaced it with his own. He put the needle through one side and out the other, before coming back round to the other side and doing it again.

He got to the end. The stitches weren't neat, the middle of the cut meandered out before coming back in; the scar would heal in the same way.

Anna shook Mikey gently. He had passed out. 'He's not waking up. Graham, is he OK?'

'He'll be fine. He'll be out of it for a while. He just needs rest.'

Graham stood and wiped his hands on his vest, leaving bloody hand marks.

'We need a doctor.'

'He's fixed. He needs rest. I saved him, Anna. Remember that. This is your fault.'

'This is not my fault. This is your fault! You are keeping us locked in here when we could be out there finding other survivors, working together as a community.'

'The air is fucking contaminated, you dumb bitch.'

'Bullshit. How did you survive then? Going outside, letting all the air in?'

Graham seemed to consider this for a second before blurting out: 'I'm immune. OK! I'm immune from the disease.'

Anna barked with laughter. 'You're immune? That's just fucking priceless. Mikey saw a car this morning, driving past our house. How do you explain that?'

Graham's face flushed, flinching away as if dodging a hit.

'How did you see outside?'

Anna was so past furious she didn't care if Graham knew everything. 'There's a crack in the shutter in here. We've been using it to look at the outside.'

Graham wiped his face, putting blood in his long salt-and-pepper beard. 'You could have compromised our entire safety by not telling me. You know that? It's a wonder you're not all dead already.'

She saw that look in his eye, the look of a madman. His appearance might have changed, his hair grown longer, his beard out of control, covered in muck and blood, but his eyes – they were what gave away his insanity. He had been losing his sanity for a while; the thought had crossed her mind even before this virus had hit but never had she imagined it could get this bad. Now she wondered if he had descended too far down that dark pit to ever come back.

'Is it even that bad? Out there, is it as bad as you say? We've never heard the radio broadcast, or seen anything to support what you said.'

'You think I made this up? I came home, covered in blood. Other people's blood. You think I made that up, do you?'

She remembered the look in his eyes that night. That was what had scared her more than anything. 'I don't...I don't know.'

'You want proof? I'll give you fucking proof.'

Graham ran downstairs; his footsteps sounded like thunder. While he was gone Anna knelt beside Mikey and stroked his hair. His face was pale, his lips looked like the colour of ash. Anna watched his chest move up and down in relief. If it weren't for that sign, she would have thought by the look of him that he was dead.

Graham came back into the room with the radio under his arm. He shook it at her in an immature school playground way and plugged it in to the wall. He sat it down on the desk and hit a button on the top.

He stood aside and put one hand on his hip. The message came out of the radio, telling them what it was like on the outside, what was happening and how bad the virus was. Telling them the survivors were at the old radio station.

'There, do you understand what's happening now?'

Anna listened intently, hearing every word that came from the speakers. She looked at Graham and nodded. 'I understand.'

Graham shook his head in disgust, ripped the plug from the wall and headed downstairs.

Anna flinched as he slammed the door. She put her head in her hands and started to laugh, laughing at her own naivety.

Her own stupidity. She had always been one to take everything on its merit. Seeing is believing and all that. She wouldn't believe in hearsay until she saw it or read about it in a reputable media outlet.

This whole time, she had taken Graham at his word, before starting to doubt him slowly. His inconsistencies, his strict rules that everyone apart from him had to follow, the man outside who sounded perfectly normal. He'd knocked on the door for God's sake, he wasn't hitting it or trying to break through, he was knocking, to see if they were in.

The voice on the radio was panicked enough, sounded sincere too. Told them things none of them in that house would know, unless of course someone in that house had made the entire thing up.

She thought of the months of planning he had been doing in that basement. Just how long had her husband been insane, she wondered? The voice on the radio was truly panicked, the things it said were terrifying to hear. What terrified her more, was that it was Graham's voice.

Chapter 54

LOCKDOWN DAY 25

The plan for Anna was a simple one. Play. The. Course.

If she was to tell Graham she knew the truth, had figured it out, that would be her signing her own death warrant. And Mikey's and Joy's in the process.

Graham was so absorbed in the lie he'd been telling them, he hadn't allowed them to take Barney outside and give him a proper burial. Instead, he had put him in a carrier bag from under the sink, and simply thrown him out of the basement doors.

Anna knew she just had to wait it out a little longer; someone would notice they weren't turning up for things. Mikey's school was out for summer, but he spent every summer out with his friends playing football and jamming with their instruments. They would come calling sooner or later.

Beverly.

Beverly had gone to Italy for four weeks. It had nearly been four weeks now, and she'd said if Anna didn't get away and go stay at hers whilst she was away, the first place she'd come was here for a brew and a catch-up on her way back from the airport.

She'd know something was wrong straight away. She'd see the shutters, and the plastic carrier bag containing their beloved family pet. She'd call the police in no time.

What if she knocks?

Anna felt her heart do a somersault. If she knocked, she was likely to get a bullet in the head, like the other guy. Beverly knew Graham was showing signs of violence, but even seeing the shutters on the windows, she'd never be able to accurately predict what was going on inside. There was no way she'd have the foresight not to knock on the door. There had to be a way to warn her so that as soon as she got here, she'd know to phone the police and stay safe.

Chapter 55

Anna had spent the past few days at Mikey's side. He was in and out of consciousness, struggling to eat food, and managing only a few sips of water a day. Graham kept refusing helping him in any other way, saying all he needed was rest to recuperate. He had done all they could.

Graham had stopped feeding them altogether. He had stopped doing anything; he didn't care about the state of the house, the jobs that needed to be done, or saving electric and gas. He would throw a protein bar for her and one for Mikey. That was to last the whole day. If she touched any other food, there would be consequences. The pain she felt between her thighs reminded her of the consequences he could dish out. Every cut or scrape, bruised flesh, none of it seemed to heal.

Whilst Graham slept, she tried the combination on the padlocks; she tried Graham's birthday, Mikey's, hers (that last one was a guess of desperation), their wedding anniversary. Nothing. She tried removing the air filter he had put back in the hole, just to block the virus getting in, he had said. She couldn't fit through, despite only consisting of skin and bone now.

She had watched for anyone passing by; she tried flashing a torch out there. On and off. On and off. Hoping someone would see it and notice it was S.O.S in Morse code. They hardly had any traffic past here, and their neighbours had to be looking in the perfect direction at the perfect time to be able to see it. No one had come, no one had seen her signal, so she had kept on going.

She fed Joy in the morning. She told Graham they were down to the last tin of formula and the way she was drinking it, it would only last for the next two, maybe three days.

'I've told you. She's old enough for solid food, she can eat like the rest of us.'

We don't get to eat! is what she wanted to scream at him. She reminded herself to play the long game. Bev would be here in three more days. That was what Anna was pinning all of her hopes on now. She would continue to keep on flashing the torchlight out of the hole in the window, and trying different combinations in the lock, but the only realistic way she could see herself getting out of this with Mikey and Joy, was Bev.

Chapter 56

Anna staggered upstairs and put Joy down on the floor of the craft room. Every step felt as though she was dragging a boulder behind her. Thigh muscles burning, hamstrings tight, hunger cramping up her stomach.

Mikey was lying in a makeshift bed, a white pillow under his head and a light sheet covering him. The first thing Anna noticed when she walked in was the smell.

She had to cover her nose with the back of her hand. She had never smelt anything like it before. It smelt rancid, like rotten shellfish and decay.

Kneeling beside Mikey she touched his brow, he was burning up. His lip was quivering and his body shivered. Sweat was pouring out of him, his lips were cracked deep.

'Shh, Mikey. There's my big brave boy.' She wet a flannel with a bowl of cold water and dabbed his head.

His eyes opened partially, enough to look at her. Her face seemed to calm him, his shivers were less violent and his lips had stopped quivering.

He opened his mouth; his tongue was white and dry like cotton.

'Mum...I'm cold,' he said.

She looked at him, confused. He was running a fever, hot to the touch and sweating profusely. She couldn't understand why he wasn't getting better.

He looked in so much pain; his eyes were looking into hers and for a second, he seemed to be five years old again, wanting a song before bed.

She couldn't think of a lullaby he would like, now he was older. Lullabies were for babies, not for rock n' roll stars like him.

She dabbed his brow with fresh water and chewed her lip in thought.

She thought of a song to sing, a song she hadn't sung since she was eighteen.

Mikey's mouth turned up in one corner as he tried to smile at her singing.

He opened his mouth; his voice was croaky and weak. 'I'm on a highway to hell.' He chuckled, which quickly turned to coughing.

Anna gave him a sip of water. He smacked his lips together and rolled his tongue around his teeth. He was drifting again. Shivering again, teeth chattering.

Anna removed the dressing that was wrapped around his cut. She had removed it and cleaned the wound every day to try and avoid infection. The redness around the cut told her she was failing. The smell that repulsed her when she first walked in was getting worse as she unravelled the bandage.

When the last wrap came off, she saw exactly what she feared she would see under it. The wound was oozing yellow pus through the stitches. The flesh had turned a shade of green, and red lines had started to reach up his arm.

'No no no no. Shit. Mikey! Wake up, I need you to sit up.' Anna started shaking Mikey's shoulders; his head wobbled but he failed to open his eyes. How could infection take hold so fast? She'd changed the dressing yesterday and hadn't noticed anything. She was panicking, her heart beat faster and the room began to swim.

Mikey's body was so devoid of nutrients his body couldn't fight the infection any longer. She knew from watching the stories from Auschwitz documentaries that many of the children died from disease and infection. Once an infection took hold, the body couldn't fight it off without medicine.

She didn't know what to do. She tried to think if she had antibiotics left over from when she'd had an ear infection.

246

She'd never finished the course. As soon as she felt better, she always forgot to take the rest of them.

Joy had crawled over to Mikey and pulled herself up so she could stand over him, her legs wobbling under her slight weight. She looked at him smiling, waiting for him to open his eyes and say 'boo' or try to tickle her. When he didn't, her smile fell.

'Ikey.'

Anna's heart broke. Joy's first word was her brother's name, out of worry, wanting him to wake up.

Anna grabbed Joy and put her in her cot in the next room. She started screaming and crying, not wanting to nap. Anna needed to look for some antibiotics. She needed to find them fast if Mikey was to stand a chance.

She ran downstairs to the kitchen and rifled through the cupboards where they kept the painkillers, aspirin, plasters, antihistamines. Boxes fell out and she pushed them aside, so they landed on the counter and the floor.

'What are you doing?' Graham stood in the door from the basement.

'Mikey's cut. It's infected, I need some antibiotics now.'

'I'll have a look. You women can be so hysterical.'

Graham went up, leaving Anna in the kitchen. She searched every cupboard and found nothing. She decided to head back upstairs. When she turned to walk back, she kicked a box along the floor. She bent to pick it up.

Penicillin.

'Yes! I've got some!' she shouted and ran upstairs, her thigh muscles aching and creaking. For the last few steps she had to put her hands on the handrail and drag herself up.

'Graham, I found some.' She ran into the craft room. Joy was still crying in the room across the hall.

Graham held out a hand, his gaze not shifting from Mikey. He opened the flap on the box and pulled out the foil pill-holder inside. He sighed and his shoulders slumped. He held the foil over his head, in the direction of Anna standing behind him.

'What is it?' she said, wandering why Graham wasn't acting faster.

'Empty. The box is empty.'

'No!' Anna put her hands to the side of her face despairingly. 'We have to do something. Graham, he's going to die! We need to get him to the hospital. He needs a fucking doctor.'

'We can't take him out of the house because of the virus!'

'There is no virus. Stop this, Graham, you made the whole thing up. You've lost your fucking mind. You need help.'

'You heard the radio! You heard what he said.'

'That was you! You recorded your own voice on tape. Graham, you're losing it and it's going to be the death of our son. Let me out. Let me take the kids, please. Please.'

Graham stood and looked sharply into space. He was breathing heavily.

'You don't understand!' he shouted. He put his hands to his head and pulled on a chunk of his hair. 'I had to keep us together! You were going to leave because you couldn't see, nobody could see what was happening right in front of their eyes! I told you this virus was coming but you wouldn't believe me, you called me crazy, you plotted and schemed to run away when my back was turned,' A loud rumbling came from outside. 'I did what I had to do to make you see, to keep you here with me!'

'You're dangerous! You need help!' Anna cried.

Graham laughed and stomped his feet in fit of hysterics. 'I need help? I need my family to do as they're told!' His face changed to fury as quick as a flash. 'This virus has taken everything from me, everything I worked for, everything that made me a man. It took my business, my

248

friends, my money –even my dad! Everything I had built and worked for was slipping through my fingers and I wasn't going to let it take you too! I did all I could to keep you with me, the only way I knew how.'

'Don't' you see how delusional that is? You've turned into your dad; he controlled and abused your mother all of their married life. And from what I hear, he most likely killed her too.'

Graham shook his head and smiled. 'Mum knew how to be, knew how to behave and trust in her husband.' He jabbed a finger towards Anna. 'You need to learn that lesson.'

The weather had finally broken. A thunderstorm began raging outside; rain poured down, sounding like a million tiny pebbles hitting the windows.

Anna looked down at Mikey, saw him declining in front of her eyes. 'Graham, we know that there isn't a virus. You need to let us go now or Mikey will die.'

Graham shook his head slowly, the smile slipped into a scowl. 'The virus is real, Anna. I just jumped the gun a bit, said it was here a bit early to stop you from running out on me.' He pointed towards the window. 'The world out there is in ruin. You can't go out there, you need to stay here with me. And do, as you're fucking told!'

Anna looked back to Mikey again and felt her heart racing. 'He's going to die!'

Graham chewed his lip in thought. 'I know what to do. I'll fix him. I've seen this done before. Stay here.' Graham walked past Anna and left the room. Before he shut the door, he fired a hateful glance at her.

'Hang in there, Mikey,' Anna whispered. 'I'll get you out of here, I promise. This will be nothing but a bad dream. You'll write songs about the time we were locked in with a psychopath. Wake up Mikey, please talk to me!'

Mikey started talking, making no sense, as though he was speaking a language only he knew. His teeth were chattering together so hard they made a sickening snapping sound that cut through Anna, making her skin turn to goose flesh.

A thud came from the hall. Graham entered the room with an iron. His face was sullen and focused. He plugged the iron in on the floor near Mikey.

'Graham? What are you doing? Burning it won't get the infection out!'

Graham looked at her.

'Graham? What are you doing?'

He shot over to her, faster than she could react. He grabbed her by the hair and pulled her to her feet. She screamed and reached her hands to her head, trying to get his hand off her hair. He yanked and pulled, dragging her into the hall.

'Graham! What are you doing?' she screamed at him as he threw her to the floor.

Graham picked up the axe he used for chopping wood for the fire. He had dropped it against the wall. That was what had caused the thud, Anna realised.

He held the axe up next to his face. 'I'm saving my son's life.' He slammed the door and turned the key, locking the door.

'Noooo!' Anna screamed. She jumped at the door, her slight frame bouncing back from it like a rubber ball. She hit it again and again with everything she had. Finally, she lay on the floor, screaming through her sobbing. Joy screamed in the other room.

Chapter 57

Graham pressed his head against the door, feeling the hits from Anna on the other side, through the wood. She had become convinced that the virus wasn't real, that outside, nothing was happening. If she truly believed that then it was all over. How could he save them? How could he show her she was wrong?

What he was doing, everything he had done, was for them, to keep them together. If it wasn't for him, she'd be dead just like everyone else.

And she thought she could survive it without him?

He thought then, maybe it would just be better to kill them all now?

Be done with it.

He stood over Mikey and looked down at his weak, decrepit body. The infection was working its way through his bloodstream until it reached his heart. Then he would die.

Graham placed the blade of the axe against Mikey's neck.

It would be so easy.

'No,' Graham said, as If arguing with himself. 'Not yet. There's still time.'

The time has come for you to do what must be done.

'Not YET!'

He grabbed Mikey's arm and squeezed; yellow pus flowed over his fingers. Mikey winced and started weeping quietly, semi-conscious to what was happening.

Graham pulled his belt out of the loops on his jeans and tied it around Mikey's arm, as close to the shoulder as he could. Cutting off the blood supply to the wound.

This is what they had to do in the war; when a soldier was down, his limb badly injured, the only way to save his life was to cut it off there and then. Graham had seen it on countless war films and TV dramas. He had his first-aid training; he could do this. No messing about, no debates - cut it off and live, leave it on and die. The axe was old. Graham ran his thumb over the edge. He couldn't remember the last time it had been sharpened, not for a few years at least. It was only used for chopping wood for the fire, but that didn't require a razor-sharp edge.

He stood, marked an imaginary line on Mikey's arm for where to aim. Just above the green, infected area. It would take a few, hard and accurate swings. If anyone could do it, he could.

'It's OK Mikey. Daddy's here. Everything's going to be OK now. Don't you worry.'

He lifted the axe up over his head, his legs spread evenly for balance.

Deep breath. Count backwards from five.

A rivulet of sweat rolled down his cheek and followed the curve of his jaw line.

He ignored the banging on the door from Anna and the cries from Joy across the hall.

Focus.

The axe came down hard, hitting the exact place above the infection where he wanted it to land. It cut through the flesh but the bone only smashed and splintered.

Mikey started screaming, writhing around on the floor, yelling and crying.

Graham, wide eyed and panicked, lifted the axe up over his head again; this time he brought it down with as much force as he could muster. With all of Mikey's thrashing he had shifted his position so that when the axe came down, it hit his forearm, this time cutting straight through the flesh and bone; it stayed connected by a string of skin. Mikey was screaming in agony; he was trying to lift his arm and get away from the pain. The blood was pouring out of his arm, the white bedsheet that covered him was now dark red. A puddle was spreading across the floor.

'What are you doing to him? Graham, please stop!' Anna was hitting the door with everything she had, kicking the panels, trying to create a hole where she could get her hand through.

'I'm saving him!' Graham shouted. He was breathing heavily, spit was flying from his mouth, sweat poured down his face, stinging in his eyes.

He had to cut again in the area he'd hit first. He stepped on Mikey's elbow to try and stop him from changing position when he screamed.

'Will you shut up! I need to concentrate.'

He swung the axe up high. Staring directly into the first incision, seeing the shards of bone fraying and splintered inside the flesh.

He brought it down accurately, cutting through the damaged bone, but failing to cut all the way through the triceps muscle still holding it together.

'Fucking hell.' Graham threw the axe to the side of the room and grabbed Mikey's arm with both hands. When he pulled it, the skin at the back of Mikey's arm stretched, looking like a piece of elastic about to twang back any second. It snapped, making Graham stumble back and fall on to the door.

Mikey was screaming – blood-curdling screaming, then he closed his eyes and fell silent.

Graham, holding part of his son's arm in his hand, dropped it to the floor. Seeing the amount of blood that kept pouring out of Mikey's severed limb, he knew he needed to hurry.

They don't show this part on the TV.

'Graham! Let me in! You're going to kill him!' Anna shouted.

He ran and opened the door. 'Come on, hold him.'

Anna swung a hand and slapped him, rocking his head back and splitting his lip in the same place she had last time she hit him. She looked across to where Mikey lay and cried out-*No-no-no-no!* when she saw him. His arm was butchered into three pieces, blood pooling around him. She ran and fell onto her knees beside him; she took his pale skinny face in her trembling hands.

'Mikey!' she shouted, trying to wake him.

'I've managed to cut away the infection, I need to cauterize the wound or he'll die. Hold him down.'

She had no choice but to let Graham finish what he'd started if Mikey was going to have any chance of survival. Anna put her hands on Mikey's shoulders. 'Hold on, Mikey. Hold on.'

Graham picked up the iron and touched the underside of it, then he snapped his hand away from the hot metal plate. 'It's ready.' He knelt down and picked up the stub that was now Mikey's arm. He struggled for a firm grip; the oozing blood was as slick as oil.

'One. Two. Three.' The meat sizzled on the red-hot iron. Mikey woke up to scream once more; he started thrashing, trying to escape from the pain. Graham held it on, steam arose from it, filling his nostrils with a sickly-sweet smell.

Curiously, he thought it smelled of pork.

He pulled the iron away; bits of stringy flesh still clung to it.

He grimaced. Anna turned away and retched. If there had been anything in her stomach she would have puked.

Graham stood over his wife and son, thinking what a messy business it was.

The things people have to do to survive.

Chapter 58

Anna cried and squeezed Mikey's hand. He was still breathing, miraculously so. She couldn't quite understand how, after all the trauma he had suffered, his body had carried on going.

Robust little things, children.

Bev had said that. Anna doubted this sort of thing would ever have crossed Bev's mind when she said it.

Joy was still crying from over the landing. She couldn't bring her in here, but she couldn't leave Mikey alone. The blood and mess had to be cleaned. She grabbed another spare sheet and started soaking up the pools of blood. The carpet had soaked up a lot. She just had to get the worst parts and then cover the carpet up with towels.

She threw the dirty sheets into the hall and put a fresh one over Mikey. His stump looked black and red, like a piece of badly barbecued meat.

'Here.' Graham threw a pack of bandages up the stairs. 'They're still in the sealed bag. So maybe he won't get an infection this time.'

Anna didn't reply. Graham walked off, suggesting he didn't expect one.

Joy cried again; her screams had turned to screeches.

'I'm coming, darling. Give me a minute.' The stress Anna was under was so high she thought there must be another name for it.

Anna wrapped Mikey's stump with the bandages, ensuring every piece of open wound was covered.

Running past Joy, who was standing at the bars of her cot, red-faced and tear-stained, Anna gave her a quick kiss and went into the bathroom and got a set of towels. She ran back to the craft room and covered the floor. It was the best she could do.

Joy started screaming again but stopped as soon as Anna came back through the door and picked her up.

'Ikey!'

'Mikey's through here darling, come on. Let's go see him.'

Anna sat beside Mikey. She looked out of the crack in the steel shutter. Two cars, both going in different directions, were on the horizon. One leaving into the distance, the other coming towards her. In two or three days, that car would be Bev, heading here to see if they were all OK. Surely, she thought, she must have tried phoning her by now? When she realised something had to be wrong, she'd be more determined than ever.

A couple more days, she thought. *A couple more days.*

And slipped the small knife into the back pocket of her jeans.

Chapter 59

The night was cooler after the storm. The air had been cleared of the humidity and it made a difference in the house. Graham must have heard Anna come down and make a bottle for Joy because he met her in the kitchen.

Anna moved her hand to her back pocket and felt the smooth plastic handle of the knife. She could stab him. She had imagined doing that very thing for days, thought about how she would carve him up, free herself from him. What stopped her was the thought of what would happen if he got the better of her. Which was a more than likely possibility. She was so weak now. Graham was big and strong; sure, she could catch him off guard, stab him once or twice, but what if that wasn't enough to kill him? What if he overpowered her, used the knife on her, slit her throat and left her to bleed out...it wasn't the thought that she might die that stopped her, it was what would happen to the children if she wasn't there. Although, could things get any worse? Things could always get worse, she thought, and moved her hand away from the knife's grip.

Graham held out a bag. Anna looked inside cautiously. Inside it was two protein bars, four apples, and a five-litre bottle of water. She didn't want anything from him, didn't want him to think she needed anything he had to offer, but she took it. Her hand grabbed the handle and tried to pull it towards her. For a second, she didn't think he was going to let go. Then he did, and the bag nearly dropped to the floor, Anna wasn't prepared for the weight of it.

'See. I'm not a monster. Or a psychopath. I'm me. I'm your husband. You can trust me, and trust me when I say that everything I've done is for this family,' Graham said, looking at Anna as if she had been unreasonable.

Anna didn't respond. If it was just them in the house, and if she had the energy, she would have beaten him until there was nothing left of his face. Like the old Anna would have done.

'Stay away from us,' Anna said through gritted teeth. 'You leave us alone or so help me I'll fucking kill you.'

Graham shook his head. 'You'll learn,' he said. Then he turned and walked back down into the basement.

Anna grabbed the ready-made bottles of formula and the bag with the food and water and went upstairs.

She closed the door of the craft room and wished there was a way to lock it to stop him from coming again. After putting the bag and the bottles down, she grabbed the knife from her back pocket and taped back underneath the desk.

Joy took her bottle and drank it desperately. Afterwards she cooed at Anna and played until an invisible force seemed to be pulling down on her eyelids. Anna wrapped Joy in the crocheted blanket she had made for her and put her down into the Moses basket. Joy fell straight to sleep. Anna smiled down at her. An exhausted tear rolled down her cheek and curled round onto her lips. Anna wiped it away, sniffed; her own eyes were growing heavy, forcing her to rub them with her fingers. She sat beside Mikey. She watched as he slept. Every time his chest rose and fell, she felt relief. It meant he was still alive, that she hadn't lost him. She stroked his face and laid beside him, watching the steady rise and fall of his chest, but the relief never lasted long. Anna didn't sleep that night.

Chapter 60

Mikey was still breathing the next morning. He was pale and unresponsive to Anna's touch and her talking in his ear, as well as Joy's jabbering and shouting his name excitedly: 'Ikey! Ikey!'

The fact that he *was* still breathing was nothing short of a miracle, with the amount of blood he must have lost yesterday, his body's energy reserve depleted from fighting the infection, as well as the lack of food.

Anna was dabbing his dry lips with a clean sponge soaked in water. He was instinctively licking his lips, his body needing to hydrate.

Anna stroked his hair whilst feeding Joy. Joy drank her bottle but was still hungry. Anna gave her a rusk biscuit, one designed for babies as it dissolved easily on the tongue. Joy ate it within minutes, using her gums to soften the edges before biting them off, smacking her lips together merrily.

Just two days until Bev would be here. Two more days. She had said it would be first thing in the morning; the plane landed just after eight. The airport was about a half an hour's drive from here. By nine o'clock, Bev would be here, she would see what had happened, and phone the police.

Anna drank some water and ate a protein bar. She was desperate for energy; lifting the gallon bottle of water and pouring it into a cup she found in the bathroom was a struggle.

She did everything she could to avoid Graham. She could hear him downstairs, playing his music, singing, grunting. It was as though she was dealing with a sadistic monster in a horror film. She woke up in the night and heard scratching at the craft room door. She was getting ready for him to try and sneak in and get her like he did before. She waited, listening to him for what must have been thirty, maybe forty minutes. God knows what he was doing out there, but eventually, he just left.

She touched her hand to the knife taped under the desk. It comforted her to know it was there, to know that if he came at her in here, she had some means of self-defence. She was under no delusion how hard it would be to stab someone and take a life, the life of someone she had spent the majority of hers with, building a home and a family together. She would do what was necessary, in the same way he was doing what he no doubt believed was necessary.

There was a knock on the door of the craft room. Both Joy and Anna looked at it with fear in their eyes. The door opened and Graham walked in.

'Morning. How is everyone today?' He nodded at Mikey.

'Fine,' Anna said through gritted teeth. Her hand was twitching in preparation for diving for the knife.

Joy crawled away from Graham and clambered up on to Anna's legs. Anna put her on her lap and wrapped her arms around her. She stared at Graham as if trying to project her hate on to him.

He smiled, seemingly soaking it up. 'If he's still resting, you should probably think of tidying up. It's a bit of a mess down there. There's still a long way to go in this lockdown, and if you think you're going to be getting out anytime soon, you can think again.'

'Fuck. You.'

'Fuck me?' Graham smiled cynically. 'Fuck me? You still haven't learnt, have you? Why can't you see it? This is the best way for us all to be together. There is another way but I'm doing my best to avoid that, Anna. Believe me when I say I'm using all my strength not to take that last option.'

'Get out.' She kept her voice as strong as she could, not wanting to show any signs of weakness. Her hand was ready to go for the knife at any second.

Graham shook his head. 'If you won't get on board, I can't rest in this house thinking that any second you might be trying to escape. We are a family, Anna. We belong together.' Graham turned to leave; he stopped in the hall outside the door and looked back at Anna, seeing the rage in her eyes. 'I'll give you some more time to think about it, before I have to take that final option. You'll notice I haven't fixed the crack in the window shutter you love so much. Call it a gift.'

'Leave us alone,' Anna said.

Graham turned and walked out, shutting the door behind him. There was a snap, like that of a deadbolt. Anna went to the door and put her ear to it. She heard him go down the stairs, whistling some tune.

She needed to get some more food; she hoped Mikey had stashed some in his room for emergencies.

She turned the door handle.

It was locked.

Suddenly, the scratching noise last night made sense.

He hadn't been scratching at it, he'd been screwing on a lock, as quietly as he could.

Chapter 61

Graham was making himself some dinner. He thought how hungry Anna must be up there.

He ate a hearty meal of six sausages, four rashers of bacon, chips and baked beans. He managed to stuff it all in, licking the grease clean from his fingers; his beard had bits of chewed sausage meat that had fallen out of his gaping mouth as he chomped his food down. He washed it down with four bottles of lager.

He sat back in his chair and slapped his bulging gut. He sank his beer and belched loud enough to shake the shutters.

He stood and put his plate in the sink. It was full of dirty water; oil spots from the greasy pan floated on the water, and burnt bits of bacon fat lifted from the bottom as they got disturbed from the plate.

He put his hand to his crotch. He needed a piss. After drinking beer, when you needed a piss, you needed it quickly.

He whacked his dick out; standing on his tip-toes, he managed to reach it over the sink. He pissed in the water, then made a game of knocking the remaining tomato sauce from his plate that had been left by the beans. Splashes of piss covered his arms and the kitchen worktops.

He put his cock away, then laughed at how Anna must be dancing around up there. He had put a lock on the outside of the door. That would teach her. Nowhere to piss in there, she would be sat up there now, choosing which corner would be best to piss and shit in. She wouldn't even be able to throw it out the window.

He roared with laughter at the thought. He belched again and felt his eyelids were heavy. He thought he'd take a nap. The living room was disgusting, he wasn't going to sleep in there. The basement was too cold, besides there was two beds in this house last time he checked. His own, or Mikey's. He hadn't slept in his own bed for about three weeks. He'd made a strange deal with himself, not to sleep in his marital bed until Anna had decided that them being together would be for the best.

He started up the stairs. Anna was knocking on the door, he could hear her now: 'Graham, let me out, Joy needs a new nappy. Please, just pass them through the door.'

'Shut up! Not 'til you've learnt your fucking lesson!' He hit the door with his fist.

He walked past the door and moved over to Mikey's room. He looked at the guitar in the corner. He looked at it sadly, realising the only dreams for the future his son had ever expressed were over. Despite how ridiculous they were, Graham still felt sad for him. All because Anna had forced Mikey to try and find a way out, making him cut himself and get an infection, leaving Graham with no other alternative then to cut it off to save his life. God she was a fucking selfish bitch sometimes. She was the crazy one.

He sat on Mikey's bed. He put his hands back, about to shuffle into position to lay down, when he heard a rustling noise from the back of the bed. He moved his hand to the gap between the bed and the wall. He pulled out an empty cookie wrapper.

He jumped up and pulled the duvet off the bed, grabbed a corner of the mattress and yanked it off the frame of the bed. Crisp packets, cookie wrappers, cake wrappers. The pile was huge.

Graham looked at it in shock. It dawned on him that Anna must have been going behind his back this entire time, giving Mikey all this junk food, even after he'd specifically said they had to stick to a strict rationing structure in order to survive.

She had undermined him at every step. No wonder Mikey was so eager to be on her side. Everything he had put in place to keep them together, to keep them together as a family, she had tried to ruin.

She had her mind set on this from day one. This was always her plan, ridicule and undermine me at every opportunity. Turn Mikey against me, my own son! She had been whispering shite in his head since the beginning. I never stood a chance with that manipulative little bitch. Well, if she wants Mikey all to herself, she can. I'll take the other one, show her what it's like to have your child ripped away.

He threw Mikey's door open. It hit the wall, knocking lumps out of the plaster. He removed the deadbolt on the craft room door and swung it open. Anna retreated to the back of the room, holding Joy.

Scanning the room, he saw a puddle of something in the corner. She had pissed over there. Like a dog, squatting in the corner of the room and messing herself. A nappy full of poo was folded up and put near the wet spot.

'I found your secret stash.'

Anna shook her head, looking confused.

'In Mikey's room. All the empty wrappers...You think you're clever, deceiving me like that?'

Anna was scared. She could see the look in his eyes, he meant to hurt her. She glanced over to where the knife was under the desk. Slowly, she put Joy down on the floor behind her. If she needed to jump for the knife, she needed a clear jump at it. 'He was starving, Graham. I was just giving him some snacks to fill him up.'

'You were playing the hero. Weren't you? Making me look like the arsehole, despite everything I was doing to keep you all safe.'

'We're prisoners! Can't you see what you're doing, You're killing us!'

Graham made a movement towards her. Anna didn't miss a beat; she dived over Mikey and landed near her desk. She put her hand to the knife and pulled it out of the makeshift holder she had made with tape. She spun on her heels, her legs bent ready to lunge up at him. He was stood at the door, half in, half out. He held Joy up with one hand. She was crying and reaching in Anna's direction. Graham smiled.

'You won't turn this one against me. Bitch.' He slammed the door. The metal clunk of the deadbolt on the other side sent a wave of fear and panic through her that prickled her skin.

'No!!!' She screamed, she jumped at the door, her fists hit the door over and over again. The knife was held firmly in her hand, she tried to stab through the wood in her desperation. The blade snapped, pinging off the handle and on to the floor. She slumped to the floor with her back against the door and sobbed. 'Don't you hurt her!'

Joy's cries carried through the house.

Chapter 62

LOCKDOWN DAY 28

When Anna woke, the first thing she did was check that Mikey was still alive. He was breathing. His breaths were shallow, but his fever had broken and his temperature had returned to normal. Cutting off his arm had stopped the infection from spreading, some sort of miracle.

She stroked his face and wiped his lips with the wet sponge, pressing a little on the inside of his cheeks, trying her best to keep him hydrated.

She looked out of the crack in the shutter and saw the day was brightening. Which put the time at something between six and seven AM.

Bev would be here soon. It was today she got back. Anna had to close her eyes and think for a second, make sure she hadn't dreamed a day away. She hadn't, it was today, it was *the* day.

Joy had cried all of the day before; the screeching sound was unbearable, torturing Anna. Which she figured was Graham's goal. He wanted to torture her. He'd wanted to torture her, punish her from day one, for even suggesting a trial separation, telling him she wasn't happy with him anymore and felt their future was being apart. She knew he would never take it well, but to do all of this just to hurt her was insane. She had no doubt that in his mind he thought it would keep them together, that she would come to her senses and see what a hero he was and fall madly in love with him.

Joy was crying as if she was starving. She hadn't stopped for even a second, which meant he *hadn't* fed her. She was still crying now. Graham was losing his mind. Last night, when exhaustion had let Anna fall asleep, she'd woken up to hear Graham screaming at Joy.

'Shut the fuck up. Shut up Shut up Shut up!'

Then he'd stormed downstairs, leaving Joy in her cot, screaming.

Anna had tried for hours to sing through the door to Joy, to try and calm her. Joy was quiet for about an hour when Anna sang 'Twinkle, twinkle, little star' over and over again. She sang until her throat was dry and so sore it felt as though her neck was lined with barbed wire. Joy began crying as soon as she stopped.

Now it was Anna's turn to cry herself back to sleep. Unable to help anyone in her position, the only thing she could think to do was try and sleep the time away, bringing today around sooner.

Graham came storming up, thudding his feet on every step. Even his footsteps sounded deranged.

'Graham, let me have Joy back. She's starving, I need to feed her.'

Graham just thumped the door as he walked past.

Joy's screams were gut-wrenching, then she stopped.

Everything went silent.

He's feeding her.

Anna, despite how much she wished Graham was dead, sat back and rested her head against the door in relief. Joy was being fed; maybe now she'd be able to rest. Bev would be here soon; Joy would wake up to police officers wrapping her in a blanket and passing her back into Anna's arms.

A deathly silence seemed to descend over the house. Until it was broken by a faint, fragile sound: 'Mum.'

Chapter 63

Mikey struggled to open his eyes; his pale complexion was a stark contrast to the dark circles around his eyes that made them look sunken, deep into their sockets. His voice was hoarse and dry but he managed to speak and lift his head from the pillow.

'Mum? What happened?'

Anna ran to his side and held his hand. 'Oh Mikey, I'm so glad you're awake.' She kissed his hand repeatedly as she cried.

He winced and sucked his teeth as a bolt of pain shot through him. 'My head hurts, and my arm is really hurting.' He lifted his stump from the floor and sucked his teeth again as pain shot up into his shoulder when he tried to wiggle his fingers that were no longer there. He looked down to where his arm should be.

He started crying and shaking his head. 'Mum? What happened?'

Anna couldn't speak. She gripped his hand tighter and pressed it against her face.

'What happened to my arm?' He was crying now – weak, exhausted sobs. 'Mum, please.'

'I'm so sorry darling,' was all she could say.

'No, no, no!'

Anna watched on as he looked from his arm to her, she could see the desperate pleading in his eyes, wanting her to tell him it wasn't true, that it was all a bad dream, of course he still had his arm. He could still be a rock star. His life wasn't over.

'I'm so sorry Mikey,' she said again.

He managed a scream, and cried as she held him.

Chapter 64

The airport was busy. The plane had landed twenty minutes ahead of schedule thanks to a tailwind that gave them a little extra 'Umph' on the way back from Italy.

The only problem with arriving home early was that the plane had to sit on the tarmac for fifteen of those gained minutes.

Bev had just finished off the second half of Stephen King's Misery on the plane and tucked it back in her carry-on bag. She pulled her phone out and flicked through her address book, trying to find the name she was looking for.

Mum.

She hit the call button and put the phone to her ear. She was desperate to hear her kids' voices – four weeks was a long time to be away from them. Who knows, there would probably be another lockdown before long to make up for the time they had lost, she thought dryly.

'Hello,' her mum answered.

'Hey it's me. The plane just landed but they're trying to find a spot to park up.'

'That's nice, you landed early.'

'A favourable tailwind apparently.'

'Do you want to speak to the girls? They're very excited to see you.'

'In a minute. Have you heard from Rob at all?' Bev asked, trying to hide the concern in her voice.

'Not since he dropped the children off with me a couple of weeks ago. Why?'

'I haven't been able to reach him. I asked him to go check on Anna after dropping the girls with you because she hasn't been answering her phone either. He said he would but I haven't been able to get in touch with him since.'

'I wouldn't worry dear, don't get yourself in a fuzz. It was probably that foreign phone reception, they don't do it as well over there as they do here. Whenever you called me you sounded really far away.'

'I was far away.'

'Funny.'

'Ok, well, put the girls on. I'm going to check on Anna on my way back, then I'll pick them up. I tell you though, Rob will be in for it when I get home.'

Chapter 65

Anna finished going to the toilet in the corner of the room. Mikey had managed to sit up with Anna's help, after he had calmed down. He averted his eyes as his mum finished her business.

'I'm going to kill him,' Mikey said.

Anna had told him everything that had transpired since he cut his arm and lost all that blood. How Mikey's hunch was right: Graham had been lying to them, he'd made the whole thing up to keep them together, to stop them from leaving him.

'The police will arrest him. He'll go to jail for the rest of his life, he can rot in there.'

Mikey drank some water from a straw. Anna had some too. If all went like she hoped it would, today would be the last day they'd be stuck in here. Bev would notice, she would have to notice. Anna had hoped there might be an opportunity to find her phone to at least send Bev a warning message. But no such opportunity presented itself.

She looked at Mikey. 'Can you stand?'

'I don't know. I feel like hammered shit all over.'

'Language.' Anna said, trying to smile.

Mikey gave her a sharp look.

'Let's try and get you up.'

Anna got behind him and put her hands under his armpits and helped him get to his feet. He groaned from the effort it took. Then yelled and sucked his teeth when her hand slipped and knocked the raw end of his stump.

'Watch it!' he pleaded.

She got him to his feet; he was shaky but it was better than keeping him on the floor.

'I feel dizzy,' Mikey said. Anna could see him trying to focus his eyes.

'Here darling, go steady.' Anna eased him into the chair near her desk.

'How are we going to get out of here?' he asked her.

'I've got a plan.'

She told how she knew Beverly would be coming round today, within the next hour in fact, and when she did, she'd realise something was wrong and she'd call the police or ambulance or whatever it was. As long as it had flashing lights, it would help.

'What if she doesn't? What if she knocks and Dad goes out and kills her like he did that guy? What then?'

'We can't think like that, Mikey. This has to work. It just has to.'

Mikey nodded. His eyes kept rolling, he complained a lot of feeling faint and nauseas. Anna told him he'd lost so much blood that it would probably be months before he felt right again. The hospital would probably have to give him a transfusion.

His head kept on lolling from side to side, as if he didn't have the strength to keep it up. Mikey asked what a transfusion was. His voice was so weak it was hard for Anna to make out the words. He was so mature and beyond his years in so many other ways, she forgot sometimes just how young he was.

He looked back at his arm and winced. He looked away; he couldn't bear looking at it for longer than a couple of seconds.

'Wait a minute. Where's Joy?' Mike scanned the room as if he had just overlooked her.

Anna wiped a tear as it rolled down her cheek. 'He's got her.'

'You let him take her!' Mikey shouted.

Anna put a finger to her lips; she didn't want Graham to hear what they were talking about. 'No, I didn't let him. He took her from me, then locked the door.'

'Is she OK?'

'She cried for nearly two days straight. She stopped this morning when he came upstairs to feed her in her cot. She must be napping now. She'll be so tired.' She walked around the room with her arms folded, chewing her lip as she worried about everything that was going to happen that day. 'My poor baby. She must be so distressed without me there. She's been on me this entire time, her whole life in fact; she must feel lost.'

Mikey had passed out in the chair.

Anna breathed deeply and shuddered. She looked out of the crack in the shutter, the day was getting brighter. Bev would be here soon.

Chapter 66

Beverly stood in the airport waiting for her suitcase to come round the carousel. The speakers in every corner rang out a cheery voice that welcomed everyone to England, and hoped everyone had a safe flight. People whistled around her; she heard music being played from a teenage girl's headphones at such a volume Bev thought it a wonder the girl didn't blow her ear drums. People from other flights walked away to the checkout desk, dragging their suitcases behind them, freshly tanned and still wearing their bright and breezy holiday gear.

While she waited, Bev tried to call her husband, Rob, again. His phone just rang out. She tried Anna and it just went straight to answer machine. Something was seriously wrong. She had thought about phoning the police, seeing if they'd send a car round just to check, but thought she was being daft. Anna had probably broken her phone taking Joy out for a walk by the lake. Thrown it in with a few chunks of bread for the ducks.

Now that she was back home, she struggled to rationalize her fears in her head like she could when she was abroad. Now she wished that she had phoned the police, even if it just gave her some peace of mind. Rob, she was less worried about. He had said he was going to be using his time to get some extra shifts in, and going out with the lads, so not to worry if he didn't call as much. Men, they can be so self-centred sometimes, she thought.

A message came over the airport speaker system, apologising about a technical fault with the carousel, they'd have it back up and running in the next twenty-minutes, and thanking everyone for their patience whilst waiting for their luggage.

'Mother-fucker.' Bev moaned, loud enough for the woman next to her to cover her child's ears and look at Bev scornfully.

'Sorry,' Bev mouthed, and moved to a different spot.

She sat on a bench. A discarded newspaper was beside her so she picked it up, thinking she'd read some actual news instead of seeing the same shit that clogged up her Facebook newsfeed every day.

She unfolded it to see the front page. The headline read: 'MANHUNT ONGOING FOR SUPERMARKET KILLER.'

She was going to move past it until she saw the first line mentioned Wymere. Seeing the name of her hometown on the front page of a national newspaper flipped her stomach.

She leaned forward and read the passage.

'Police in Wymere are still searching for the man dubbed 'the supermarket killer'. Four weeks ago, an unidentified man killed five people, one of which was a two-year old boy.

For reasons unknown to many horrified witnesses in Wymere that day, the suspect rammed his truck into a man while he was putting groceries into the back of his vehicle. He then went on a rampage, attacking everyone who wasn't wearing a mask. He was heard to be screaming, 'The end is coming. You're all gonna die.'

He was said to have been average height. He wore a military-style gas mask and a white vest with a logo on the front. No witnesses recognise the man and with a lack of CCTV in the area, there has been no ID on the truck. The camera in the supermarket car park managed to get the suspect in shot, but with no clear images of his face, it has been impossible to form a possible ID. The police ask anyone with any information regarding the whereabouts of this man to please get in touch and alert the authorities. They also ask, under no circumstances, is anyone to approach this man; he is believed to be extremely dangerous and armed. The search continues with officers going door to door and conducting thorough searches of homes and abandoned buildings. Drones are being used to scan the dense woodlands that run towards the coast.

Many believe the suspect has left Wymere, the police, however, are acting on the suspicion that he is in hiding within the town.'

The story continued on the other page but Bev couldn't bring herself to read any more. A grainy picture of a man, obviously zoomed in, accompanied the piece. The gas mask was covered in blood, his eyes were wide and crazy, looking straight into the lens of the CCTV camera. That was the day she'd left so Rob couldn't have been one of the victims, but could Anna? It couldn't be because it would have mentioned Joy. She suddenly felt like crying. She needed to get to Anna's now. She stood and walked to where the conveyor belt appeared from beyond the wall. She hit it with her hand, willing it to work. As if by magic, the belt started moving and the luggage started to come through. Someone was willing her to get there, she knew it. She knew it more when her bag was the first one to appear.

Chapter 67

Mikey was still asleep. Anna checked he was still breathing. He was. She kept watch out of the crack in the shutter, hoping to see the salvation of a light bouncing off the hood of an oncoming car. Twice she had been duped into thinking one was coming for it just to be her eyes playing tricks.

She could hear Graham now. He was downstairs banging and crashing around. He sounded drunk. He probably was drunk. There was no concept of time in this house any more. She heard his footsteps as he came up the stairs. It sounded like he was taking one step at a time, as though he was unsure about every step.

She watched the door. Her heart thumped in her chest. She scanned the room looking for a makeshift weapon. She had scissors. They were in her desk drawer. She moved over to get them, when there was a thud at the door that made her yelp.

Mikey stirred, opening his eyes for a second before shutting them again.

'Aaannnaa.' Graham said from behind the door.

Anna walked over and sat against it.

'I can feel you against the door, Anna.' He was breathing heavily.

'What do you want?' she said, keeping her voice as strong as she could.

'You know. We've been married for sissteen years. Sixteen. That's a lonnng time. You, were all I ever wanted. I would have died for you, killed for you. I would do any fing to save our famly.' He was slurring his words. 'But you! You would throw it all away. I just wanted to keep us together. Bond.'

'You could never have made me love you again Graham.'

'I thought, you needed a real man. I was too soft. My dad always said I was too soft. Pushover. Little, cunt. So, I did. I was strong, I was the man of this house like he was the man of my house growing up.' He paused. Probably to drink more, Anna assumed. 'Why couldn't you respect me, like my mum respected him!' He hit the door with his fist.

'She didn't respect him. She was afraid of him. Your dad was a horrible man.'

'Fuck you! Bitch. Whatta you know? You never knew what you wanted; vat was your problem. You needed a stronger man, but also someone who was sensss-itive and bought flowers, and who made the big decishons, and who washed pots and appreciated the flower smells int' washing powder. A man who would be masterful in the bedroom. I bet you decided you didn't like that either.'

Anna took a deep breath. Her lip shook as she tried to hold back the tears. 'You raped me. Graham. That wasn't masterful or passionate. That was rape.'

'Rape? Pah. Don't make me laugh. You're my wife. A man can't rape his wife.'

'You're a monster. And when the police get here, they'll take you away and lock you up for the rest of your miserable life.'

'Police? There won't be no police coming here, dumb bitch!'

They started shouting at each other on either side of the door, hitting it, getting so loud their words stopped making sense. They stopped when there was a knock on the front door.

Chapter 68

The gate at the end of the drive was open, so Bev drove straight up. She knew she was right to be worried as soon as she saw the post-box at the gate overflowing with mail. She drove towards the house slowly, the gravel crunching under the weight of the car.

There were three cars in the drive: Graham's pick-up, Anna's Ford and... a Mercedes.

Her husband's Mercedes.

It was red and had that hideous neon-green steering-wheel cover she had loathed since the day he got it. She'd said it was embarrassing, like he was trying to be a forty-year-old boy racer.

She stopped the car and got out. She wanted to run to the door and knock it down, find out what the hell was going on. Why was no one answering their phone, why was Rob here? What the fuck was happening? But her legs had other ideas; she was walking at a steady pace. Fear and uncertainty had set her muscles like stone. Something was wrong, something was *really* wrong. Each step made her heartbeat quicken.

She looked at the windows; her first thought was that all the curtains were drawn. Looking closer, she thought it looked like steel shutters were blocking them from the inside, like they had on the outside of shops to stop people getting in when they were shut. A square hole had been cut in the glass of the living-room window and a fan had been stuffed in the hole.

'What the fuck is going on?'

She moved over to the door; she could hear voices. They were muffled, but she could tell they were shouting.

She knocked on the door with her fist, adrenaline making her lips shake and her jaw clench.

'Hello! I know you're in there. What's going on?' She hit the door again. The voices inside had stopped.

She listened carefully to the door, expecting to hear footsteps. She heard nothing and decided to try the back door.

Walking round the side of the house, as quick as her legs would carry her, she heard something coming from inside the house. She looked up at the windows. On this side there was a single window on the first floor, the one which belonged to Anna's craft room, she knew. It had the same steel shutters on the inside. The noise was coming from up there. Banging and yelling.

It was hard to decipher what it was the voice was saying, but she could tell it was Anna. And she sounded desperate.

'Anna?! It's me. Bev. I'm going to call the police-'

Then the basement doors flung open. Graham emerged slowly.

He climbed the steps to the outside, his eyes fixed on Beverly. She saw the gas mask, but that wasn't what drew the initial connection to the story she'd read in the paper. It was the eyes. The eyes that had sent a chill up her spine when she saw them in print, were now in front of her. They scared her to death.

Chapter 69

Anna hit the steel shutters, over and over again, rattling them in their brackets.

'Run, Bev! Call the police!' She was screaming at the top of her lungs. Mikey stirred in the chair. He lifted his head from his shoulder and smacked his dry lips together.

'Mum, what's going on?'

'Bev's here, Mikey. I think she's in trouble. Your dad's gone out to meet her.'

'Has she called the police?'

'I don't know. I've tried shouting.' Anna ran her hands through her hair.

'Do you think she heard you shouting?'

'I don't fucking know!' Anna started hitting the shutters again. 'Bev!' She ran to the door and started pulling at the door handle, kicking at the bottom panel, hoping it would kick through.

She kicked again and again until she heard a crack. She looked round at Mikey, with something that was close to a smile pasted on her face. She kicked again and again. The wood cracked down the middle, and a shard fell out, creating a hole big enough for her to put her hand through. She grabbed it with her fingers. The sharp edge of the splintered wood cut her fingers. She hadn't noticed the blood smearing over the door panel. She pulled and yanked with everything she had until the rest of the panel snapped out of the frame. She reached her arm out of it. She was so focused on feeling for the bolt on the other side, she hadn't noticed she was laughing. She'd managed to break through the door, Bev was here and she'd phone the police, they'd all be saved.

She slapped the other side of the door, blindly trying to find the deadbolt. She tried to fit her head through, get a look at where the lock was, but couldn't.

She was stretching as far as she could, her face pressed uncomfortably against the door.

A gunshot from outside shook the house, rattling the steel shutters.

Chapter 70

Graham walked towards Bev slowly, the gun gripped firmly in his right hand, down by his side.

'Graham, what are you doing? What has happened here?' Bev slowly backed away, holding her hands out in front of her, palms open. She could see how crazy he looked; his beard had grown long and untamed, his hands and arms were covered in dirt and grime like he hadn't washed. His fingernails were black with muck.

'You!' he shouted. 'You want to try and take them away from me! Don't you!' he screamed at her, jabbing the gun in her direction. Walking towards her, forcing her back towards the garden.

'Graham. You need help.' She glanced over her shoulder; something was sticking out of the ground. She tried to step around it.

'I don't need help. We were fine. It's because of people like you! Meddling in business that has nothing to do with you.' He raised the gun and fired.

The bullet blew a hole in Bev's shoulder. She spun and fell to the ground, her face landing in the mud. She lifted her head and screamed in agony. Her hand crawled to her jeans pocket where she kept her phone. She pulled it out. She could hear Graham's breathing as he got closer to her, his footsteps loud and steady. He wasn't rushing, like this wasn't the first time he'd done this.

She opened her phone and hit the emergency call button; she dialled the first two numbers then shifted her body to get whatever it was that was jabbing her out of her stomach.

It was a shoe. Rob's shoe. She knew because she had bought him a brand-new pair of running shoes because he had gone on relentlessly about how he was going to take up jogging with his buddies this year.

His foot was sticking out of the ground, a bright orange Nike Air. She looked across the dirt and saw a hand poking out with a gold wedding ring. She reached out and grabbed his fingers, then screamed again.

Graham stood over her; his shadow blocked out the sun. His foot splashed in the pool of blood collecting under Beverly's shoulder.

'You shouldn't have come here. You should have just left Anna alone. We were fine before you started meddling. Putting ideas in her head.' He pointed the gun at Beverly's head. 'I'm doing you a kindness by killing you where I killed him. You can rest together. Forever.' With that, he pulled the trigger.

Bev flopped lifeless into the dirt; her fingers were entwined with her husband's.

Graham picked up her phone that was still clutched in her other hand.

'Hello, which emergency service do you require?' said the nice-sounding woman on the other end of the line. He hit the hang-up button and dropped the phone back to the dirt.

Blood poured round his feet, soaking between his toes. He removed his mask and dropped it to the floor. He looked up at the blue sky, the birds flying in front of the golden sun. He realised then that maybe the virus hadn't hit yet. It would, there was no doubt about that, not in his mind. A wave of acceptance washed over him. It was over. The police would track the call and send a car. Maybe an ambulance too. They'd have heard the gunshot. Armed response were probably five minutes away.

Anna would get her wish; she'd be free of him and he'd be thrown in jail or a mental asylum because they'd make out that he was crazy to do all of this, because none of them would understand that this is what had to be done. He'd rot in a cell somewhere. Alone. Weak. Pathetic. He'd die before he let that happen. He looked at the gun and thought he could end it all right now. Save everyone the trouble. Just put the barrel into his mouth and squeeze. It would all be over.

Then what?

Anna just takes the kid and gets on with her life? Meets someone else, someone else for Mikey to call Daddy?

Not a fucking chance.

If he couldn't have them, nobody could. It was time to do what needed to be done. He had tried to avoid it; he had given them every opportunity to save themselves. Now it was too late.

Chapter 71

Anna and Mikey sat in silence. Both of them looking anywhere but each other, knowing if they did, they'd both have to come to terms with the fact that the second gunshot probably meant Bev was dead.

Mikey's head flopped down, resting his chin on his chest. 'We're fucked.'

Anna ran to the desk and frantically started looking for something, anything, she could use as a weapon. She found a pair of scissors, the ones with the extra-long blades for cutting fabric. She put them in Mikey's hand, wrapping his fingers around the handle. She didn't have time to think about what would or wouldn't happen if she didn't kill him, this was their only chance to get out.

'When he comes in, stab him. Wherever you can.'

'I can't. I'm too weak.'

'You'll find the strength. You have to. When he comes in, he'll come straight for me. When he has his back to you. Do it.'

'What if he comes for me first. He won't. But if he does...' Every word seemed to take a monumental effort from Mikey.

She reached back into the drawer. 'I always have a spare pair of scissors.' She snipped the air twice.

They heard Graham shouting downstairs.

'That's it Anna. You've really done it now!'

THUD! THUD!

His feet hit each step hard, as if he wanted them to know what was coming.

Anna looked at Mikey, nodded a silent understanding. Mikey nodded back. She moved over to the other side of the room.

'You win. It's over!' He sounded like he was crying. 'I've lost everything. *EVERYTHING!*'

THUD! THUD!

There was silence. Anna could feel her pulse in her temples. Every breath she took felt laboured.

BANG!

The gun went off in the hall, echoing round, piercing Anna's and Mikey's ear drums.

Anna didn't know if it was ringing in her ears or the cries of Joy.

'You have fucked me, time and time again. You want to leave? Fine. I'll let you fucking leave. You can leave in a fucking body bag!'

BANG!

The gun went off again; this time a bullet hole appeared in the door. The bullet ricocheted off the wall and landed on the floor next to the desk. Anna let out a sharp yell.

THUD!

He was outside the door.

Anna could hear his breathing, heavy and rattling. She was holding her breath; her heart was throbbing in her ears. She looked across and saw Mikey had spun the chair around. He nodded at her and seemed to visibly swallow down a lump of fear. Tears were running down his cheeks. He was gripping the scissors out in front of him.

'Mikey. Daddy's here.'

Anna took a step towards the door. She lifted the scissors up in the air, holding them up like a dagger, ready to bring it down when he came in.

She looked at Mikey, checking he was ready.

The room was deadly silent. Only the heavy panting from Graham could be heard.

She moved forward again. The hole in the door seemed to change. Graham was looking at them through it, watching them getting ready for him.

'I see you!'

BANG!

He shot through the door; the bullet hit Anna's left elbow. An explosion of fire ripped up her arm. She fell to the floor, screaming.

The door burst open and Graham ran in. He ignored Mikey and jumped straight onto Anna. He wrapped his fingers around her throat and squeezed. He watched as her face turned red, and then purple. The vein in her forehead was bulging like it was about to pop.

She slapped at his hands feebly.

'I could have just shot you. But where's the pleasure? Huh Anna? Where's the fun in that? I wanted to watch the life drain out of you. Watch you be silenced. The way you've silenced me over the years, the way you've drained me of everything I could have been, everything I would have been. I fucking loved you and you wanted to leave me! To take my children away and destroy me!'

He stopped shouting and his eyes shot open as wide as Anna had ever seen them. He let go of her neck and lifted his hands over his head, desperately trying to grab at something in his back. Mikey stood behind him; his face appeared from behind Graham's shoulder, his hand holding onto the pair of scissors he had planted in his dad's back.

'Fuck you, dad!'

Anna clawed herself away over to the desk. Gasping for air, feeling her throat burn. Her face tingled and her eyesight blurred as oxygen made its way back into her system.

Graham fell to the floor; Mikey hobbled over to the desk and fell into the chair, his hand covered in blood.

Anna sat herself up; she was sat on something that was digging into her leg.

She didn't care. She glanced over at Graham, laid face-down in the carpet, just the plastic handle of the scissors sticking out of his back. It was over.

Mikey fell to his knees next to Anna and hugged her. They both started to laugh and cry with the relief.

Graham groaned. Mikey fell off Anna and turned. Graham was stood over them. He swung a back-hand at Mikey and sent him crashing into the door. He bent for Anna and grabbed her throat. Anna reached blindly for anything that she could use to stop him. Her hand touched something, the thing that had been digging into her leg. She grabbed it, not knowing what it was and swung it round towards his face.

It was the crochet hook Graham had bought her last year, with the engraving: 'To my darling wife Anna, Get Crafting,' written on it.

The small metal hook went straight through his eye, piercing the eyeball with an audible 'pop' noise. He screamed and fell back, holding a hand to his face. Blood and gore streamed over his hands and down his vest. His belly jiggled over the crotch of his pants.

'RUN!' she screamed at Mikey. Mikey got to his feet as quickly as he could and headed down the stairs.

Anna tried for the door, holding her arm where the bullet had torn a chunk of flesh away; it still dangled from the crook of her elbow.

Graham grabbed her leg and tripped her, making her fall to the floor.

'You won't leave me! Bitch!'

He started pulling her closer to him, then started climbing on top of her. He got his face over hers, blood and spit dribbled from his mouth onto her face, stinging her eyes. She hit at him; his body felt solid and her hands stung with every blow.

He spat at her, then raised a fist in the air. She grabbed the scissors she had dropped and drove them into his stomach.

He fell to the side of her. This time, she would make sure. She straddled him and yanked the scissors from his gut.

She lifted them high and drove them down into his chest. Lifted them and drove them down again.

And again,

and again.

She left the scissors in and pulled out the crochet hook, bringing plenty of eyeball with it, and drove it back into the other eye.

Graham didn't react this time.

His chest and stopped rising; the grating sound of him breathing had ceased. If he'd had any eyeballs left to speak of, they would have been rolled into the back of his head.

Anna stopped. She cackled, wiping the sprayed blood from her face with her blood-soaked hands. She got to her feet, exhausted, on the verge of collapse.

Then she heard the sirens.

They were here, they were here to save them. She ran, desperate to get out of the house, she didn't stop to think. She grabbed Joy from the cot, wrapped in the blanket she had made her, and ran down the stairs, clutching Joy to her breast. The police were banging on the door.

'In here!' Anna shouted, laughing and crying at the same time with relief.

She ran for the basement, praying Mikey had got out without falling down the basement steps. She got into the kitchen and saw the stairs to the basement were clear. She stumbled on the steps but kept upright. As she ran into the basement, she saw Mikey's foot as it left the basement door to the outside world. She climbed the stairs and ran out on to the gravel driveway. Armed police vans, two ambulances, and a helicopter circled above them.

'Please, check my children!' she screamed, holding Joy out to the onrushing paramedics.

The armed response unit smashed in the front door; they swarmed inside the house, seeing the carnage that had gone on in there.

A paramedic, a nice young lady with brown hair and green eyes, took Joy from her. Another one put a foil blanket over Mikey and took him to a different ambulance. Anna fell to her knees and watched as everyone buzzed around her in a mad panic.

She was relieved to see that none of them were diseased, she knew none of them would be. The whole thing had been made up in Graham's twisted paranoid brain. They would think she was really stupid when they found out what she thought had been happening.

Sharing her husband's belief in something so ridiculous.

But they had survived. That was all that mattered in the end. They had survived.

'*Miss? Miss?*' A paramedic was shaking Anna by the shoulder. He was kneeling beside her.

'*How long, Miss?*'

Anna couldn't understand what he was saying. The light of the sun was blinding her; the birds were flying overhead in pretty patterns as if the past four-weeks hadn't happened. The cool breeze kissed her neck and blew strands of her greasy hair off her face. She saw people running around, talking on radios, running their hands over their heads like they were in disbelief.

'*Miss, can you answer me?*'

Anna looked over her shoulder. She saw a bunch of cops gathered round in the garden. One of the police officers moved, holding his hands over his mouth. The gap that created in the circle of police let Anna see Bev's body. Her face was covered in blood and her hand was holding what looked to be another hand from someone else, coming out of the ground. A young officer was doubled over, puking into the garden, using a tree for support as another officer slapped his back. Bev had saved them; it had cost her life, but she had saved them.

'Miss! How long has the baby been unresponsive!?'

Anna looked at the man who was talking to her. 'What do you mean?' she said. Anna looked over at the pretty, green-eyed paramedic she'd handed Joy over to. She had Joy on a gurney. Being on a full-size bed like that made her look so small and fragile. The rainbow blanket had been thrown on the floor. The paramedic was pressing Joy's chest with her fingers, pushing hard, over and over.

Again and again.

Then she was putting a mask over her face and squeezing a little plastic balloon that made Joy's chest move up and down.

'Joy. My baby's name is Joy.'

'When did Joy stop breathing, Miss?'

'I-I don't know.'

The man left her side and helped with the CPR on Joy's little body.

Anna watched on in a haze of unreality. When did Joy stop crying? First thing this morning. That was when Graham must've fed her, that was right, Graham fed her, so she stopped crying. Anna thought she should probably tell them. In case Graham gave her the wrong milk.

Joy had come so far, she was getting so strong – crawling, learning to stand up. She'd said her first word just a few days ago.

A flash of images filled Anna's head. Each one of Joy smiling, furiously flapping her arms around playfully, giggling at Anna when she pulled funny faces, crawling around the living room with Mikey chasing after her.

She had to be fine.

She snapped back when the two paramedics looked solemnly at each other.

'Time of death. 9:13 AM.'

Chapter 72

THREE MONTHS AFTER LOCKDOWN.

Anna stood staring in the mirror of her rented apartment. They'd find a new place to buy once the old one had been renovated and sold; until then they had to manage in a shitty two-bed flat above a convenience shop. That was OK, it was better than the alternative of going back to the house. Mikey was in agreement; they couldn't go back there.

Her skin was returning to something like it used to be, she had managed to put on ten pounds. They'd weighed her in at eighty-five pounds after they found her and took her to the hospital. She had been a hundred-and-twenty before.

Her ribs were still sticking out and she could feel the lumps of her spine. She had tried eating more, but her appetite was zilch. She struggled to eat anything at all. The only reason she did was because Mikey needed her.

She stayed as strong as she could for Mikey, but when he went to bed, she had nothing left for herself. She just curled up in a ball and cried until she fell asleep.

Crocheting was a thing long forgotten, she couldn't bring herself to pick up a hook and a ball of wool any more. The baby hats she had made had been given to the neo-natal unit at the hospital. The nurses were very grateful, they always needed hats and mittens for the new-borns. Some people couldn't afford them.

'What a talent,' the staff nurse had said. 'I wish I could do that.'

Anna had watched as the parents in the unit took the hats, and put them on their babies when they were ready to leave. The husband pushed the pushchair whilst the mum walked beside them, smiling at each other, happy to be taking their baby home.

The coroner declared Joy's death as murder. She had been suffocated with the rainbow blanket Anna had made for her. They'd found small fibres of it in the back of her throat from when Graham had stuffed it in her mouth to shut her up.

When they buried her, they wrapped her in it. Hoping, in some way, that it would feel like she was being held by her mum.

Mikey had struggled tremendously with the death of his sister, and the loss of his arm. They had measured him up for a prosthetic which he would be having fitted in the next month or so. His dreams of being a rock star were over. Unless he found his singing voice. He'd lost interest.

A doctor told him there was a rock band with a one-armed drummer. He didn't care.

At first, they thought they would have to take the top of the arm off as well, all the way to the shoulder, due to the hack job Graham had done. Fortunately, they were able to trim off the rotten flesh and fix it up without taking more off.

He was going back to school soon. They needed to try and get back to normal. Something that Bev's girls would never be able to do.

The police identified the body buried in the garden as Rob Cage, Beverly's husband. They'd found Bev with a gunshot to her head and shoulder; she had died holding her husband's hand that was protruding from the garden. Their children now lived with their grandmother.

Anna went back into the living room and sat beside Mikey on the stained and worn sofa. The window that overlooked the street below them was small and single-paned, letting in all the voices of the passers-by outside. She thought she'd get used to the voices of strangers talking about her and what her husband had done. She didn't know when she'd get used to it, but she was sure she would.

She tucked her legs up on to the sofa. Her elbow still ached where she had been shot: they had grafted the flesh back on to the bone, but the muscle damage would never heal fully. The joint cracked if she tried to fully extend her arm.

They sat watching the TV mindlessly, like they did most nights. Not talking, thinking about how it would maybe have been best if they had died? She couldn't speak for Mikey, but it was how she felt. By how reclusive and depressed her son seemed, she guessed he felt the same.

It didn't help that everyone knew they were related to Graham. A lot of the town were sympathetic to them, but some, like the people who egged their windows and spray-painted the walls of their house, weren't.

When it became apparent the person responsible for killing all those people at the supermarket was Graham, Anna may as well have painted a target on her back.

The police told her Graham had gone to the supermarket, seen a few people weren't wearing masks, and lost his mind.

He'd lost his mind alright, Anna thought, but didn't say.

The TV programme they were watching was interrupted by a news-night special. The Prime Minister stood at a podium in the centre of a large room; the walls were mahogany and the shelves filled with leather-bound books.

He proceeded to tell them that the new variant of the virus that they were extremely worried about was getting out of control. 'Regrettably' was the word he used. 'Regrettably, the government would need to impose a new national lockdown for the next three months.'

Another lockdown. A new variant forcing them to stay indoors.

It couldn't be worse than the last one.

End

July 2020 – July 2021, Axl Malton.

Acknowledgements

First of all, thank you to Conrad Jones and Red Dragon publishing for taking a chance on a new author like me. Karen Ankers, my editor, did a fantastic job of helping me fine tune this novel. The whole team has been invaluable in helping Cries of Joy get out into the world.

A big thank you has to go to my wife, Haley. Without her support and encouragement, I wouldn't have been able to put this book together. She's always there to push me on when I'm feeling stuck. She's my rock, and I'd be lost without her.

Thanks to my family and friends for all of your support, I love you all.

And a thank you to everyone who buys and reads this book. I hope you enjoyed it. It's dark and it's gritty, but sometimes, unfortunately, that's just how life is.

Axl Malton

Printed in Great Britain
by Amazon